Also by Jennie Marts

A *Cowboy* COUNTRY CHRISTMAS

JENNIE MARTS

sourcebooks
casablanca

Published by Sourcebooks Casablanca, an imprint of Sourcebooks
P.O. Box 4410, Naperville, Illinois 60567-4410
(630) 961-3900
sourcebooks.com

Printed and bound in Canada.
MBP 10 9 8 7 6 5 4 3 2 1

This book is dedicated to everyone who loves Christmas.
To the ones who love cookies, carols, and candy canes.
To the ones who adore sparkly lights and get
choked up singing "Silent Night."
To the ones who have faith in the spirit of
Christmas and still believe in Santa Claus.
To the ones who carry Christmas in their hearts.
This book is for you.

CHAPTER 1

HOLT CALLAHAN HATED CHRISTMAS. EVERYTHING about it set his teeth on edge—from the cheery carols to the too-sugary cookies to the obnoxious yard displays and strands of twinkling lights decorating everything from porches to pickups.

He used to love it, but not anymore. That's what happens to an already surly cowboy who gets ditched twice on Christmas Eve, the most recent time with a proposal on his lips and a ring in his pocket.

He turns into a grinch. And not the cute grinning version whose heart grows two sizes, but the grumpy, ill-tempered, sulking version who liked to hole up by himself in a cave.

Holt's current circumstances were far from a cave. He'd recently moved into the bunkhouse on his cousin's ranch. The ranch had originally been his grandparents', but they'd passed it down to his cousin, Bryn Callahan, who'd turned it into the Heaven Can Wait Horse Rescue ranch. He'd been bumming around Durango when Bryn and her fiancé, Zane Taylor, had found him and brought him back to the ranch and the small Colorado mountain town of Creedence.

With Bryn's sunny spirit and eternal optimism, Holt had never been able to say no to her. Which was also why he had two boxes of those annoying strands of lights he hated sitting in his living room with instructions from her to string them over every corral fence and porch railing he could manage. At least she'd brought him a box of doughnuts to soften the ask.

Might as well get on with it. He dumped the remains of his already cold coffee into the sink and switched off the radio as it started to play another sappy carol. Geez, he must be losing it. Even with the radio off, he swore he could still hear the sound of sleigh bells.

Nope. They were gone.

Wait. There they were again. He cocked his head, listening, as he opened the front door and stepped out onto the bunkhouse porch. The sun was out, but a light snow was falling, covering the ranch in a dusting of white and giving it a magical feel as the flakes sprinkled like diamonds in the air. A typical day in the Colorado mountains.

He pulled on his Carhartt jacket and grabbed his cowboy hat from the peg inside the door. His sunglasses were in his coat pocket, and he slid them on, cutting the glare of the sun off the snow. He snatched another doughnut from the box and stuffed it in his mouth.

A large pig wearing a silk poinsettia around her neck lay on the front porch, and she lifted her head to offer him a friendly snort.

"Mornin', Tiny," he said to the pig, who thought of herself as more like a dog, as he leaned down to scratch her behind the ear. He *dis*liked Christmas, but he liked animals, and it wasn't the pig's fault he was grumpy and imagining he heard Santa's sleigh bells.

The pig leaned in to the scratch, and he swore she smiled up at him. Try as he might, he couldn't help but smile back as he passed her the other half of his doughnut.

His head jerked up as the jingle of bells rang through the air again. He looked in the direction of the sound, then blinked at the sight of a huge black horse galloping across the field, a yoke of sleigh bells around her neck. The mare looked like some kind of mirage, the way she suddenly materialized out of the snow and trotted into the farmyard, her thick black mane floating around her neck as the bells jingled.

"Whoa there," Holt said, holding up his hand as he stepped down off the porch and toward the horse. A decade spent rodeoing and cowboying had taken away any fear of horses, but he still had a healthy respect for them, especially ones this big.

The horse came to a stop in front of him, and Holt reached for the red-and-green halter around her neck. Two silver tags were affixed to its side. One read "MERRY," which he assumed was the mare's name. The other tag read "Mountainside Ranch," and seeing the name of the farm hit him like a punch to the gut. He'd thought about the place— *and her*—a million times since he'd been back in Creedence. How could he not?

Lainey McBride and Mountainside Ranch were as much a part of the town and the time he'd spent here as a kid as his own grandparents' ranch. Bryn and her brother, Bucky, and he and his brother, Cade, all got dumped on their grandparents every summer. They didn't mind. They all loved it—riding horses, swimming and going fishing in the pond, eating wild strawberries and their grandmother's peach cobbler. They all helped around the farm too, but their grandparents always seemed to make it fun, teaching them how to tend the chickens, feed the cows, and help put up hay at the end of summer.

They'd met Lainey the summer Holt turned ten. She'd come galloping up to the ranch on a horse that seemed too big and like it should've been too wild for her, but she'd handled it as if they were one being. She'd introduced herself, told them she was spending the summer with *her* grandparents, Walter and Elizabeth McBride, at the ranch next door, and invited them over that night for homemade ice cream.

She was so friendly, so carefree with her big smile and spray of freckles across her pert nose. She'd been wearing cutoff jean shorts, her long legs golden tan, a halter top, purple Ropers, and her wild mane of dirty-blond hair was tied back with a piece of bailing twine.

Holt had fallen in love with her that day.

They all had. They'd gone to Mountainside for ice cream that night and been inseparable the rest of that summer and every summer they were all in Colorado together. Especially that last summer, their junior year, when he and Lainey had become more than friends. Then it was like the two of them were joined at the hip.

Until she'd left. She'd stood him up on Christmas Eve with no explanation, then sent him a "Dear Holt" letter two weeks later telling him they were over and to let her go. Then he'd never heard from her again.

"Come on," he told the horse, leading her toward the barn. "We'd better get you back." It would be easier to saddle one of Bryn's rescues and lead the mare back across the pasture than to hook up a trailer.

He'd been riding Bristol lately, a quarter horse who'd been rescued from a livestock auction, and the mare whinnied at him as he walked into the barn. It was probably more for the sugar cubes he liked to slip her than at seeing him.

It didn't take long to saddle her and hook a lead rope to Merry, and he gave both horses a sugar cube before leaving the barn. Bristol liked to gallop, and he gave her a little lead as they headed into the pasture. Merry—ugh, she was a sweet horse, but what an unfortunate annoyingly cheerful name— kept pace with them, seeming to enjoy the snowy morning run as they raced across the fields and toward the small creek crossing where the Callahan property met Mountainside's.

Memories swirled around him—as vivid as the silvery, shimmery flakes of snow. This had been *their* place, his and Lainey's, halfway between the two ranches. The huge cottonwood tree marked the spot, standing tall on the Callahan side of the creek, its exposed roots spreading out like spindly legs that looked as if they were reaching toward the water.

He surveyed the bridge they'd built over the creek, the structure now fallen apart, the slats broken, and the remaining wood rotted from years of neglect.

Kind of like me and Lainey.

The horses didn't need a bridge, and their feet splashed through the water, breaking through the occasional thin layers of ice. The creek was deep enough that it hadn't completely frozen over, and he could hear the water trickling over the rocks and through the holes in the ice. At one time, this had been his favorite place. He and Lainey had spent hours here and left notes and trinkets for each other in the crevices of the huge tree. He remembered coming to his grandparents for Christmas one year and building a snowman in hopes she'd see it when she visited Mountainside.

But he hadn't been here for years, and the thoughts of what could have been seemed to swirl around inside him, making his throat tight, and it was hard to swallow.

Forcing the memories behind him, he pushed the horses harder. The snow whipped in circles around their hooves as they galloped across the fields of the McBride land. Then he pulled up short as he rode into the ranch.

He hadn't been here in years, but today the place looked like it could rival the North Pole. Garland and twinkle lights adorned every gate and section of fence, the pine trees were all hung with colorful glass balls, and Christmas music was somehow being piped through the air.

For as long as he could remember, Mountainside had had the tradition of holding an annual Christmas festival and a dance on Christmas Eve, but he had no idea it had gotten this extreme. It looked like Santa's workshop and Disneyland at the holidays had had a Christmas baby. He could feel the scowl tightening his face.

He looked toward the house and let out a groan. If the decorations all over the ranch weren't bad enough, what looked like one of Santa's elves paced back and forth across the front porch of the farmhouse.

As he galloped up to the house, the elf turned to him, and he almost fell off his horse.

Dressed from head to toe in red and green, the elf wore a red coat with a white fur collar and shiny green leggings tucked into red pointy-toed cowboy boots adorned with bells and glittery snowflakes.

Even though he hadn't seen them in a decade, he recognized the flash of emerald eyes, almost the same color as the green in the red-and-green felt cap sitting atop a mess of familiar curly blond hair.

Lainey?

CHAPTER 2

FULLY OUTFITTED IN THE COSTUME OF ONE OF SANTA'S elves, Lainey McBride paced the wide front porch of her grandparents' two-story farmhouse, the bells on her pointy boots jingling with each step.

Where did that dang horse go?

At any minute, a family of five would be showing up to the ranch, ready to embark on a horse-drawn sleigh ride through the mountains. Except now she had no horse.

Everything has been going well, nice weather, it was even snowing. She was feeling good as she'd brought Merry out of the barn, in her mind replaying the instructions her grandfather had given her for hitching the horse to the sleigh. Maybe too good, *too* confident, since she'd apparently not been holding the halter tightly enough and the horse had pulled free and taken off running across the pasture.

Lainey bit her bottom lip to keep from crying. This was the first year they'd held the Mountainside Country Christmas Festival without her grandmother, and she'd promised her grandpa that she could handle the festivities without him. And there was no way she was going to let him down—even if she had to pull the dang sleigh herself.

A pounding of hooves mingled with the jingle of bells,

and she looked up to see a horse and rider galloping across the field, towing the big black horse with them. Like a hot cowboy mirage, he'd come out of the trees then through the swirling mist of snow blanketing the pasture.

The cowboy pulled up to a stop in front of the porch, and something tightened in her chest. There was something familiar about the set of his broad shoulders, the sandy-blond hair, the way he rode in the saddle. He wore a gray Carhartt jacket, a black cowboy hat, and aviator sunglasses and looked like a cross between a fighter pilot and a bull rider.

He got off his horse and walked up to the porch steps. The wave of familiarity washed over her, but not like the gentle wave of a mountain lake. This felt more like one of those giant tsunami waves that takes out entire resort communities.

It was in the way he moved, the way he walked, the slow saunter in his steps. Then he took off his sunglasses, and she couldn't think at all. Couldn't think. Couldn't move. Could barely take a breath beyond that first sharp inhale.

It couldn't be.

But it was.

"Holt Callahan." She breathed his name. "As I live and breathe."

He was shaking his head. Not in denial, but in what seemed like the same disbelief she imagined was mirrored on her face. "Lainey?" he croaked, then cleared his throat. "What are you doing here?"

"I'm…um…" She swallowed. *Good thing I'm not the only*

one having trouble getting my words out. "I'm helping out my grandpa. This is the first year he's tried to put on the Christmas festival without my grandma."

"I was sorry to hear about her passing," he said. "I always liked her."

"You liked her macaroni and cheese."

A grin tugged at the corner of his lips. "Yeah, that too."

"Gramps fell off a ladder trying to put up all these dang lights by himself and broke his hip." She gestured around the ranch, trying to focus on anything other than the twinge in her stomach that she'd felt at the sight of Holt's grin. "He said he was going to have to cancel the festival, and I couldn't let him do that. It's too important to him, and the farm counts on the proceeds from the month of December too much. So I told him I would come back to finish putting up all the decorations, then stay through Christmas and help with the festival."

"You did all this?" he asked, his eyes wide as he took in all the decorations.

"Yeah. Isn't it great?" She was proud of what she'd accomplished in the few days since she'd arrived. "I think I turned the ranch into the next closest thing to the North Pole itself. I put up all those evergreen wreaths and garlands and stapled up what felt like a million icicle lights and colored bulbs. Then I covered it in fake snow. Which is now all under the real snow. Teach me to check the weather next time. If I'd known we were going to get real snow, it sure would have saved me a lot of trouble."

Oh. My. Gosh. Why was she rambling? *Stop talking.*

"Come back from where?" he asked.

"I'm sorry?" She shook her head, not understanding the question or connecting what it had to do with the decorations.

He was looking down at his boot, but he raised his head and tilted it to the side, an action she'd seen him do a hundred times. "You said after your grandpa got hurt, you decided to come back to help with the festival. Come back from where? Where have you been?"

She swallowed again, knowing the question had a lot more behind it than just the mere inquiry into her last address. "Oh, well, I've been living in Montana. I went to college there." *Community college. And only for two semesters.* But she didn't need to tell him that.

"What—?" He started to ask something more, but Merry cut him off as the big horse stamped her feet.

"Where did you find her?" Lainey asked, happy to change the subject *and their focus* to the mare.

"She found me," Holt said. "I'm staying at Bryn's place. You know she inherited the ranch from our grandparents and she and her boyfriend turned it into a horse rescue?"

"Yeah, Gramps told me. It seems she's really made a place for herself in this community."

"She has. They haven't been doing it that long, but she and Zane have already helped a lot of horses." He nodded toward Merry. "This one just ran up to the bunkhouse where I'm staying. Tiny and I were sharing a doughnut on the porch when she came galloping across the field."

"Oh, is Tiny your…um…girlfriend then?" She couldn't

believe she'd asked that, but she couldn't have stopped the words from coming out if she'd tried.

"She'd like to be. She tried to get in the shower with me last week." Holt's lips curved into another grin; then his shoulders shook with a chuckle.

"Oh" was all Lainey could think to say, not sure what was so funny about that. "Well, thank you for bringing Merry back. She's supposed to be giving sleigh rides around the ranch today, but she got away from me as I was trying to hitch her to the sleigh." She turned at the sound of an engine to see a blue minivan coming down the driveway. It had stuffed reindeer antlers affixed to the front grill and small excited faces peered out the back windows as they took in the ranch.

"Oh heck. The Hendersons are here. They're the cutest family, but they paid for the deluxe sleigh ride, and it was supposed to start ten minutes ago, and I don't even have the horse hitched to the sleigh." She started to run down the porch steps, then stopped midway and headed back up. "Or the hot cocoa made. And I forgot the welcome sign."

How had she made such a mess of the first morning she was in charge?

She looked at Holt. "I hate to ask, but I need your help."

———

Holt shook his head, still in shock that he was standing here having a conversation with Lainey McBride. She looked good, even dressed as an elf. But he knew what she was asking, and he wasn't about to get sucked into the holiday cheer happening around this ranch. "No way. I hate Christmas. I just brought the horse back."

She jerked her head back. "What do you mean you *hate* Christmas? You used to love the holidays."

He turned his head away. "That was a long time ago."

"Well, regardless of your aversion to the season, can you just help me hitch the horse to the sleigh? Then give me a quick lesson on how to *drive* a sleigh?"

It was his turn to jerk back. "'*A quick lesson on how to drive a sleigh*'? What the hell were you going to do if I hadn't shown up?"

She pushed out her bottom lip in a pout, a gesture so familiar to him that it made his chest ache. "My grandpa told me what to do, and it didn't sound that hard. And I was going to watch a YouTube video. Then I planned to practice around the yard a little before the first family showed up. And I would have had time to do it if the dang horse wouldn't have run off."

He stared at her incredulously, already knowing what he was going to do.

"Please, Holt," she said, lowering her voice. "I need you."

He shook his head again. He'd never been able to resist that. Not when he was ten years old, not when he was sixteen, and apparently not today. "Yeah, okay, fine."

"Yay," she said, clapping her hands and jumping up and down a little, which made the bells on her boots jingle and a growl of annoyance hum in his throat. She pointed toward the barn. "The sleigh's in there. You can leave your horse in one of the open stalls. I'll greet the family over by Santa's workshop and get them to sign their waivers, and then we'll meet you back out here."

He led both horses toward the barn, still not sure how she'd just talked him into this. It didn't take him long to stable his horse and hitch Merry to the sleigh. He'd driven plenty of wagons, and he figured a sleigh wouldn't be much different. It was all about controlling the horse.

A YouTube video? He hadn't seen Lainey McBride in over a decade, and she still killed him.

He clucked at Merry and drove the sleigh from the barn, much to the delighted cheers of the Henderson clan. He assumed the tiny shed where they were gathered was Santa's workshop.

Holt cringed as he took in the Christmas-crazy family. Every single one of them was decked out in holiday gear, from ugly holiday sweaters to snowman-covered tights. The mom and two young daughters all had glittery gift-wrap ribbon tied in bows like headbands around their hair, and the dad and the son wore necklaces of Christmas tree bulbs that blinked on and off. The kids all looked to be in grade school, young enough to still believe in the magic of Christmas and still carry the hope that Santa was real.

He might hate Christmas himself, but he wasn't an asshole—not all the time anyway—and he wasn't going to ruin the day for this family just because he was a big, fat grinch. "Hop in," he told them as he pulled to a stop in front of them.

"Hey," shouted the youngest girl with a pout. "Where's Santa? I thought Santa was driving our sleigh."

Hmm. He was starting to like this family a little less.

"I thought so too." Mrs. Henderson frowned. "We did pay for the *deluxe* package."

"Yes, of course you did," Lainey said, reaching into the hut behind her and pulling out a bright-red coat and hat. "But Santa's a pretty busy guy this time of year, so he sent us, his best helpers, to take you on your sleigh ride. I'm Lainey, and this is Holt. He just hasn't had a chance to put his Santa's helper coat and hat on yet."

He looked down at the coat and hat she was holding out to him, then back up at the pleading look in her eyes. The Santa hat was bright red and had a huge puff of white fur on the end.

He shook his head. There was no way in hell he was going to wear that.

"Please," Lainey whispered, stepping up into the sleigh with him.

Two seconds later, he was shoving his arms into the sleeves of the coat. "I'm not wearing the hat," he growled in a low voice.

"You have to wear the hat too," one of the little girls said as the family climbed into the sleigh. These Henderson kids were really starting to get on his nerves.

"They did pay for the *deluxe* package," Lainey reminded him.

He put his cowboy hat on the floor of the sleigh, then grabbed the hat from Lainey's hand and tugged it on his head, realizing too late that a bell was hidden inside the white puff of fur. It jingled merrily as he turned around to make sure his passengers were all safely inside the sleigh.

"Everyone, please keep your hands and feet in the sleigh at all times," Lainey instructed them, sounding like an amusement-park ride operator. "And stay in your seats until the sleigh has come to a complete and final stop."

She sat down in the seat next to him, so close her thigh rested against his. "And we're off," she said with a flourish.

Holt snapped the reins and gave Merry a cluck, and the sleigh burst forward, the runners gliding easily along the freshly fallen snow. Lainey laughed with delight, and he knew he would do just about anything, even wear a stupid jingling Santa hat, to hear her laugh like that again.

Or so he thought, until the Hendersons broke out into a rousing rendition of "Jingle Bells," followed by a hearty performance of "Santa Claus Is Coming to Town," in which he was pretty sure they bungled over seventy-five percent of the actual lyrics. He spent the rest of the ride thinking of ways to get his revenge on the chipper elf sitting next to him.

He drove them around the farm and up a path that led through the trees behind the ranch. Lainey pointed out trees and rocks along the way, giving them cute names and stories that made them sound like the whole ranch was part of Santa's village. She could barely contain her excitement when they came upon two deer standing off to one side of the path, nibbling on a mountain mahogany bush. He would have thought they'd ridden up on two of Santa's favorite reindeer the way they all carried on about how amazing they were.

They finally made it back to the barn, then Lainey showed them the Christmas tree maze they'd created in the field of pine trees next to the house.

"I'm going to run into the house and make the hot cocoa while the Hendersons are in the tree maze," Lainey told him. "You want a cup? It's your favorite."

He frowned. It had been so long since he'd had hot chocolate that he couldn't even remember what kind his favorite was. And he was taken aback that Lainey did.

She nudged his shoulder. "You know, the kind with the crushed-up candy canes stirred in and then sprinkled on top of the marshmallows."

"Oh yeah," he said. "I'd forgotten about that."

"I haven't forgotten anything," she said quietly, but she'd turned away and was climbing out of the sleigh as she spoke, so maybe he'd just imagined she'd said it.

"I'll just unhitch the sleigh and get the horse put away," Holt told her.

"Oh…actually…" she said, shifting from one foot to the other. "Another family is scheduled to be here for *their* sleigh ride any minute." As if on cue, a red SUV pulled into the driveway. "I'll bet that's them now."

CHAPTER 3

"*Another family?*" Holt stammered. "Now wait a minute."

"I'll pay you with the most delicious hot chocolate ever," Lainey said, before hurrying toward the SUV. "You're the best, Holt Callahan," she called over her shoulder.

"The best at being a sucker for a pretty girl," he muttered to the horse.

Merry stamped her foot as if she agreed.

But he knew Lainey wasn't just some pretty girl. She was the pretty girl. The one who had stolen his heart, his first love, and the one against whom he measured every other woman he'd met.

He'd thought he'd found someone in Talia. They'd met on the rodeo circuit. She was a buckle bunny, but she kept showing up and he kept winning, and she'd somehow convinced him that she was his lucky charm. *Some luck*. Right after she'd moved herself into his apartment, he started losing. And not just losing but failing *hard*. One night, he fell off the bull right out of the gate; another night, he'd barely lasted six seconds, then almost gotten his head stomped on. It had been a whirlwind romance, all fire and passion, and in the beginning, all she talked about was getting married and how in love she was with him.

He'd fallen in love with her too. At least he'd thought he had. She wasn't Lainey, but she was sweet and funny and shared his interest in the rodeo, and he'd thought they could eke out a happy life together. Enough to buy her a ring and book a trip to a resort in Aspen to celebrate their engagement and spend their first Christmas together. But apparently, she'd found another cowboy whom she'd rather hitch her wagon to, probably just a coincidence that he was number one on the circuit.

Holt's losing streak had continued after Talia left him, then his horse had broken her leg halfway through the summer and had to be put down. He'd barely left his apartment since then, wallowing in grief and self-doubt. If he were honest, he was grieving more for his horse than Talia, but that was how his cousin had found him. And it took all of four minutes for Bryn to decide he was moving back to the ranch with her.

The new family had exploded out of the SUV, like a Christmas piñata bursting open with four kids in red-and-green-colored clothes. The mother of the festive bunch held a toddler dressed in a tiny elf suit, and it let out a loud shriek, derailing Holt's train of thought into the past and bringing him crashing back into the present.

Lainey corralled the whole family in front of the little shack, passing out candy canes to the kids and clipboards with forms to sign to the parents. She disappeared into the shack and must have prepared the hot cocoa inside because she reappeared a few minutes later and traded the clipboards for festive paper cups that she handed out to the family.

The mother got in exactly one sip before the toddler in her arms whacked the cup and spilled the whole thing down the front of her jacket. At the same time, one of the little girls dropped her candy cane in the dirt and her older brother accidentally stepped on it, sending the girl into hysterics.

He wondered what kind of work Lainey did that made her seem completely unfazed by the drama, laughing as she raced back into the shack and out again with a handful of paper towels and a replacement candy cane.

Was that part of the *deluxe* package too?

Then he didn't have time to wonder anything else because Lainey was leading them toward the sleigh and the rowdy bunch was piling in and fighting over who was going to get the best seat and what they thought the horse's name was and if they thought the horse would poop while they were in the sleigh and, if it did, would Santa's helper have to get out and use a pooper-scooper to clean it up.

"I don't care if it *is* part of the deluxe package," he told Lainey as she scooted into the seat next to him. "I'm not scooping that horse's poop."

He'd thought he'd said it quietly, but the kids must have heard it because his comment sent them into gales of laughter, hysterical giggles, and more talk of poop as the mother tried to reprimand them for the potty talk while keeping the toddler from grabbing the jingling puff at the end of Holt's Santa hat.

"And here we go," Lainey called, nudging his leg as she snatched the Santa hat off his head and out of the toddler's reach.

He clucked to Merry, and the horse took off, jolting the

family into a few seconds of silence before they embarked on excited chatter about what they were seeing around the ranch. He thought he was getting lucky with no longer having to wear the Santa hat, but instead, Lainey had picked up his cowboy hat and affixed the Santa one over the top of the crown, then handed it back to him.

He settled in on his head, then cocked an eyebrow at her. "Normally a cowboy doesn't let any woman touch his hat."

She grinned in response, a flirty grin that had his insides flipping upside down as she lowered her voice. "What would a cowboy let a woman touch?" Her eyes widened, and she clapped a hand over her mouth. Pink rose to her cheeks. "Oh my gosh. Pretend I didn't say that."

"Too late." He chuckled as he maneuvered the sleigh through the trees. "I heard you say it."

"So did I," the mother of the kids said, leaning her head toward them.

Dang. Moms hear everything.

"Sorry," he said, but he couldn't keep the grin off his face. It had been so long since he'd smiled like that. He wasn't sure his face had still known how. Apparently, all it took was a flirty comment from Lainey McBride to rekindle the long-unused muscles.

Lainey settled in next to him, the narrow seat of the sleigh bringing them closer together, but she didn't say anything more. Probably because the kids were now singing "Rudolph the Red-Nosed Reindeer" at the top of their tiny lungs.

What was up with this sleigh ride inspiring the singing of carols?

The day flew by, with three more families and a group of rowdy teenagers arriving for sleigh rides. Holt had been a pretty good sport about the families, but Lainey thought the teenagers were going to do him in.

He did agree that he loved her hot cocoa, once she finally got him a cup, but she didn't think there was any amount of hot chocolate to make listening to the teenagers sing "Grandma Got Run Over by a Reindeer" seven times in a row worth it.

Lainey had known the day was going to be hectic, so she'd put some chili in the Crock-Pot earlier that morning.

"Good chili," Holt told her as they each snuck a bowl in between two of the families' arrivals.

"Thanks. It's my grandma's recipe."

He nodded, but she caught the flicker of something in his eyes, not quite anger, but maybe definitely annoyance. "I remember." Then he blinked and turned his gaze toward the ranch as if purposely cutting off any other discussion about what they remembered from when they were kids. "You've done a great job with all this. Everyone seemed to have fun."

"Gosh, I hope so. I worked so hard to set up all sorts of things for them to do around the ranch, like coloring pages and a Christmas craft in the barn."

"They all seemed to like the outdoor games too. I saw them playing what looked like cornhole in the yard."

"That was my Christmassy version. I called it 'Down the Chimney.' I sewed little Santa patches onto the beanbags, and then they had to toss him into the 'chimney holes.'"

"Clever."

She smiled as she drew her shoulders back. "All part of the deluxe package, you know."

He groaned. "If I hear 'deluxe package' one more time today…"

She laughed. "I loved it. Every time I heard those words, I heard dollar signs *cha-chinging* in my head. That was my idea too—to offer a 'special' package that cost more and gave them a few extra amenities, like sugar cookies with their hot cocoa and caroling during the sleigh ride." If the delighted laughter she heard throughout the day was any indication, she'd say her ideas of games, activities, and deluxe offerings were a success.

"They paid *extra* for that? Now it makes sense why every group spontaneously broke out into song once the sleigh started."

"Wasn't it fun?"

"If you think fun is listening to two cats screech-howling at each other, then yes. Because that's all I heard."

"You really have gotten grouchy about Christmas," she said.

He shrugged and stood up, collecting their empty paper bowls and dumping them into the trash can next to Santa's workshop shack. His walking away effectively curtailed the conversation, and she was pretty sure that had been his intention. Which was okay with her. She was still angry and hurt that he'd abandoned her, but she was also intrigued with and curious about the man he was now. And they had been having fun together, she and *Holt Callahan*, the first boy she'd ever fallen in love with.

And the first boy who'd not just broken but *shattered* her heart.

She'd never understood why he hadn't shown up to meet her or ever tried to find her. She'd thought they meant so much to each other. They'd made plans to run off together the day after they graduated from high school and to get married that summer. They'd even talked about what they wanted to name their kids—Joshua and Emily. But apparently, all those conversations had been the whispered dreams of two kids, or maybe the drama of her situation had been too much for him because after she'd left that last time, she'd never heard from him again.

Until today.

She inhaled a deep breath, the scent of him still on the sleeve of her coat. Aftershave, laundry detergent, leather, and cinnamon. She loved that he still chewed the same cinnamon gum. She'd never been able to buy a pack without thinking of him.

She had so many questions, wanted to ask him so many things. Where had he been for the last decade? What was his job? Had he ever thought about her? And who was this woman named Tiny who shared his breakfast and wanted to shower with him?

An old pickup pulled into the driveway, cutting off any chance for her to interrogate him. She laughed as she watched as an elderly man dressed in full Santa gear get out and circle the truck to open the door for a woman decked out as Mrs. Claus. "You all look great," she said, clapping her hands as they walked toward her and Holt.

Santa, a.k.a. Doc Hunter, had been the primary physician for the town of Creedence for the last forty years. Now retired—from his medical practice, not his Christmas duties—he had been friends with her grandfather for as long as she could remember.

"Thank you, honey," the woman dressed as Mrs. Claus said, giving Lainey a hug. Her name was Cassandra James, and she was the real-life aunt to the James brothers who had a ranch across the road, but most of the town knew and loved her as Aunt Sassy. In her early eighties, she was still spry and healthy enough to attend line-dancing lessons at the town's pub and restaurant, the Creed, every Thursday night and could be counted on to know most everything happening around town.

Lainey gestured toward the frowning cowboy standing behind her. "Holt, do you remember Doc Hunter and Aunt Sassy?"

He nodded. "Of course. Known Doc since we were kids. He used to hire Cade and me to do yard work for him in the summer." Lainey caught the ghost of a grin trying to escape his mouth as he turned his gaze to Aunt Sassy. "And this one just snuck a baked ziti into my oven a couple of days ago. Although I didn't know you moonlighted as Mrs. Claus," he told Sassy as she pressed a kiss to his cheek.

"There are all sorts of things you don't know about me," Aunt Sassy said with a playful wink and a flip of her short silvery curls. "I'm a woman of mystery." She peered up at his hat and poked the fuzzy ball with her finger. "What's this? Are you trying to put Doc—I mean, Santa—out of a job?"

"Not even close." Holt tilted his head toward Lainey. "I just somehow got roped into helping one of his elves."

Lainey smiled, unfazed by his grumpy comment as she gave Doc a hug. "It's so fun to see you both, but what are you doing out here?"

"We just finished up our shift as Mr. and Mrs. Claus in the park downtown and thought we'd come out to check in with you about our official duties for the festival," Doc told her.

"And I was hoping we might sneak in a romantic sleigh ride while we were here," Aunt Sassy said. "We just saw the Henderson kids, and they couldn't stop talking about how much fun they'd had."

Lainey grinned at Holt, then nodded at Sassy and Doc. "I think that could be arranged," she told them before Holt had a chance to decline.

They spent the next few minutes talking through the plans for the festival. Doc and Aunt Sassy, a.k.a. Mr. and Mrs. Claus, would spend several hours at the ranch during the main festival on Friday, the twenty-third, then come back on Saturday night, Christmas Eve, to help pass out toys to the kids that night at the annual Ho-Ho-Hoedown.

"That works," Doc said. "We've got an appearance booked at the Elks Lodge the day before, and we're helping with another toy drive that morning, but we've got the time scheduled to make sure we're here for the festival."

"Thank you," Lainey said. "That means so much to me *and* my grandfather."

"You two are pretty busy," Holt told them as he helped Aunt Sassy climb into the back of the sleigh.

"Yes, we are," Aunt Sassy said, patting his arm in a gesture of thanks. "But it's all for the kids, and every second is worth it. You should see the way their eyes light up when they get to sit on Santa's lap and tell him their Christmas wish."

"I can imagine." Holt climbed into the front of the sleigh and picked up the reins. "What's the hot item this year that everybody wants?"

"Oh, lots of requests for bicycles and video games and Barbie dolls and Legos," Doc said. "Those are easy ones. Especially when I get a wink from the parents telling me that they've already made the purchase. The hard ones are when kids ask me for nongift things like bringing their dad home from jail or wanting a job for their mom. I had one little girl this morning who asked me to help find her lost horse. Cute as a button, big blue eyes, lots of blond curls, couldn't have been more than three or four years old. But she knew everything about that horse, from the white star on its forehead to the single white sock on its leg. She called it a 'palminio,' which I assumed was toddler talk for 'palomino.' She didn't give a wit about toys. All she wanted was for me to bring Goldie home."

"Wow. That is a tough one," Lainey said, her heart aching for the little girl.

"How about you?" Doc nudged her shoulder. "Any Christmas wish you're hoping for?"

"Just for this festival to go off without a hitch and to make the money needed to keep my grandpa's farm afloat for the next six months."

"I think I can manage that one," he said with a wink. "I'll

give it a little of my Christmas magic, but I know the event is going to be a great success. Everyone in town is talking about it, and Walt always gets a great crowd."

Aunt Sassy nudged Holt's shoulder. "What about you, handsome? Do you have a Christmas wish for Santa? Or do you just want to come over and sit on Mrs. Claus's lap?"

He let out a grunt accompanied by a small grin. Aunt Sassy was known for comments that lived up to her name. "My only wish is for this sappy dang holiday to be over."

Lainey bumped his shoulder with hers. "Don't be such a grinch. Or I might be forced to get the song sheets out."

"Song sheets?" Doc asked, leaning forward. "I didn't know there would be caroling."

"Doc's got an excellent voice," Lainey said. "He sings in the church choir."

Holt fixed her with a steely stare, but she just laughed in return. Those mean stares of his had never worked on her. She knew he was a softie on the inside. Or at least he had been.

"We're not singing carols today," Aunt Sassy said. "This is supposed to be a romantic sleigh ride. So you two just focus on driving and keep your eyes forward in case Santa wants to give Mrs. Claus a smooch and we make a little Christmas magic of our own happen back here."

Holt almost choked, but he kept his eyes on the horse as he clucked for her to pick up the pace.

Lainey laughed again, then let out a contented sigh as she breathed in the crisp mountain air. Holt could be as grumpy about Christmas as he wanted, but she loved everything about the season. Although, as she snuck a quick glance at the handsome cowboy grinch next to her, she couldn't help but wonder if she didn't have another Christmas wish after all.

CHAPTER 4

THE NEXT MORNING, HOLT WAS SITTING ON THE FRONT porch sharing the last doughnut with Tiny when he heard a small sound under the floorboards. It was like a scratching followed by a soft whine. He tossed the last bite to the pig, who was much more concerned with the chocolate-frosted doughnut than any mysterious sound, and climbed down the steps to investigate.

Cedar lattice had been used to skirt the bottom of the porch, but one section had fallen off where the slats had broken and come loose. He heard the scuffling sound again. Using the flashlight on his phone, he knelt down and shined the light under the porch, praying it wasn't a raccoon or skunk that had gotten under there.

A pair of sad brown eyes stared back at him. Not a skunk or a racoon, thankfully, but what looked like a small scruffy brown dog. Its fur was matted and dirty, and it shivered against the cold shadows of the porch. He held his hand out to the dog, wishing he wouldn't have given his last bite of doughnut to Tiny. "Come here, girl," he called gently. It only whined again and scooted further under the porch.

"Suit yourself, then," he told it. "You can stay under there for all I care."

Like most days in Colorado, the sun was out and the snow from the day before was already starting to melt. It was close to nine, and Holt had already fed the cows, mucked out the stalls, and fixed a loose hinge on Bryn's chicken coop. He still hadn't put up the lights and felt a little guilty for finishing off the bribery doughnuts before he'd completed the task, so he trudged into the bunkhouse to get the boxes and get it done.

Once inside, he picked up the first box, determined to complete the odious task, then set it back down, then picked it back up again. He talked a big game, but his conscience was getting to him. "Aw hell," he muttered before setting the box down once again and going into the kitchen. Rummaging through the cupboards, he came up with a couple of old butter tubs and filled one with water and one with the slice of cold meat loaf he'd planned to eat for lunch.

Going back outside, he knelt down next to the broken section of porch and slid the containers inside. The dog had wiggled even further under the porch, but maybe the smell of Bryn's meat loaf and fresh water would lure her out. He called to the pup again but only got another whine in reply.

He stood at the sound of a car coming down the driveway and was surprised to see a blue compact SUV pull up in front of the bunkhouse. The SUV itself wasn't the surprising part; the Christmas tree that was bigger than the vehicle and wobbling haphazardly on the roof and Lainey in the driver's seat were.

"You're lucky that tree didn't fall off on the drive over here," he told her by way of greeting as she climbed out of the car. "That twine looks like it's ready to snap."

"I know," she said, blowing her bangs out of her eyes. "That's why I'm here. I need your help."

She was no longer dressed as an elf. Today she had on a red down jacket over a black sweater and worn black cowboy boots on her feet. She wore a blue-and-white stocking cap with a puffy ball on top, and her hair was twisted into one braid that lay alongside her neck. The Lainey he'd remembered was a tall, gangly girl with long legs and bony elbows. This Lainey was a woman, still tall, but now shapely and soft and curvy in all the best spots, as evidenced by the snug jeans that hugged her hips perfectly.

"I think I helped enough yesterday," he said, leaning casually against the porch railing.

"Yes, I agree, you were great yesterday, but seriously, if you don't help me now, this tree is going to fall off and cause an accident, or I'll end up dragging it into town and all the needles will be gone by the time I get it to its destination."

"Which is…?"

"The assisted-living center where my grandpa is staying. I thought since he can't come home to see all the Christmas at the ranch, I'd bring some Christmas to him. And to the other residents."

"Are you sure they want you bringing this huge tree in there?"

"Yes, I'm sure. You think I'd just show up with an eight-foot Douglas fir and a box of tinsel without checking with someone first?"

He shrugged.

"I called this morning, and they said they hadn't had a

chance to put up a tree in the common room yet, so they'd be thrilled to have me bring one in and decorate it."

He produced a growl in his throat. He hated to think a group of old folks would suffer because he was too grouchy to help her tie a few knots. Apparently, he was destined to be putting up Christmas decorations one way or another.

Although… he thought as an idea came to him. "How about we work out a trade?"

She cocked an eyebrow and shot out her hip. "What kind of trade? Because I'm not into any of that kinky stuff."

He barked out a laugh as she dropped her head into her hands. "Good to know. Disappointing, but still good to know."

"What is wrong with me?" she said, talking into her hands that were still covering her face. "I swear when I'm around you, everything I'm thinking just seems to pop right out of my mouth." She spread her fingers and peered at him from between them. "Can we please forget I just said that?"

He laughed again. "Not likely. But for the sake of our getting this tree into town, I'll say I will." He stepped away from the porch and walked around her car, examining the way she'd tied down the tree. She'd strung bailing twine around the trunk and tied it to her luggage rack, but half the knots had come loose, and it was barely hanging on. "It's a miracle this tree didn't fall off on the way over here."

"I know." She reached inside the car and pulled out a Christmas tin. She popped the lid and tilted it toward him. "But I did bring you some sugar cookies for your trouble."

"You think plying me with home-baked goods is going to make me bend to your will?"

"I'm hoping so," she said, grinning across the car at him. "Otherwise, I baked all these cookies for nothing."

"Fine," he said. "Give me a cookie."

She pulled one from the tin and started to hold it out when she let out a little shriek. "Um, Holt, I need a little help here."

"What's wrong?" he said, already coming around the front of the car.

"There's a hog trying to steal your cookie," she said, her voice raising as she backed up against the car. She held the tin higher as Tiny sniffed at her legs.

"Don't worry, she's friendly. Although, she apparently doesn't like being called an H-O-G," he said, coming up and gently nudging the pig out of the way. "She won't hurt you though. She's a sweetheart. Aren't you, Tiny?" He scratched under her chin, and she gave him an adoring look accompanied by a snort of agreement.

"Wait," Lainey said, relaxing against the car door. "*This* is Tiny? The one who wants to be your girlfriend and take a shower with you?"

He grinned at her, unable to keep a straight face now that the jig—or, in this case, the *pig*—was up. "Yep, this is her. She and the ranch goat like to watch television in the bunkhouse, but I must have left the bathroom door open last week because she came in and tried to climb in with me. Bryn has all these fancy soaps and shampoos in there, and I think she smelled the orange-scented one."

"So she was more interested in getting a good meal than in being with you?" Lainey asked, grinning back at him.

"You'd be surprised how often that happens on my dates."

She snorted out a laugh, and he had to chuckle with her.

"Nice to meet you, Tiny," Lainey said, handing the pig a cookie. "I'm taking that one out of your paycheck just for teasing me like that."

He arched an eyebrow. "What did you care about who wanted to shower with me? Were you jealous?"

"Of a pig? Not likely," she said, but she kept her head down and wouldn't meet his eyes.

That's interesting. And weird. And kind of awesome. But still weird.

Why would she be jealous of another female being interested in him? She'd had her chance with him, and she was the one who'd left him behind.

"So what do you think we should do?" she asked.

It took him a second to realize she was talking about the tree. *Of course she was talking about the tree, you idiot.*

"Yeah, right, so, um, I don't think we're going to be able to really secure it to the top of your car. It's bigger than your roof. I think it would be easier if we just loaded it into the back of my truck and I drove you into town. It's not like you'd be able to carry it into the center on your own anyway."

"That would be great. Really, Holt, thanks so much."

"Don't mention it."

"This place looks great," she said, walking up the porch steps. "I can't believe this used to be the run-down bunkhouse we weren't allowed to play in. I remember it being full of old junk and more than one family of mice."

"Cade came back last year, and he renovated and updated

it into two side-by-side apartments," Holt told her, surveying the building as if through her eyes.

It had the look of a log cabin with a long covered front porch and thick cedar posts. Galvanized steel buckets that overflowed with pink trumpet flowers in the summer sat on either side of the stairs, and a blue-and-white quilt was folded over the back of a blue-cushioned glider swing. Two rocking chairs looked out over the ranch with a small wooden table between them. Flower boxes, which Bryn had recently filled with bright-red fabric poinsettias, hung below the two wide front windows, and identical red welcome mats sat in front of the matching screened doors that opened to each apartment.

"If the inside looks anything like the outside, he did an amazing job," she said. Was she fishing for an invitation to go inside? Or just making conversation? "How's Cade doing these days?"

"He's doing good. Lives on a nice little farm just west of here with his daughter, a new fiancée, and way too many barn cats." He answered with a light tone, but the phrasing of her question had seemed odd to him, like maybe she knew about the car accident that had taken his brother's ex-wife's life and brought his estranged teenage daughter back into his life the summer before. But how would she know about that? Unless she'd kept tabs on Cade.

Did that mean she'd kept tabs on Bryn and Bucky, and him, too?

The question—one of *so many* questions—was on the tip of his tongue, but he couldn't bring himself to ask it. There would come a time to get into all of that, but now wasn't it.

"I'd better get that tree loaded up," he said, already turning and heading toward his truck.

It took him less than ten minutes to bring his rig over and transfer the tree to the bed of his pickup. He secured it in place with some ropes, just so it wouldn't slide around the back end and cause any more of the needles to fall off. Wouldn't want to get to the center with only a Charlie Brown Christmas tree left in the back.

He finished tying the last knot and came around the front of the truck to find Lainey trapped on the porch by Tiny; Otis, the ornery goat who acted like he ran the ranch; and Shamus, a mini-horse Bryn had rescued the year before. Lainey was standing on one of the rocking chairs and holding the cookie tin over her head. "Help," she called to him. "I gave them each a cookie, and now they won't let me down."

"You must make great cookies," he told her as he shooed the animals away from the porch and held out his hand to help her down. His mouth went dry as she slipped her hand into his. It wasn't romantic—he was just helping her off the chair—but still, the feel of her palm sliding perfectly into place against his brought to mind a million times he'd taken her hand before.

"Thanks for saving me," she said, climbing off the chair. "Again."

Now that she was steady on her feet, he pulled his hand away and crammed it into his front pocket, suddenly unsure of what to say. "We should probably get going."

She nodded, then followed him off the porch. "You said something about a trade?"

"Oh yeah. So my cousin... You remember Bryn?"

"Yeah, of course."

"She's been bugging me to put a bunch of Christmas lights up. I was going to say that I'd help you with this tree if you help me string the lights."

"Deal. That was easy. I love putting up lights."

"Somehow, I knew you'd say that."

"Is it okay if I leave my car here?"

"Sure."

"Just let me grab my purse. And the decorations."

He groaned as he peered into her back seat at the two large tubs marked TREE TRIMMINGS. "You've got *more* decorations?"

"Of course I do. We need stuff to trim the tree. I've got strings of lights and colored bulbs and a bunch of ornaments."

He groaned again but grabbed the boxes and stuffed them into the back seat of the truck. It was going to be a long day.

Lainey was so thankful she'd asked Holt to help her with the tree. She would never have been able to get it into the assisted-living center on her own. Or into the tree stand.

They'd strung the lights and put on the decorations together, all under the watchful eyes of several of the residents. Two older men offered plenty of advice, things like "You want to put that bare spot to the back" and "You've got too many lights bunched up in that one section," while three little old ladies had dragged their chairs up to basically ogle

Holt and cackle at each other's inappropriate comments that they somehow acted like he couldn't hear.

"Wish Santa would leave a stud like that under my tree this year," one of them said.

"You wouldn't know what to do with him if he did," the other chided. "A man like that needs a *real* woman."

"You've had so many hip and joint replacements, the only thing *real* left on you is your eyeballs," the third one chimed in.

"My eyeballs are all I need to check out that hunk of hot cowboy meat."

"All right," Lainey said. "Down, ladies. Leave Holt alone or we'll never get this tree up."

"Fine by us," the first one said. "We're in no hurry. He can stay here all night."

"He can sleep over," the second one said, nudging the third. "He can sleep with me."

Holt seemed to take it all in stride, even occasionally flashing a grin at the women or teasing them back. Which they ate up like ice cream. At one point, Lainey was worried one of them might swoon right out of her chair.

Although she got it. Holt *was* pretty swoony. It was crazy how they hadn't seen each other in over a decade, yet at times, they seemed to fall right back into their easy banter, teasing and joking around with the other one.

Then something awkward would happen. Either they would get too close, like earlier when Holt had held her hand to help her off the chair, or some reminder of their past would pop up and then they'd both shrink back into silence.

"You want to do the honors?" Holt asked, drawing her out of her reverie.

"Hmm?"

"The angel?" he said, holding out the tree topper. "You want to put the angel on top?"

"Yeah, sure." She took the angel from him, then took the hand he held out to help her up onto the chair he'd placed next to the tree.

"Careful now," he said, holding tight to her hand. He reached an arm around her legs to steady her as she struggled to get her balance.

"Watch your hands, mister," one of the ladies called out.

All too aware of his warm arm pressed against her legs, Lainey quickly plunked the angel on top of the tree, then climbed off the chair. "There. Got it," she said, her voice coming out a little breathy.

"Let's see how she looks," one of the older men said, already grabbing the free end of the string of lights and plugging the cord into the wall.

The tree lit up to the *oohs* and *ahhs* of the assembled group in the community room. And it really was pretty.

She and Holt took a step back to admire the lights, and she wondered if he realized he was still holding her hand.

"Uh-oh," one of the ladies called out, pointing to something above their heads. "Looks like you two are in trouble now."

Lainey and Holt looked up at the same time, then back down at each other.

Hanging from the arch above them was a big sprig of mistletoe.

CHAPTER 5

HOLT GROWLED. OF COURSE THERE WAS MISTLETOE.

It was bad enough that he was still holding Lainey's hand. Why *was* he still holding her hand? Now they were standing under a stupid plant—one that was actually *poisonous* for animals to eat, by the way—with three old ladies peer-pressuring him and Lainey to kiss.

And the worst part, even worse than the memory of his neighbor's dog eating mistletoe and barfing for two days, was that he *wanted* to kiss her. With everything in him. He'd been wanting to kiss her since he'd first laid eyes on her the day before—even in that silly elf costume. And now, even with the thought of the Charlestons' dog ralphing all over their yard, he still wanted to pull her into his arms and feast on her delicious pink lips.

But he was also irked as all get out—hurt and pissed off that she'd left him all those years ago without even a backward glance. He recognized now that they'd only been kids, but he'd still loved her. And when they'd talked about getting married after high school, he'd meant every word. He'd envisioned a life with Lainey by his side and completely believed that she shared that vision, so he couldn't for the life of him figure out why she'd left one day with no warning and he'd never heard from her again.

He wanted to just ask her why the hell she'd left, but now didn't seem the best time for that discussion.

Besides, Lainey was back in his life, and it felt like old times when he made her laugh and she flashed that big smile at him. He didn't want to change that by pressing her about why she'd left and where the hell she'd been for the last decade or so. Yeah, maybe that made him a coward, but he didn't care.

At least for today, he'd rather be an oblivious coward with Lainey *in* his life than hear something that would crush his soul and take a chance on losing her again. But they *would* talk about it. They had to.

"Do it," one of the older ladies called out.

"Kiss her," one of the others said.

The final one spoke more to her companions than to Holt and Lainey, but they heard just the same as she said, "I heard mistletoe is good for arthritis *and* fertility."

Holt gulped. He didn't have a current need for either of those remedies. Now if she would have said it was good for getting rid of that nervous feeling in his stomach that made him feel as nauseous as the Charlestons' dog, *then* he'd be interested.

The two older men walked over and were getting in on it too. "Just kiss the girl," the taller one instructed. "What are you waiting for?"

"Come on," the other one said. "Give her a big Christmas smooch."

Lainey looked up at Holt, her eyes wide and round. "I think we'd better just do it. Just to get these guys off our case."

That didn't feel like the best reason to kiss the girl he'd been pining over for the last decade or so, but at least it would give him an excuse to feel her in his arms again, to taste her.

"Okay," was all he could manage to say. And even that came out in a hoarse whisper.

He let go of her hand so he could slide his arm around her waist and pull her to him. They'd both changed from those gangly teenage bodies, but she still fit perfectly against him.

Why was he so nervous? It's not like he hadn't kissed a woman before, for Pete's sake. But he hadn't kissed *this* woman. He'd kissed her as a girl, but that had been a long time ago.

He bent his head, leaning closer, and watched as her gaze dropped to his mouth. He caught the flicker of desire in her eyes before she brought her gaze back to his. Her lips parted, like an invitation, and he bent closer still.

Lifting his free hand, he cupped her cheek and felt the small inhale of her breath as he grazed his thumb over her bottom lip. Then he couldn't take it anymore. He tilted his head and pressed his mouth to hers.

Her lips were soft, pliant, and just as sweet as he'd remembered. He could taste peppermint and a hint of cherry flavor that must have been in her lip gloss.

It was supposed to be one kiss, just a quick peck to satisfy the elderly observers, who he'd completely forgotten about now because he was lost in the essence of Lainey. As he pulled back, just the barest amount, he couldn't help himself. He had to take another kiss. Then another.

She leaned into him, her fingers clutching a handful of his shirt as she kissed him back.

It took every ounce of his willpower to break away, and his breath was a bit ragged as he pulled back and let her go.

He was relieved to see she looked a bit dazed herself. At least he wasn't the only one who felt like he'd just been picked up by a tornado and was left hanging in a tree.

She blinked up at him, her eyes wearing that same familiar soft glow they used to after he'd kissed her. Then she released his shirt, her hand fluttering to her mouth as she pulled away, but she still held his gaze, as if unable to tear her eyes away.

Suddenly remembering they had an audience, Holt turned his head to see the whole group of their elderly encouragers staring at them. One of the women had her mouth hanging open, and one wore a chaste expression, while the other grinned at them with a saucy smile.

One of the men started a slow clap, nodding and winking while the other joined in the applause and added an attaboy with a small fist pump.

"What's all the commotion about?" a man's voice called from behind them. "I doze off for a few minutes and apparently miss out on a party."

"Gramps," Lainey called, pulling away from Holt and trying to catch her breath as she recognized the man's voice. The group of onlookers parted as she hurried forward to hug the man sitting in a wheelchair.

"Good to see you, honey," Walter McBride said, smiling up at his granddaughter. His smile fell as he turned and must have recognized Holt. "Well now, young Mr. Callahan. Haven't seen you in a long time."

"Not so young anymore," Holt said, extending his hand to shake. "How are you, Mr. McBride?"

"I've been better," he said, nodding toward his legs. "Didn't know you were back around these parts."

"I got back a few months ago. I've been living down in Durango."

"You still on the circuit?"

Holt shook his head. "Nah, my rodeo days are over. At least for now. I came up to help my cousin, Bryn, with the horse rescue ranch."

That was more information than Lainey had been able to get out of him.

"I'm familiar with it," Walt said. "We've helped each other out a time or two and have a few joint projects in the works. That's quite an outfit she's got going over there. Your cousin has taken in and helped place a lot of animals. And not just horses. I heard she had at least a dozen baby goats over there this summer. They were doing some kind of newfangled yoga or some such where they'd let those goats walk all over them while they did some kind of doggy-style nonsense."

Lainey pressed her lips together to keep from laughing. "I think the yoga move you're thinking of is downward dog, Gramps."

"That's what I said. This newfound generation is always getting up to the most foolish guff. For the life of me, I can't figure out why anyone would pay good money to roll around on the ground and let a goat trample all over 'em. Especially when there's a good chance they'll crap right on their fancy yoga britches. But to each their own."

"I don't get it either," Holt agreed. "But it seems to be weirdly popular. They were doing a bunch of those classes in the late summer when I first got here, but they seem to have dropped off this winter."

So he'd been here since late summer? A little more information. If only her grandpa could keep him talking, she might find out what Holt had been doing the last decade.

Walt squinted as he looked from Holt to Lainey. "So what are you two doing here? Together?"

Great question. And an even better one was how in the world was she still standing when that kiss from Holt had made her knees go so weak, she thought she'd melt to the floor in a puddle. "We brought a tree over," she told her grandfather, pointing to the Christmas tree. "Got it all decorated and lit. I wanted you to have a piece of Christmas from the ranch here with you."

He patted his granddaughter's hand. "Well, that's awful sweet of you, honey. But I'm doing my dangdest to get out of here before Christmas rolls around. I hate leaving you with all the work on the ranch. It gets so gol-dang busy during the festival."

"No rush, Gramps. You just worry about getting better. I've got everything under control," she assured him, already knowing there was no chance his hip would be healed in time. "And Holt's been helping me."

Walt looked up at him, a question in his eyes. "Oh yeah?

Why would you want to do that? That cousin of yours not got enough to keep you busy around her place?"

"Oh no," Lainey said, grinning over at Holt. "He's just helping out because he loves Christmas."

One of those growl sounds came from Holt's throat, but he also offered her the slightest wry grin. The sight of it sent butterflies skittering through her stomach. She hadn't seen him since she was seventeen, but being around him still left her breathless.

A buzz emanated from his pocket, and he pulled his phone out and checked the screen. "I should take this. It's Zane, so he might need me at the ranch." He nodded down at her grandfather. "Nice to see you again, Mr. McBride," he said, before backing into the hallway to answer the call.

Her grandfather looked up at her. "Holt Callahan, huh?"

"I'm just as surprised as you are," she said.

"I was under the impression you two had lost touch."

"We had. I haven't spoken to him in twelve years. I had no idea he was even in town. It was just a fluke that I ran into him yesterday." She didn't want to admit to her grandfather that the horse had gotten away from her when she'd been trying to hitch it to the sleigh.

"And another fluke that you ran into him today?"

She shrugged. *Fluke or fate?* She wasn't sure. But she'd known he was the first person she'd thought of to help her this morning when she'd failed so miserably to tie that dumb tree to the top of her car.

Her grandfather arched an eyebrow. "You sure you know what you're getting into, Granddaughter?"

"I'm a big girl, Gramps. I know what I'm doing," she assured him. Although she honestly had *zero* idea of what she was doing. Seeing Holt again had thrown her emotions into a tailspin. He'd been *the one* for her, but he obviously hadn't felt the same way because he'd never tried to contact her after that terrible night when she'd had to leave her grandparents' ranch so suddenly. She'd done her best to let him know how to find her. But since she'd never heard from him, she could only assume she hadn't been worth the effort or the wait.

But he was here now. And if that kiss was any indication, he still had *some* feelings for her. Not that she had time for any kind of romance in her life right now. She had hours and hours of planning and scheduling and organizing ahead of her to make sure that the Christmas festivities at Mountainside went off without a hitch.

She peered down at her grandfather, and the love she felt for him filled her heart. He had been her rock growing up, and she and her mother would have been lost without the support of him and her grandmother. This festival had meant everything to them, and it had the financial means to support the ranch for the next six months. She had to make sure it was a success.

Which meant she didn't have time for old flames, no matter how hot they looked in a black cowboy hat or how much fire burned in their kisses.

"Sorry, but I need to get back to the ranch," Holt said, coming back into the room. "That was Zane calling to say that wet snow yesterday downed a big tree in the west pasture and took out a big section of fence. I need to help him fix it before half the herd decides to escape."

"Yes, of course. I'll come with you," Lainey told him.

"I hate to take you away from your visit," he said.

Walt waved a dismissive hand. "You go on, honey. I'll be fine."

"I'll call you later," she told him, bending to press a kiss to his cheek, then following Holt from the building.

"Sorry to rush you out of there," Holt said as they pulled out of the parking lot and turned toward the highway.

"It's okay. I've got plenty of work I need to be doing at Mountainside. But I do feel a little guilty."

He kept his gaze on the road, but she caught the frown he made. "You mean about the kiss? I'm sorry if I took advantage."

"No, I wasn't talking about the...about that. And you didn't take advantage." She paused, knowing that what she said next could make or break this new...*friendship* they'd found with each other. "In fact, if we wouldn't have had a room full of people watching us, I might have taken advantage of *you* because I thought that kiss was pretty amazing."

The curve of his lips changed from a frown to a small grin. "Good to know."

She looked down at her lap, unable to keep the smile from her face. "I may even be inclined to watch for *more* mistletoe opportunities when I'm around you."

His grin widened. "Also good to know."

They rode in silence the short drive to the ranch. But it was an okay silence. Not exactly comfortable, but not completely *un*comfortable either.

"So what was it that you were talking about earlier?" Holt asked after they'd arrived and she was heading toward her car. "When you said you felt guilty. Guilty about what?"

"Oh, yeah," she said, opening her car door. "It was because now that you're going to be working this afternoon, I feel bad that I can't hold up my end of our deal and help you string the lights today."

He looked thoughtful as he pushed back the brim of his hat and regarded her. "I guess there's always tomorrow."

A little flicker of something that felt like hope bloomed in her chest, and she couldn't keep the smile from broadening across her face. It had been a lot of years since she'd flirted with Holt Callahan, but it still felt as easy as falling into a mountain lake on a hot summer day.

She flashed him a coy grin and called out to him as she slid into the front seat of her car. "I'll bring the mistletoe."

CHAPTER 6

THE REST OF HOLT'S AFTERNOON FLEW BY IN A BLUR.

Zane hadn't been exaggerating about the downed tree taking out a huge section of fence. Not only did it cover a large portion, but the weight of it had also pulled several posts down on either side. It took them hours and the help of two chain saws to cut the tree apart and repair the damaged fence.

Thankfully Bryn had packed them a big lunch, complete with meat loaf sandwiches, thick kettle chips, and hearty chicken noodle soup. The hot soup and thermos of coffee she'd also sent went a long way to warming them up on the brisk afternoon.

His cousin was a great cook and had the philosophy that feeding people was equal to loving them. She had a shift at the diner where she waitressed part-time that night but had left a Crock-Pot of chili on the counter for him and Zane when they returned with a full truck bed of fresh firewood.

He and Zane had filled their bowls and eaten while they caught the tail end of a hockey game. The Colorado Summit was their favorite team to root for, and it was even more fun to watch since one of the starting defensemen was Rock James, a guy they'd known since they were kids and whose family had a ranch up the road from theirs.

Holt checked under the porch as he headed back to the bunkhouse later that night. The meat loaf and the dog were gone.

She must have found her way home, he figured as he turned around and walked toward the barn. Although that dog was too dang scrawny to be eating regularly at anyone's home. Maybe she'd been lost. Whatever the dog was, Holt knew it *wasn't* his problem. And he *wasn't* going to worry about it, he told himself as he grabbed an old horse blanket, took it back to the bunkhouse, and placed it under the porch.

Nope. Not his problem at all.

He wouldn't give it another thought. Especially since he had enough other things to occupy his mind, like a certain blond who wore cherry-flavored lip gloss and the hope of another mistletoe opportunity.

─────

Holt had just finished pulling on his boots the next morning when he heard a knock on his front door. He growled at his chest, reprimanding his heart for leaping at the hope that it was Lainey already, showing up to hang Christmas lights or to ask him for another favor that might entail them spending the day together again.

"Good morning, Cousin." Bryn smiled at him and held up a covered plate when he opened the door. "Can I come in? I made cinnamon rolls this morning and brought you some."

"I would never turn away a woman carrying a plate of cinnamon rolls," he told her, opening the door wider.

She swept in, and her tripod dog, Lucky, hopped in after her. Holt bent to scratch the dog's ears. He and Bryn were a perfect match, both dog and owner seeming to always have the sunniest dispositions, going through life seeing the good in people and radiating happiness wherever they went.

"Good," she said, already pulling a plate out of his cupboard and dishing a roll onto it before passing it to him. "Because this was an excellent batch.…and it's definitely *not* a bribe."

Uh-oh.

He took the roll, leaving the plate in her hand. It was still warm, and he groaned as he took a bite. The cinnamon and sugar combined with the butter and warm, yeasty bread brought back memories of being in his grandmother's kitchen. "Dang, that's good," he said around a second bite. "Just like Grandma's."

Bryn smiled at the praise. "I always use her recipe. Remember that time we'd gone sledding and got into that huge snowball fight and we were all frozen and soaked to the skin and we got back and she'd made us hot chocolate and these same rolls?"

He nodded, smiling with her at the memory. "We sat by the fire in those matching flannel pajamas she'd made us, and Cade made Bucky laugh so hard he snorted hot chocolate out of his nose."

"Ha. I'd forgotten that part. That was so gross."

"I remember the next day we went out and made that cool snow fort."

"*We* made the cool snow fort," she said. "You were too

busy making that huge snowman with Lainey to help us." Her smile fell. "Sorry, I know you don't like talking about her."

"It's okay," he said, swiping another roll. "She's back, you know."

"Who's back?"

"Lainey."

"McBride?"

He cocked an eyebrow in her direction as he stuffed the rest of the second roll in his mouth. "What other Lainey is there?"

"Oh my gosh," Bryn said, her eyes going round as she shook her head. "Lainey's *back*? After all these years." Then her shock must have started to wear off as she peppered him with questions. "Where is she staying? Where has she been? What's she doing here? Have you seen her?"

Holt held up his hand. "Calm down there, Sherlock. I only know about half the answers to those questions. I have no idea where she's been all these years—sounds like Montana for the last few, at least—but she's here helping her grandpa with the Christmas festival at Mountainside."

"Oh crud," Bryn said, the edges of her mouth turning down in a frown. "Then you're bound to run into her."

"Why's that?"

"Because we partnered with Walt to help out with some of the Christmas festival stuff. We're supposed to help with some of the decorations, and we partnered with him for the Ho-Ho-Hoedown this year. We found a great band that agreed to play for cheap, and I was going to ask you to take some straw bales over there and help set up the stage and the dance floor, but I didn't know about…" Her voice trailed off.

"Don't worry about it. I've already seen her. I was over at Mountainside yesterday and helped her with the sleigh rides."

Bryn blinked up at him. "*You* helped with the sleigh rides? That sounds like way too much of a Christmassy activity for you. How did you get roped into that? And how did I not hear about it?"

He shrugged. "I'm still not quite sure how I got roped into it either. And I'm surprised you hadn't heard about the sleigh rides *or* that Lainey was back. Seems like you hear everything in this town."

"Usually I do, but I hadn't heard about this." She studied him, moving her mouth from side to side as if considering if she should say something or not. "I don't think I ever told you this, but I've looked for her too."

"What do you mean?"

"Just every once in a while, I'll do a search for her on social media. You know, look her up on Facebook, check to see if she has an Insta. Sometimes I just google her name."

"And?"

"And nothing. I've never found any kind of profile for her or anything on Google. It was like she just disappeared off the face of the earth. I used to wonder if she'd been kidnapped or was an actual missing person."

"That's what I used to think too." He was ashamed to have thought that if Lainey had been taken, that would at least be a reason for her to have disappeared instead of just the simple choice that she'd left him behind.

"I'm sure she wasn't," Bryn said. "Because I've asked her grandparents about her several times over the years, and they always just say she's doing fine. It's weird though because they don't usually offer up much other information." She offered him a conspiratorial grin. "I've even tried to dig a little. You know how I can get."

"Yes, I know." He'd been on the other side of one of her "digs," and she always got more information out of him than he'd wanted to give. Which was how she'd ferreted out the information about him losing his fiancée and his horse. And how he ended up back in Creedence.

"But even my best detective skills didn't work. Walt always acted like he couldn't quite remember, and Elizabeth was always very skilled at changing the subject and focusing the conversation back on me. So I'd ask her about Lainey, then end up telling her about *my* latest dating fiasco. This was before Zane came into my life."

"But doesn't that seem weird to you?"

"Yes, totally weird. But it also makes me feel like there was more to the story of what happened back then. I *know* she loved you, Cousin. She loved all of us. So it just never made sense to me that she'd disappear like that. Without a word. And then never have her try to contact any of us."

"She never reached out to you?"

Bryn shook her head. "No. Never."

He leaned back against the counter. "I've never admitted this out loud, but I've done the same thing, looked for her on social media. And the only reason I have a Facebook account is to have a place for her to find me."

"I thought it was to show off all your rodeo prizes and your gorgeous girlfriend."

He huffed. "I never posted any of that crap. Talia was the one who was always posting pictures of us or bragging when I took a purse. She'd just tag me or whatever, so it showed up on my page. I swear, sometimes she acted like she was the one who'd won a buckle instead of me."

Bryn wrinkled her nose like she'd smelled something rotten. "Good riddance to that one, Holt. I know you loved her or whatever, but I never thought she was right for you."

"You met her one time when you came to see me ride at that rodeo in Fort Collins."

She shivered. "Once was enough. She just always seemed kind of fakey nice to me. Remember that was the night you dislocated your shoulder when you fell off the bull? And she kept giving you advice on how you could have had a better ride. She just acted like she cared more about your rodeo success than she did about you."

He shrugged. "She did. Which is why she left me for the guy who *did* stay on the bull longer that night."

"You're better off without her." She passed him the plate of rolls. "Want another one? I always like to feed my sadness with sugar and carbs."

He chuckled. "I'm not really sad anymore. I've gone from depressed to annoyed to mad as hell and have now settled into bitter and grumpy. But I'll still take another roll." He took a small one from the offered plate.

"I get that," Bryn said. "But you're not gonna win Lainey back being bitter and grumpy and anti-Christmas."

Her statement took him off guard, and he worked to swallow his last bite. "Who said I was gonna try to win her back?"

"No one, but the sappy look on your face when you told me about helping her with the sleigh rides sure implied it."

He wasn't about to admit that yet. Not even to himself. "I don't know *what* I'm going to do about Lainey yet."

"You need to talk to her. Ask her what the heck happened. I adored Lainey, but I love you more, and it always made me mad the way she broke things off with you. Mad and confused. It didn't seem like her to use her grandma to break up with you and then just write you a stupid letter."

"I agree. But that's what happened," he said, remembering that terrible Christmas Eve when Lainey had stood him up for the dance and her grandmother had told him she didn't want to see him anymore. He wouldn't have believed it if he hadn't gotten the letter from her a few weeks later saying basically the same thing.

"So you're going to talk to her, right?"

"Yeah, of course I am. Believe me, I want to know what happened just as much as you do." Although he had to ask himself if he wanted to start that conversation with Lainey more than he wanted another chance at kissing her. He nodded to the plate in her hands, ready to change the subject. "You said these rolls definitely weren't a bribe. What are you *definitely not* bribing me to do?"

"Oh gosh, with all this talk about Lainey, I almost forgot. Zane and I got a call this morning from an outfit in Montana that has taken in a bunch of rescued horses. Some slimeballs had been stealing horses and buying them supercheap from livestock auctions so they could take them out of the country to one of those slaughterhouses where they pay by the pound for old horses and then sell off the horse meat. The sheriff busted them, but now this rescue group has all these horses, and they need help taking care of them and tracking down their owners and getting them returned. They've got funding, so we'd actually get paid to help, which would be really nice for *our* rescues. They just don't have the manpower of folks trained to deal with this."

Holt nodded. "Yeah, you guys should go. I can take care of things here."

"I know you can. But I really do need you to help with the Christmas festival stuff too."

He raised an eyebrow. "I'm not sure you brought enough rolls for that."

"I know it's a lot to ask. But I already committed to Walt, and we need the funds the festival brings in just as much as Mountainside does."

Holt let out a resigned sigh. As much as he hated all this holiday crap, a small part of him recognized that helping out at Mountainside meant more time with Lainey. "Yeah, okay. I'll do it."

"Really?"

"Yeah, really."

She threw her arms around him and hugged his neck. "Thank you so much, Holt. And don't worry, I'll rope Cade and Nora and some of my friends into helping too."

"Why? Don't you trust me?"

"I trust you to haul straw bales over for seating and to

drive the sleigh, but you have to admit, your decorating skills *are* a bit lacking." She glanced at the still-full boxes of Christmas lights he'd yet to put up.

He lifted one shoulder in a shrug. "Yeah, all right, you make a valid point. But I won't let you down." His cousin had done a lot for him, and he owed her way more than a little help putting on a holiday festival. "When do you need to leave?"

"We're hoping to get on the road this afternoon. We've got to get packed up, but I think if we leave by three, we can make it to Casper by nine, spend the night there, then head on to Montana tomorrow."

"Makes sense. What can I do to help?"

———

It was just after three when Bryn and Zane pulled out later that afternoon. The ranch seemed quiet with them gone, even though plenty of animals were still there, including an adorable mini-horse standing on the front porch of the bunkhouse. It was a mystery how he, the goat, and the pig always seemed to get free.

"Shamus," Holt said, tipping his hat in greeting. "What's the good word?"

The horse let out a whinny and stomped his foot.

"I know the feeling," Holt said, opening the front door. "Would a carrot make it any better?"

The horse stamped his foot again.

A familiar blue SUV had pulled up in front of the

bunkhouse by the time Holt had retrieved the promised carrot and come back out to the porch. His breath caught at the sight of Lainey climbing out of it with a warm smile on her face. She wore a sage-green down vest over a white thermal shirt and jeans tucked into short Sorel snow boots, and her mass of curly hair hung loose around her shoulders. He remembered her as a teenager, so vibrant and full of spit and vinegar.

She'd been cute then, with the spray of freckles across her pert nose, but now...as a woman with lush hips and a new kind of wisdom and playfulness in her eyes, she was downright gorgeous.

"Hey there," she called with a wave. "You still need help putting up those lights?"

He nodded, unable to find his voice. He still couldn't believe Lainey McBride was standing right in front of him. Swallowing, he finally managed to say, "Yep."

You're a real charmer, Callahan.

Nobody said he was trying to charm her. But his heart knew he'd do just about anything for her. She'd shredded his emotions and pretty much wrecked him for years. Maybe still. But she was here now, smiling up at him, and that was all that mattered.

He finally passed the carrot to Shamus, who had been trying to nibble it out of his hand, then nodded toward the bunkhouse door. "I've still got the coffee on. You want to come in?"

Her smile widened, but she also tucked her chin a little as if she suddenly felt shy around him. Which was funny because Lainey had never had a shy bone in her body. "Yes, I do."

CHAPTER 7

"You still take it with milk and enough sugar to cause a cavity?" Holt asked as he poured coffee into a red Christmas cup.

She laughed. "Ha. No. I can't drink, *or eat*, like I did as a teenager. But it's nice that you remembered."

He remembered everything.

She glanced toward the refrigerator. "But I do love a little flavored creamer. Any chance you've got some of that?"

He nodded. "Sure. I've got peppermint mocha, pumpkin spice, gingerbread, and sugar cookie," he said, naming every ridiculous Christmassy creamer he could remember Bryn offering him the week before at the diner.

Lainey's eyes widened. "You do?"

He chuckled. "Hell no. Of course I don't. But I have some sugar and some milk that may not be expired."

She shook her head. "Half a teaspoon of sugar and a splash of questionably fresh milk. Although if a chunk comes out of the carton, I'm going to have to pass."

He laughed again as he pulled the milk from the fridge and checked the date. "Still good," he told her as he passed her the carton.

She doctored her drink, then held up the cup. "You've got

some pretty festive dishes here for a guy who proclaims to hate the holidays."

He raised one eyebrow. "I do hate the holidays. And those are *not* my dishes. Bryn pulled a fast one on me last week and exchanged my regular dishes for these when I was out in the pasture." He opened the cupboard to display a set of red-and-white dishes covered in a country Christmas setting, complete with a barn sporting an evergreen wreath, horses, a decorated tree in the yard with a snowman next to it and woodland creatures around its present-filled base, and Santa's sleigh flying through the starry sky. "Do you really see me picking these out?"

"They're so cute," she said with a teasing grin. "They're country-themed, and I love the snowman."

"You would," he said. "You still collect them? Snowmen, I mean?"

She'd started her collection when they were twelve. Holt had given her a stuffed one for Christmas after they'd made one in the yard, and she'd loved it so much, he'd turned it into a tradition and gave her at least one or two every winter after that.

"I do," she said, her smile wistful, as if revisiting a memory. "Most of them are packed away in the attic at Mountainside, just to keep them safe since we moved so many times, but there are a few I've kept with me and put up every Christmas. And I still use the little snowman tray on my dresser for my jewelry." She said the last part quietly before taking a sip of coffee.

He tried to keep his expression neutral. He knew exactly

what "little snowman tray" she was talking about. He'd given it to her, along with a snowman necklace, for her sixteenth birthday. The thought of her still using it and seeing it on her dresser *every day* had a flurry of emotion swirling through his stomach.

He sat his half-empty cup down, unable to recall even drinking from it. Being around her got his thoughts all jumbled up and had his nerves feeling wonky. He needed to get his focus on something other than the emerald-green color of her eyes and the shiny pink lip gloss that he wanted to kiss from her mouth.

"We might as well get this over with." He turned his back to her as he crossed the room and picked up the box of lights. Hefting the box into one arm, he held the door open for her.

He'd worried his voice had come out too gruff, but she didn't seem fazed at all as she put her cup in the sink, then clapped her hands like a little kid as she practically skipped out the door, leaving him in a heady scented wave of her floral perfume. "Yay. I love putting up lights, and I can't wait to add some cheer to this porch."

He nodded to Tiny, who was sunning herself in a patch of sunlight by the steps. "How much more cheer do you need when you've got a pig on your porch wearing a poinsettia tucked into her collar?"

"You make an excellent point," Lainey said, laughing as she crossed to give Tiny a chin scratch. The pig grinned up at her as she leaned contentedly into the scratch. Stepping off the porch, Lainey rubbed her hands together in anticipation. "Where should we start?"

He chuckled. "You look like an evil villain plotting some kind of takeover."

"More like world domination. But with a Christmas theme." She gave a villainous laugh. "Covering the planet with cheer, one strand of lights at a time."

"You're killing me," he said, shaking his head and chuckling as he followed her down the steps, then pointed to the front of the bunkhouse. "Let's just start with this part of the planet. Bryn said to do the bunkhouse first, then if we have any lights left, to try to frame the barn door with them. So I was thinking we should start by stringing them along the roofline." He dropped the box of lights on the steps, then set up the ladder he'd left sitting by the house a few days earlier when he was supposed to have started this job.

"Yes, good," Lainey said, then gestured to the front of the porch. "Then we can bring them down the cedar posts and run them along the railings."

Holt frowned. "That seems a little excessive."

"There's no such thing as excessive when it comes to Christmas lights," she said, pulling a thick strand from the box and passing it to him.

A staple gun was also in the box, so he pulled it out and started up the ladder.

"Wait," she said, pointing to the outlet on the front of the bunkhouse. "First you've got to plug them in to make sure they all work."

He passed her the end, and she plugged it in. The massive bunch of lights sprung to life in his hand. "Oh goody. They all work," he said with feigned enthusiasm.

"That *is* good," Laney told him. "It's much more of a pain when you have to test and replace a bunch of bulbs."

"If you say so," he said, climbing up the ladder again. He fixed one end to the edge of the roofline and stapled the strand to the wood. He passed her the jumble of lights. "You want to untangle this while I staple the next section up?"

"Yep." She worked the strands, pulling them over and under the bundle, then passing the next untangled set up to him.

Every few feet he'd move the ladder, giving her time to connect the next strand before he climbed up and stapled the next section in place. Working together, they didn't take long to string the lights across the roof and then start circling the cedar posts and going along the railings with them. The work wasn't hard, but Holt's heart pounded like a jackhammer every time she handed him a string and her hand brushed his.

"What about the rest of your place?" she asked, nodding toward his door as she held up the next section.

"What about it?"

"It's kind of blah in there. I mean, it looks amazing—Cade did an awesome job with the renovations—but don't you want some decorations inside? Or are you going to wait to do that until you put up your tree?"

"What tree?"

She raised one eyebrow as she planted her fist on her hip. "I know you're a little cranky about Christmas, but surely you're going to put up a tree."

"Don't call me Shirley," he muttered, suddenly focused on stapling the last section of lights.

"Holt."

He sighed. She wasn't going to let this go. He knew by the way she'd said his name. One word. Full stop.

"So I don't put up a tree. Who cares? It's not like I have any ornaments, and we're already using all the lights to be found on the ranch. And trees are for stacking gifts under, so how pathetic would that be if I just wrapped something up for myself and put a lone present under the tree. No thanks."

"They're for more than just presents," she said. "And you can *buy* lights. And ornaments."

He shook his head. "Not worth the time or the money. Bryn and Zane don't even know if they're going to be back for Christmas, so I'll be spending the day alone anyway."

"But—"

He cut her off, flashing her a stern look and hardening his tone. "Let it go, Lainey."

"Fine," she said with an exaggerated sigh. "For now," she muttered.

He needed to get the topic of conversation off him and his sad plans for the holidays. He really just wanted them to be over. "So what do you do in Montana?" he asked her, trying to put the focus on her. And maybe hoping to find out more about where she'd spent the last decade without putting her on the defensive by straight out asking her what the hell had happened to her.

She offered him a casual shrug, but he caught the tenseness in her shoulders. "Not much, really. I like to hike, and I try to sneak in a bike ride every few weeks."

"I mean for a job," he said. "I always thought you'd be a

great teacher. Or some kind of counselor or maybe something in HR. Or maybe marketing. You've always been great with people, but you're creative too."

"Thank you." She'd been fidgeting with the last strand, but she stopped and stared down into the lights. "I'm kind of *between* jobs now. But that's nice of you to say. And kind of funny too because I did spend a year teaching at a preschool. And also worked in a human resources department. I haven't done anything in marketing, but I have worked as a waitress, a bank teller, a salesgirl, and spent a fun summer as a magician's assistant."

"Wow. That's a lot of jobs. In a lot of different fields." He didn't ask her *why* she'd had so many jobs. But he hoped by staying quiet and keeping his focus on the task at hand, she might just tell him. From the corner of his eye, he could see her shift from one foot to the other.

"All right. To tell you the truth, I've been feeling a little lost. I can't seem to stay at one job for more than a year, sometimes for more than a few months. They just don't feel right, and while I'd be working at each one, I couldn't help feeling like I should have been doing something else. I just didn't know what that something else was. I can't figure out *what* I want to do." She let out a weary sigh. "Or who I want to be."

He climbed down the ladder and stood in front of her. She had her eyes cast down into the lights in her hands again. He took her chin and tilted her face up so her gaze met his. "You don't have to have *everything* figured out. Sounds to me like you're figuring out a lot of things that you *don't* want to do. And that's part of the process too. But as far as *who* you are. Why can't you just be Lainey? From what I remember, she's pretty great."

"I think you have a distorted memory."

He shook his head. "Nah. You've always been something special. You have this light in you that shines out and makes people want to be around you. And to have a little of that light shine on them."

She stared up at him, her eyes wide as she blinked back tears. Leaning her cheek into his hand, she closed her eyes and whispered, "Thank you."

With every fiber of his being, he wanted to kiss her. To lean in and capture that perfect mouth. He wanted to wrap her in his arms and tell her everything would be okay and beg her to stay here with him forever.

He swallowed. When had he turned into such a sap?

Since Lainey McBride had shown back up in his life apparently.

She opened her eyes, and then he wasn't sure if she moved toward him or he pulled her in, but suddenly her arms were around his waist and her body was pressed against his in a hard hug. He wrapped his arms around her and held on tight, trying to convey the feelings he couldn't say out loud in the strength of his hold.

He wasn't sure how long they stood there like that. It could have been minutes or hours. All he knew was that he didn't want to let her go. When she finally pulled back to look up at him, the desire to kiss her again overwhelmed him. This time he leaned in and pressed his lips to hers. It started out as a soft kiss, just the barest graze of his lips, then deepened as he relished the sweet taste of her mouth. It was the kind of kiss that held a promise of something more.

She jerked back like she'd been shocked as an annoyingly loud and way-too-cheery version of "Frosty the Snowman" burst from between them. The ringtone was jarringly irritating, but the buzzing generating from her hip pocket was a little too pleasant considering all the feelings already happening in that general area.

"Sorry," she said, blinking as if she'd just stepped into bright sunlight as she pulled the phone from her pocket. Glancing at the screen, then back up at him, she offered an apologetic look. "I've got to take this." She tapped the screen, then backed away as she put the phone to her ear. "Hello."

Holt turned back to their task, not only to give her privacy for her call but to collect himself. He sucked in a deep breath. That kiss had rocked him to his soul.

Trying to focus on something else, he stapled the final length of lights to the railing, then took a few steps back to inspect their work. Not half-bad.

"Okay, I'll see you in thirty minutes," Lainey said, before disconnecting the call and walking over to stand by Holt. "Sorry, I had to take that. It was the president of the Women's Club in town. I'm planning their Christmas brunch on Thursday, and they need to meet with me today to finalize some details."

"You're planning the Christmas brunch for the Women's Club? How'd you get talked into that? Haven't you only been in town a few days?" Had she been here longer and he just hadn't known?

"I've been here a week, but that's beside the point," she said. "Their event planner went into labor last week. She was two weeks early and just had the baby, so I guess they were desperate. The president of the club knows my grandpa, and he suggested that they ask me to fill in."

"And you said yes?"

"Heck yeah. I love this kind of stuff. And I've already added a few things to make it better. No offense to the other planner—I get that she had other things on her mind—but she was just putting together a simple brunch. I've added stuffed mushrooms, mini quiches, and a chocolate fountain and gotten several businesses in town to donate items for a raffle."

"But why would you do it at all?"

She gave him a confused look. "First of all, they're *paying* me. Which is important, since if you recall our earlier conversation, I don't currently have a job, and a girl's gotta eat. And secondly, I love this kind of stuff. It's been really fun."

"It sounds about as fun as a fork in the eye."

She laughed as she nudged his arm. "You are such a grump."

"Maybe. But I'm a grump who doesn't have to order a chocolate fountain or plan a Christmas brunch."

"But you do have to get these lights up, and I only have thirty minutes before I have to be in town for this meeting. So we need to get crackin' and finish."

"I just put the last one up while you were on the phone."

He pointed to the railing where he had stapled the final strand.

"Oh yay." She took a step back to admire their work. "They look great. Are you ready to turn them on?"

Interesting choice of words since a few minutes ago she'd been totally turning *him* on. He couldn't help wondering what would have happened if they hadn't been interrupted by the phone call. "Yeah, sure."

She skipped back to the other end of the house where they'd first started and picked up the cord they'd left hanging down to plug into the socket. "Oh no," she said, her shoulders sagging inward.

"What's wrong?"

She showed him the end of the plug. It was missing two key elements to make the lights work—the prongs. "We started with the wrong end." She slapped her palm to her forehead. "And I'm the one who handed it to you like that. I can't believe I did that—what a rookie mistake."

"It's not that big a deal."

"Yes, it is," she said. "We're gonna have to take them all down and start over."

"Like hell we are," he said, turning and heading toward the barn. "I'll be right back." He found what he was looking for in the tack room, then hurried back to the bunkhouse. "Problem solved," he said, holding up a thick green extension cord. He went up the ladder on the opposite end from her, plugged the extension cord into the lights, then dropped it and ran the cord along the front edge of the bunkhouse until he got to Lainey.

"You're just going to have that ugly extension cord hanging down like that?" she asked, pointing to the offensive cord.

"Hey, it's green, so it's at least kind of Christmas-ish." He plugged it into the outside outlet and the lights popped on. "See? It might not be perfect or the way we planned it, but it still works."

"True. And I'll bet we've got just enough lights left over to frame the barn door," she said, pulling another mangled handful from the box.

He groaned but had to smile at her impish grin as she held up the lights. "Fine. Let's do it."

It took them less than fifteen minutes to string the final lights around the outside of the barn door. This time they put up the end of the string with the pronged plug first.

"We did it," Lainey said. "And with a few minutes to spare. We make a good team." She held up her hand for a high five.

Holt slapped her hand, then turned away to walk into the barn. They *had* made a good team. Once upon a time, they'd made a *great* team. So why had she left and then broken up with him?

Pushing down those thoughts—the five minutes she had left before she had to leave wasn't enough to start *that* conversation—he found another extension cord and plugged the lights into an outlet just inside the barn.

Lainey clapped her hands together as the lights came on. "Yay. They look beautiful."

Holt squinted at the twinkling colorful lights. "They look *up*, and that's all that's important to me. Now I can get my cousin off my back."

"And you have beautiful lights up for Christmas," she said, heading toward her car.

"Yeah, that's what I was gonna say next." He offered her a wry grin as he opened the driver's side door for her. "Hey, speaking of my cousin, Bryn said our ranch is partnering with you on some things for the festival, and I promised her I would do my part. So let me know if you need my help with something."

She tilted her chin as if trying to ascertain if his offer was genuine. "Really?"

"Really." He nodded and pointed to his chest. "Holt Callahan, at your service, no job too big or too small. Hay bale hauler, sleigh driver, car parker, and I'm pretty good with a hammer and screw gun."

"Wellll, I could use your help tomorrow. I have to set up the kids' crafting corner, the holiday-card photo booth, and a station for writing letters to Santa. Plus, I need to pop some popcorn for the children to string on garlands, and I want to get some signs put up for the weekend. And I need to collect some pine cones for a craft project I'm doing with the kids. Would you be able to help me with some of that?"

"I can help with all of that."

A goofy smile creased her face. A smile that had his stomach doing a little flip. "Wow. Thank you. How about I feed you lunch, then we can spend the afternoon knocking some stuff off my list?"

"Sounds good. I'll be there at noon."

"Bring the screw gun."

CHAPTER 8

THE NEXT DAY, LAINEY WATCHED HOLT'S FACE AS SHE SET the plate in front of him holding two grilled cheese sandwiches and a steaming bowl of tomato soup. It had been his favorite lunch when they were kids.

She was rewarded with the smallest quirk of one side of his lip as he peered down at the plate, and she felt like she'd won first prize at the county fair. Getting a smile out of Holt hadn't been this hard when they were younger. Now it seemed as if he offered them less freely. Which made it all the more valuable for her to win one.

"Good sandwich," he said after demolishing the first half in just a few bites. "I haven't had grilled cheese and tomato soup in a long time. Makes me think about how your grandma used to make this for all us kids. She'd call us in and have a huge stack of sandwiches on a plate in the middle of the table. She'd make us line up at the sink to wash our hands, then hand us a mug of soup as soon as we finished." He took a sip of the soup, then smiled. "Just as good as I remember."

"It should be," Lainey said. "It's her recipe."

"She was a neat lady," Holt said, tucking into his lunch. "I'll bet you miss her."

"I do. Everything about being here reminds me of her.

And she loved the Christmas festival. It was one of her favorite times of year. That's why I have to make sure I don't mess it up. It meant too much to her. And my grandpa."

"You won't mess it up."

"I don't have the best track record when it comes to following through." She was getting jittery just thinking about all the ways she could screw this thing up. One of those ways was sitting right in front of her, but she couldn't let seeing Holt Callahan again derail her from her mission of making the festival a huge success. Which meant she could hang out with him but still needed to keep a healthy distance between them. Holt reached out and put his hand on top of hers, settling the nervous jitters bouncing around her belly. "It's all going to be fine. Even if it's not perfect, it's still going to be fine. And I'm here to help."

She turned her palm over and twined her fingers with his, then squeezed his hand. "Thank you. That means a lot." So much for a healthy distance. Unless distance somehow entailed holding hands.

He looked at her for a hard second, narrowing his eyes as he stared into hers, either trying to convey a message or searching for an answer to a question hidden there. She had questions too. *So many questions.*

But when it came right down to it, she was a coward. Maybe that was why she had a hard time sticking with a job. That was for sure why she wasn't facing down Holt—asking him what happened all those years ago and demanding to know if he had ever really loved her.

It felt easier this way. Safer. They were on solid footing

and having fun together, and she liked being with him. She didn't want to screw things up with him by pushing for answers to something that happened over a decade before. See? *Total coward.*

She knew they would eventually have to talk, but that conversation and his reasoning, or excuses, for deserting her could take hours and send her spiraling into that dark place where she'd been years ago. And she didn't have the time, the mental energy, or the courage to revisit that heartbreak today.

"Speaking of helping," Holt said, releasing her hand to point to the shopping bags he'd carried in with him and set on the counter. "I brought you something."

Her curiosity was piqued. What could Holt have brought her that filled up two shopping bags? She crossed to the counter to peer inside, then grinned up at him. "There are six gallon-size bags of popcorn in here. Did you pop this?"

"Would you believe me if I said Tiny did?"

"No," she said with a laugh. "But I can't believe *you* did either. You just gave me back at least an hour out of my day."

"I get up early, so I had some time," he said with a casual shrug. But she was sure she caught a small smile playing at the corners of his lips. "Is it enough?"

"Yes. It's perfect. Thank you." She grabbed her notebook and a pen. "I'm crossing it off my list."

He peered over at the full page of items. "You have a whole *page* of things to do?"

She huffed out a laugh. "This is just for this afternoon. I have a page just as full for every day leading up to the festival."

"Dang. Bryn wasn't kidding when she said you needed my help." He mopped up the last of the soup with the remains of his sandwich, then shoved it into his mouth and pushed up from his chair. "We'd better get started then."

They spent the next several hours working together to prep the kids' activity stations and build the selfie photo booth. Then they drove up and down the main highway and placed signs at strategic points to direct folks to the festival. It was close to four by the time they made it back to the ranch.

"What's next?" Holt asked.

Lainey looked through the windshield at the waning sun. "I don't know how much daylight we have left, but I still need to collect several bags of pine cones for the peanut-butter-pine-cone-bird-feeder craft, and I have to pick out a tree and get it delivered tonight."

"Where did you want to go to get the pine cones?"

"I was thinking up the ridge between our ranch and yours. You know that old logging road that goes up between all the pine trees?"

"Sure." He nodded to the toolbox in the bed of his pickup. "I've got a saw to cut down the tree and a box of garbage bags to collect the pine cones. Do you need anything else?"

"Yes, but it will only take me a few minutes to grab it." She pushed open the truck door and called over her shoulder as she hurried up the porch steps, "Be right back."

She raced around the kitchen, filling one bowl with water and popping it in the microwave while she dumped several packets of hot chocolate mix into a pitcher. Pouring in the heated water, she quickly mixed up the cocoa, then transferred it to a thermos. Grabbing a box of candy canes and the thermos, she dumped them into the box she'd prepared the night before. On a whim that she didn't want to think too much about, she grabbed a bottle of her grandpa's peppermint schnapps from the pantry and tossed it into the box too. Covering the bottle with her scarf and a pair of mittens, she picked up the box and hurried back outside.

"Geez, what all do you need to collect some pine cones?" Holt asked, taking the box from her and stowing it in on the floor of the cab while she climbed back into the truck.

"Don't worry about it. I may have a few surprises in there."

"Oh good," he said, putting the truck in gear as she buckled into her seat belt. "Nothing I like more than surprises. I can only hope it's something full of cheer and Christmas magic."

"Sarcasm does not become you, Holt Callahan," she said in her best attempt at southern primness.

Holt chuckled softly as he maneuvered the truck down the pasture lane. He knew the way, and they both got quieter the closer they got to the logging road. The turn up the mountain was just past the cottonwood tree where they used to meet, where she'd left him the letter that last night—the night that changed everything.

She'd known something was wrong when her mom and stepfather had shown up at her grandparents' that night. They weren't supposed to come until Christmas Day. Her stepdad hadn't been able to get off work until Christmas Eve. They arrived in a flurry of excuses about the weather and some schedule changes at Randy's job, but Lainey had smelled the alcohol on her stepdad's breath and recognized the too-fast way her mother was talking, the breathy, breezy tone she used that tried to make everything sound all right and keep anyone from asking about her swollen eye, the scrape on her cheek, and the bruises on her arms.

Lainey was supposed to meet Holt that night at their tree, but something told her that she wasn't going to make it. She'd tried to call him several times, but there'd been no answer at the ranch. And none of them had had cell phones then.

She knew she needed to get him a message, just in case. She'd written the letter in a hurry, but her message was clear. If she and her mother had to disappear, she'd meet him on her eighteenth birthday at the Sunrise Cabins at the base of Pikes Peak, the place they'd always talked about going to on their honeymoon. She'd written for him to bring a pink rose if he still wanted to marry her. It seemed a silly thing to say now, but she'd only been seventeen and the idea had seemed romantic at the time. She'd put the letter and a few mementos of their relationship in a cigar box and sealed it in two zippered gallon bags, just in case they got wet from the snow. Then she wrapped those in a pink plastic shopping bag so there was no way Holt could miss it.

She'd known she wouldn't have much time, so she snuck out while the news was on and raced across the pasture. Her shoes were muddy as she climbed the tree, up to their favorite limb, and crammed the box into the space where the branch met the trunk. Racing back to the farmhouse, she prayed that everything would be okay, that her stepdad would just pass out on the couch or that her grandparents would be able to protect her and her mother.

If that happened, she could always retrieve the box in the morning, and Holt would never have to know. She'd told him her stepdad was a real jerk, but she still wasn't sure why she'd never shared the extent of the abuse her mother had suffered at his hands. Shame, mostly. And the time she spent on her grandparents' farm, with Holt and the other Callahan kids, felt like an alternate reality, one in which everything that happened with Randy couldn't touch her.

She remembered sometimes thinking if she told Holt about the things that happened in her other life, the fear and anxiety would somehow bleed into the perfect time she spent in Creedence with him and his family.

"You okay?" Holt asked, gently touching her leg and pulling her out of her memories.

"What? I mean, yes, I'm fine," she answered, letting out a shaky breath.

"You looked about a million miles away," he said as he pulled to a stop in a clearing filled with pine trees.

More like a decade away. "Sorry. I just got lost for a second."

He nodded, his expression solemn. "Easy to do. Lot of memories here."

She shook her shoulders, as if physically shaking off the memories. Thinking about all that old stuff wouldn't help with getting all the work done that they needed to do. "Lots of new memories to make," she said, pushing the past and her time with Holt back into the tiny space where she usually kept it locked away.

He pointed to the clearing. "This okay? Looks like there are plenty of pine cones."

She peered through the window at the abundance of them littering the ground surrounding the pine trees. "It's perfect."

"And what do you need all these pine cones for?"

"They're for that craft table we set up with the birdseed and the yarn. The kids tie a piece of yarn to the top of the pine cone, then slather it in peanut butter and roll it in birdseed, then hang it in a tree as a bird feeder."

"Didn't we make those one time with my grandma?"

She nodded, pleased that he remembered. "That's where I got the idea. Remember, we were eleven or twelve, and we all acted like we were too old to care about doing a dorky craft, but she'd packed all the stuff and brought a picnic and took us all up to the lake."

"I remember. It was hot that day, and we rode up in the back of the truck. We went swimming, then sat on the rocks and ate my grandma's cold fried chicken. Dang, she made the best fried chicken."

"I remember Bryn and I working so hard to make the bird feeders, and then we hung them all up in that little clearing by the waterfall."

Holt laughed. "I don't remember working hard to make them or hanging them up. I just remember Cade and Bucky and me using those tongue depressors to slap each other and fling gobs of peanut butter at you girls."

She'd forgotten that part but laughed with him as she remembered it now. "Oh my gosh. Bryn was so mad that Cade lobbed a gob of peanut butter into her hair. Then your grandma got him back by smooshing a handful into his. Then she made us all get back in the water, and she swam out into the lake and had us all float on our backs with her. Your grandma was awesome."

"Yeah, she was." Holt turned his head away, but Lainey caught the expression of sadness on his face before he opened the truck door and stepped out. "So how many pine cones do you need?"

"I'm hoping we have a couple hundred kids show up, so I'd say we need at least two hundred, maybe three."

His eyes widened. "Three hundred pine cones?" He pulled a couple of trash bags from the toolbox in the back of his truck and passed one to her as she came around the front of the truck.

She pulled on her gloves before taking the bag, then offered him a playful grin. "I'll race you to see who can collect a hundred the fastest."

"You're on," he said, already running toward the trees.

She let out a shriek as she raced after him, then dropped down next to where he was shoveling pine cones into his bag. "You're not even counting," she cried as she grabbed three at a time and dumped them in her bag.

"I'm guesstimating," he said, laughing as he tossed one into her bag.

"That's not even a word." A light snow started as they continued to fill their bags. "Thirty-seven, forty, forty-five." Lainey counted out loud as she threw handfuls in.

"Seventeen. Eighty-nine. Omaha," Holt shouted, trying to mess her up.

She wasted a pine cone by tossing it at him. "You're only doing that because you know I'm winning."

"No way," he said, holding up his bag. "This has to be at least a hundred."

She loved having fun with him, laughing as they played around and teased each other. By the time they'd filled their bags, the snow was coming down in big fluffy flakes and starting to cover the ground.

Holt held his stuffed bag next to her smaller one. "I have no idea how many I have, but it's twice as many as you and I heard you counting in the nineties, so I'm sure I'm the winner."

She smiled sweetly up at him. "Ah, but I think I'm the *real* winner here."

"How do you figure?"

"Because look how fast we collected three hundred pine cones!"

He laughed with her, and the sound of his deep chuckle ignited something inside her belly. He didn't do it as often as when they were younger, but his laugh now had a deeper, more manly timbre that made her think of rich melted caramel.

He took their bags and secured them in the bed of the pickup.

She rubbed her hands together to keep them warm. "I brought hot cocoa," she told him, holding up the thermos. "You want a cup?"

"Sure. Since you brought it."

She took off her gloves, then pulled out two mugs that were shaped like Santa heads, the tassel of each Santa's hat forming the mug's handle.

He frowned at the cup. "Are you really gonna make me use that? Can't I just drink mine straight out of the thermos?"

"No way," she said, pushing the mug into his hand, then dropping half a candy cane into the warm cocoa. She sheepishly held up the bottle of schnapps, not knowing how he would respond to the offer of an afternoon drink. "You want yours with a little kick?"

He raised an eyebrow in her direction, and a grin tugged at the corner of his lip. "Sure. But just a small one. I've still got to get us off this mountain."

She twisted the lid off the bottle and poured a splash into his cup, then added a bigger splash to hers. Because she knew what was coming next, she added another big splash, then stirred the alcohol into the cocoa with the end of the candy cane before taking a sip. The schnapps sent warmth down her throat and into her chest. "Wowza. That's got *quite* a kick." She took another drink.

Holt was watching her, amusement dancing in his eyes, but he didn't comment on her slight wheeze from the strength of the alcohol as he took another drink of his. "What's next on the list?"

"We need to find a perfect tree, then deliver it to someone special. Once we find it, I may collect a few more pine cones while you chop it down."

He pulled a battery-powered Sawzall from his toolbox. "Okay, but we'll be *sawing* it down, not chopping it. One, because I didn't bring an ax, and two, because I'm not a lumberjack."

"If only," she muttered softly. "With your scruffy beard

and rugged jawline, you would make a great lumberjack." Dang. She hadn't meant to say that out loud. The schnapps must be kicking in already.

His eyes widened in surprise, and he huffed out a small chuckle. "I heard that. But somehow, I don't think a jawline is what makes a good lumberjack." He rubbed his hand thoughtfully over his jaw as he teased her. "But it's nice to know you appreciate my five-o'clock shadow. And I guess I do have *some* lumberjack skills. I can wield an ax, and I'm good with my hands."

She swallowed at the memory of his hands on her body. If he could make her feel that good as a teenager, she could just imagine what he could do to her now. And she *was* imagining it. *Stop.* She ordered her brain to think of something else but couldn't seem to keep the flirty tone out of her voice as she playfully nudged him with her shoulder. "Let's go find that tree and then you can show off all your lumberjack skills."

She was blaming it on the booze.

They downed the last of their cocoa, then put their cups back in the truck before setting off into the trees. The snow was falling harder now, and she couldn't help feeling like they were walking through a wintry forest-filled snow globe.

"This one looks good," Holt said, stopping at the first tree they came to that was under seven feet tall.

She shook her head. "Nope. The branches are too scraggly. Good height though. Five or six feet tall is perfect."

"Okay, less scraggly," he muttered as they walked deeper into the trees. "How about this one?" he asked, pointing to a wide tree that looked to be barely five feet tall.

She shook her head again. "Too short. And too round and bushy. No room for ornaments."

"Geez. Who is this tree for? The head of the town council?"

"Ha. No. If it were, then that tree would be perfect because it kind of looks like him," she said, thinking of their rotund councilman with his abundant white beard and thick, erratic eyebrows.

"Short, round, and bushy?"

"Exactly." It wasn't that funny a joke, but she giggled anyway, which had to mean she was really feeling the effects of the schnapps now.

They trudged on, and Holt pointed out several more trees that Lainey also vetoed.

"It has to be just right," she said, hurrying a little to catch up with him. Her foot caught on an exposed tree branch, and she pitched forward.

Holt reached out and grabbed her as she fell, catching her in his arms as if they'd been dancing and he'd dropped her into a dip. He held her that way, almost as if in midair, for an extra beat as he stared down at her. His gaze traveled from her eyes to her mouth, then to the exposed skin of her neck where her jacket had come open. She saw the hunger in his eyes just before he dipped his head and brushed his lips softly against her neck.

Her head dropped back, and her eyes fluttered as she relished his warm breath on her skin. She caught sight of a small group of trees behind her, just as he pressed a tender kiss to her neck, and cried out, "Yes, that's it."

She felt the rumble of Holt's laughter against her neck. "I like your enthusiasm, darlin'. But I haven't even gotten started."

"No…I mean, yes, I do like it…that…very much…but I meant…that's it," she said, pointing over her head to the spot behind her. "That's the perfect tree."

CHAPTER 9

LAINEY CRINGED AS HOLT HAULED HER TO HER FEET. *That's the perfect tree?* How could she have noticed *any* tree when Holt Callahan had just kissed her neck. Her *neck*—one of her favorite spots to be kissed. Did he remember that? Or was that just one of his moves now?

It didn't matter. He'd let her go and was striding toward the tree she'd pointed to. "This one?" he asked. "You sure this is the one?"

She couldn't read his perfectly even tone. Was he upset or annoyed that she'd flubbed up his kiss or amused that she'd found a tree while he was focusing his attention on her? "I'm sure," she told him. "That's the one."

Using the Sawzall, he only took a minute to cut the tree down. Then Holt picked the whole thing up by the trunk and started back to the truck. "Can you grab the saw?" he said over his shoulder.

"Yes, I got it." She picked it up, careful to hold it by the handle. That was all she needed, to saw off one of her fingers. "I just love pine trees," she said, hurrying after Holt. "I think they're so cool. They can withstand heat and cold, and they can grow in all sorts of climates. They're survivors. And I read somewhere that they represent wisdom and longevity. Isn't that cool?"

"Sure," Holt said.

"*And* they ensure their own survival by making pine cones." She was rambling. She could hear herself doing it, but she couldn't seem to stop. "Did you know it takes a tree two to three *years* to create *one* pine cone? I mean, that's something right there."

"You sure know a lot about pine trees," Holt said, lifting the tree higher and setting it in the back of the truck. He held out his hand, and she passed the saw to him. He secured everything in the back of the pickup, then held the door for her.

She slid into the truck, and her mouth started up again once he'd climbed into the driver's seat and started the truck. "I know a lot about pine cones too. Because they contribute to the regrowth of the pine tree by protecting and nurturing their seeds, they're known as symbols of rebirth and renewal and everlasting or eternal life." Gah. She sounded like a textbook. Or her grandpa, since he was the one who'd taught her all that stuff.

"I see," Holt said, steering the truck back down the logging road. The snow had made the road much slicker than when they'd gone up, but he was going slowly and keeping the truck in the ruts even when the back end tried to slide out. "Do you know anything else about pine cones?"

"Yes. I know that if you put a silver pine cone on your mantel during the holidays, it will bring you good luck in the coming year."

"I had no idea pine cones were so fascinating." He snuck a glance at her, and she caught the amused smile playing around his lips.

"Are you teasing me?" She nudged his shoulder again. "You're teasing me. Here I am, sharing my fount of wisdom about all things pine cone, and you're just laughing at me."

"Not laughing *at you*, darlin'. *With* you. And your knowledge of pine cones and pine trees is impressive."

They got to the bottom of the road, and she pointed left instead of right. "It's shorter if we go through your ranch."

He turned left, and they bumped through the pasture and came out between the barn and the bunkhouse. She pointed to his porch. "You can just park over there."

He pulled the truck up to the porch and cut the engine, then turned in his seat to level a cool stare at her. "Any chance all this pine-cone talk was just a distraction?"

She widened her eyes with what she hoped looked like innocence. "A distraction for what?"

"You want to tell me who this *special person* is that we're delivering this tree to?"

"Sure." She offered him an impish grin. "We're delivering it to this friend of mine whose kind of a grinch and needs more Christmas spirit in his life."

He shook his head, then leaned it onto the top of the steering wheel. "You've got to be kidding me."

"Christmas trees are no joking matter," she said, hopping out of the truck. "Now come on and help me get your new tree inside. It's cold out here."

He reluctantly climbed from the truck and lifted the tree from the back end. She grabbed the box she'd packed and ran up the steps ahead of him to hold open his front door.

"I don't even *want* a tree," he said, hauling it inside and leaning it up against the wall. "And besides that, I don't have a tree stand or any lights or any ornaments. So it's basically like we're putting a giant houseplant in my living room. That will die in a matter of days because there's no way to water it."

She huffed as she set her box down on his sofa. "Do you think I would let a Christmas tree die on my watch? I brought you an extra tree stand we had in the barn *and* some lights *and* a few decorations," she told him, pulling each named item out of the box and setting them on his coffee table.

He groaned and dropped his head back. Then he reached for the bottle of schnapps still in the box. "I think I'll take that spiked cocoa now. Or better yet, I'll just drink this straight." He unscrewed the lid and took a healthy swig, then passed the bottle to her.

When in Rome… Or in this case, when in your old boyfriend's living room forcing him to put up a Christmas tree… She knocked back a swig, then choked at the burn in her throat. "That goes down much easier when it's in cocoa," she wheezed.

"Then you'd better pour me another cup," he said, reaching for the tree stand. "If I have to put this dang tree up, then it isn't the only thing that's gonna get lit."

"That's the spirit," she said, laughing as she grabbed the thermos and made them each another spiked cocoa.

An hour and a few more drinks later, they had the tree up, the lights on, and the few decorations Lainey had brought hung on the tree.

"Aww, it's so cute," Lainey said.

"It's pathetic," Holt said, regarding the measly number of

ornaments and the lone Christmas ball. "It's got fewer balls than I do."

She barked out a laugh, then covered her mouth. But once she started, she couldn't stop the laughter, especially when Holt joined in.

"It's true," he said. "And having only half a dozen ornaments is just sad."

"Oh no. This tree is supposed to bring you Christmas joy, not make you depressed. I'll get you some more ornaments. We can check in our grandparents' attics. I'm sure one of them has some extra Christmas stuff."

"I know my grandparents' attic does. Bryn sent me up there to find something last month, and it's still packed. But you've already done more than enough for me. And you have plenty of other things to worry about rather than the quantity of my Christmas balls."

She snorted again, then clutched her middle. "Stop it. You're making my stomach hurt from laughing so hard."

"Mine too. I can't think of a day in recent years when I've laughed so much." He offered her a sheepish grin. "As much as I hate to admit it, I had fun today."

"Yay," she said, clapping her hands. "And the fun's not over yet. Just wait until we light this thing. You won't even notice the lack of ornaments." She smiled again but couldn't bring herself to say *Christmas balls*. "Sit down on the sofa and get ready," she told him as she reached for the cord. They'd laughed at themselves earlier when they'd made a point of starting to string the lights with the correct end this time. She liked the fact that they were making new inside jokes between them. "Ready?"

"As I'll ever be." He sat down on the center cushion and stretched his arms out across the back of the sofa.

"Wait." She dropped the cord and ran around to turn off all the other lights in the room. The moonlight glinted off the snow and bathed the room in a silvery light that shone through the big picture window. She gingerly made her way back to the tree, stepping carefully and trying not to sway. She'd had way too much schnapps and not enough cocoa, which probably accounted for why she'd laughed so hard at Holt's dirty joke.

She pushed the plug in and gasped as the colored light from the tree filled the room. "It's beautiful," she said, crossing the room and sinking onto the sofa next to him. As captivated as she was by the lights on the tree, she was still hyperaware of the press of his thigh against hers and the fact that she'd just nestled into the crook of his outstretched arm.

"You're beautiful," he whispered as he lifted a lock of her hair and rubbed it between his fingers.

She turned to him, surprised that he was looking at her instead of the tree, but what she saw in his eyes had nothing to do with the tree. It was longing and desire, feelings she recognized well, having had them herself every time she'd been around Holt the last few days.

His gaze dropped to her mouth, and heat like molten lava swirled through her chest and into her belly. He let go of her hair, and his fingers trailed softly over her neck and along her jawline. Her lips parted, and she sucked in a quick breath as his thumb grazed her bottom lip.

Every nerve in her body was going haywire with heat

and shivers, tingles and trembling. How many nights had she lain awake thinking about Holt? How many times had he appeared in her dreams, fulfilling the very thing she was imagining now?

She swallowed, her mouth suddenly dry, as she tightened her hands into fists, curling her thumbs over her fingers to keep them from reaching up and yanking Holt down on top of her. Her head tried to argue all the reasons this was a bad idea—she should be focused on the festival, he'd broken her heart, she had questions she needed answers to—but her schnapps-steeped body couldn't care less about all that stuff.

Her body yearned for Holt with a fierce ache that had been brewing for over a decade. They could talk another night. *This* night, all she cared about was feeling the hard press of his body against hers and touching him again.

He leaned in, and she inhaled the scent of him: woodsy aftershave, leather, pine, and a hint of chocolate and peppermint. Uncurling her fists, she reached out and pressed a hand to the spot over his heart on his chest. It was a thing they used to do, swearing that they could feel each other's hearts beating, just for them. They'd been stupid teenagers then; they were all grown-up now, and the stakes were even higher than they'd been back then.

He closed his eyes and dropped his chin as if her touch caused him physical pain. She started to pull her hand away, but he caught it in his and held her fingers to his lips, pressing a hard kiss against them. "I've missed you so much," he whispered against her palm, his voice husky and raw with emotion.

Her heart ached for the lost years, and she yearned to touch more of him, to have his lips on hers, to feel the weight of him over her again. "I've missed you too," she whispered back, her throat dry at the same time she blinked back the tears filling her eyes.

His other arm went around her, and she sucked in another breath at the feel of his palm on her waist. He leaned closer, letting go of her hand to cup her cheek. She breathed him in, and it was as if her inhale pulled his lips closer to hers. She yearned for him to kiss her, with every fiber of her being.

Closer still, his palm tightened on her cheek as he tipped her face up and then...finally...his lips grazed hers. Just the softest touch, but it was enough to send swirls of heat coursing through her veins. Another kiss, soft, tender, then another, this one more urgent, another, more demanding.

She felt the slightest pressure from his hand on her waist, drawing her closer. Then she wasn't sure if he pulled her in or she scooted toward him, but suddenly she was straddling his lap with her arms around his neck and his hand under her shirt, skimming across her skin and sending delicious shivers racing through her.

The kiss deepened until she couldn't tell whether she was breathing out or he was breathing in. His hands moved over her, touching, caressing, holding. He trailed hot kisses down her neck and across her chest as his fingers worked the buttons of her shirt free. His breath was warm against the tender clefts of her breasts as he skimmed his lips over the lacy edge of her bra. Her nipples tightened, aching with need and begging for his touch.

She arched her back, giving him more of her to feast on and letting out a moan as he pulled down the cup of her bra and grazed his teeth over her taut nipple. She needed more, needed his skin against hers. As if reading her mind, he drew back for just long enough to pull off his flannel shirt, then tug his T-shirt over his head and drop them both to the floor. With deft hands, he unsnapped her bra and the lacy fabric slipped away.

He flipped her over, so she was on her back on the sofa, and she reveled in the feel of his weight on top of her. She couldn't get enough of kissing him, touching him, of his hands on her body.

Yes, the alcohol was probably playing a part in how quickly things were moving, but it was more than the schnapps. She felt drunk on the essence of him, of being with him, of feeling the scruff of his whiskers against her neck, the callouses of his palms raking over her waist. She didn't care that they'd only just reconnected a few days ago. Her body, no, her *soul* knew his, and this felt exactly right.

She wanted him, *all of him*, and she could feel the same ravenous hunger and yearning coming from him. The growling sounds he made in his throat as he cupped her lush breasts in his hands, the sharp intake of breath when she kissed his neck and brushed her fingers lightly over his bare chest.

The rest of the world melted away as they rediscovered each other, exploring with their hands and mouths, kissing and touching in the soft glow of the lights on the Christmas tree. She still believed in the magic of the holiday, and this felt like a Christmas wish come true to be back in Holt's arms, to hear his sweet murmurs of affection in her ear.

They weren't teenagers anymore, but it felt like the crazy intensity of teenage passion in the way they shimmied out of their jeans while still kissing. Holt's hands shook as he fumbled for his wallet, dropping it, then swearing as he dug out a foil packet and almost dropped it too.

She stared at his body, taking in the changes. His shoulders were broader, and the muscles of his arms were harder. She loved a guy's arms, and Holt's were drool-worthy, the way they stretched against the fabric of his sleeves, but holy hot cowboy, they were even more amazing with his shirt off. His hands were big, and she loved the feel of them on her body. Her heart melted a little at the way those big hands were shaking now as he struggled with the tiny packet, finally ripping it open and covering himself.

Was he as nervous as she was? The booze was culling the majority of her nerves, but she still felt trembly inside as he positioned himself above her. She had no idea who Holt Callahan had become over the decade they'd been apart. He could have turned into a serial killer or a vampire.

Well, she knew a little about him, but just things she'd gleaned from his meager social media account. She knew he'd spent years on the rodeo circuit and had been involved with a gorgeous blond. If he *had* turned into a serial killer, it wasn't evident in his posts. Or in the way he'd treated her since they'd reconnected. He'd been grouchy and sullen, yes, but he'd also treated her with gentle care, as if she might break or disappear. And he'd laughed with her. And that mistletoe kiss had conveyed he still had *some* feelings for her.

Stop. She didn't need social media to tell her who Holt was. She *knew* him. Had known him since they were ten years old. Had loved him almost since the day they'd met.

He braced himself on one elbow, his face inches above hers, and the lights from the tree reflected in his eyes. His voice was low, his tone full of concern and care. "You okay?"

"Yes." She breathed out the word.

"You sure? I know we've been drinking. I don't want you to regret this in the morning."

"Yes, Holt, I'm sure. I want you. I want this."

He touched her cheek, and she melted at the way his fingers trembled against her skin. "No regrets?"

"Not from me," she whispered. "You sure you're okay?"

His lips curved into a roguish grin. "Oh, I'm sure."

Her smile turned coy. "No regrets?"

"Not one."

"Then kiss me like you mean it." The words had popped out of her mouth before she'd had time to think. It was what they used to say to each other. *Maybe he won't remember.*

His arms stiffened, and he blinked. *He remembered.*

The words were already out there. She didn't know how to take them back—didn't know what to say.

But apparently she didn't need to say anything because Holt knew the right words, the response they'd always used. "I always mean it when I kiss you."

Her chest tightened as she caught her breath, and she blinked back sudden tears. Her throat stung with the emotion of missing this man maybe more than she'd even admitted to herself. But she didn't have time to think about that because he leaned in and captured her mouth in a kiss that affirmed he meant *everything*.

She kissed him back with a hunger that she hadn't known was inside her, burying her face in his shoulder as they moved together in a dance both new and familiar. Their bodies still seemed to fit perfectly together, and she reveled in the feel of his hands skimming along her skin, alternately caressing and stroking, then gripping her to him as soft, rumbling moans came from deep in his throat.

She gave herself to him, every part of her, as she surrendered to the passion coursing through her. The sweet sensations built inside her, spinning and swirling, until shudders ran through her and she cried out as her world shattered and she fell apart in his arms.

Afterward, they lay curled together on the sofa, their legs entwined, the small space drawing them closer together, but she was all too happy to be wrapped around him with her head snuggled into the crook of his shoulder.

She didn't want to mess up this time they'd spent together. Everything about it had felt perfect. *Almost* everything. There was still the underlying question of why he hadn't shown up to meet her.

But there would be time to talk about all that later. Best to just leave it for tonight and enjoy this feeling. That's what her head was saying. Then her mouth blurted out, "Hey, Holt, did you ever get my letter?"

CHAPTER 10

LAINEY CRINGED AS SHE FELT HOLT'S SHOULDERS TENSE, and he looked away. It felt like the air in the room had just shifted, and not in a good way.

Why couldn't she keep her big mouth shut?

"Yeah, I got it," he said, his tone flat with an edge of defensiveness.

She wasn't sure why he suddenly seemed angry. "*And?*"

He let out a sigh. "And…I don't know what you want me to say. We were dumb kids back then."

"I know that. But I just thought—"

He cut her off before she could finish her sentence. "I know what you thought. But things didn't work out for us. And now I just want to leave the past in the past. You're here with me tonight, and that's all I care about. I like being with you. Spending time with you." His gaze dropped to her mouth and a roguish grin curled his lips. "Kissing you."

His response was vague at best, but she couldn't help smiling back. His grin made her insides feel like jelly. "I like all that too."

"Then let's not drag all that old stuff back out. You know how much I care about you. I always have and always will."

She shook her head. "How would I know that?"

He gave her a look, one she recognized, the kind of look that used to pass between them that meant they got what the other one was thinking. "Come on, Lainey."

"Okay. Yeah, I know."

"So can't we just forget about what happened all those years ago and move forward?"

Before she could answer, they were interrupted by a noise at the bunkhouse door. It sounded like something was scratching at the bottom of the wood and then let out a small whine.

Holt lifted his head, twisting his head as if to listen more intently. "Did you hear that?"

"Yeah, I did. Was that an animal?"

"I don't know. It was something." He pushed off the sofa and shimmied into his briefs and jeans before crossing to the door.

She picked up his flannel shirt and pulled it on as she followed him. He opened the door, and she looked down to see a small brown scruffy dog shivering on his doorstep. "Oh my gosh, you poor thing."

Holt peered down at it. "So you finally decided to come out from under the porch?" He opened the door, and the dog ran inside, raced around the living room, then huddled against the throw blanket they'd knocked off the couch.

"Is this your dog?" Lainey asked, taking a few tentative steps toward it.

"Not hardly. I'm guessing she's a stray. I found her cowering under my porch a few days ago."

"Oh no. Poor baby. She must be starving."

"I don't think so."

She gazed back at him, the way he'd said that last thing carrying an odd tone of…humility, maybe.

He shrugged off her look. "I put a blanket under the porch, and I've been setting food out for her a couple of times a day."

"That must be why she came to your door. She trusts you."

"I don't know about that. She's probably just hungry."

Lainey regarded him with a raised eyebrow. "So you're not such a grinch after all."

He huffed a laugh. "Oh yeah, I'm still a total grinch. About Christmas. But not when it comes to animals. Then I'm just a big pushover." He crossed the room and sat down on the floor a few feet away from the dog. He held out the back of his hand for the dog to sniff.

She hesitantly stretched out her neck to sniff at his knuckles, then gave his hand a quick lick.

"It's okay," he told the dog, his voice gentle and coaxing. "Nobody's gonna hurt ya."

Lainey held perfectly still, afraid to break the spell of the connection he was making.

The dog gave a low whine but scooted a few inches toward Holt.

"That's it. Come on, girl," he said, patting his leg.

She scootched forward a little more, then paused to look up at him, her eyes wary. He gave her a small nod, then she stood up and ran forward, leaping into his lap and curling against his chest.

"Aww," Lainey whispered, her eyes tearing at the trusting look the sweet dog was giving Holt as he stroked her sodden back.

"She's just filthy," he said, running his hand over her neck. "Her hair is all matted, and she's got dirt and ice caked in her paws. She needs a bath and a warm bed."

"How can I help?"

He nodded toward the kitchen. "There's some dog food in a Ziploc bag under the sink and some plastic bowls. If you want to give her some fresh water and a dish of food, I'll go out to the barn and see if I can't find a box and an old blanket."

"I'm on it."

The dog left his lap when Lainey set down bowls of food and water, and Holt stood and pulled on his boots and T-shirt. "I should probably check on all the animals and get them fed too," he said, reaching for his coat and cowboy hat. "You okay with her for a few minutes while I go take care of some stuff?"

"Yes, of course. We'll be fine." She was actually a little thankful to have a few minutes to herself to take a breath and collect her thoughts over what had just happened. She hadn't seen Holt Callahan in over a decade, and he'd just taken her to O-Town on his living room sofa. *Twice.*

He'd also told her he'd always cared about her and always would. He hadn't made any excuses or offered any reasons for why he hadn't shown up at the meeting spot. Instead, he just said he wanted to forget about all that and move forward.

Yeah. There was a lot for her to think about. Except her

brain seemed to go on vacation when Holt was around, especially when he was kissing her. And when he was doing that thing with his mouth…sigh…then there was no thinking at all.

―――――――――

It took Holt less than twenty minutes to toss some hay bales to the animals in the corral and feed the horses in the barn. By the time he'd found a cardboard box, an old blanket, and a bottle of flea and tick shampoo and then made it back to the bunkhouse, it seemed that Lainey and the stray had become best friends.

Or at least that's the way it looked when he walked in to find the dog curled in Lainey's lap. "Looks like you've made a friend," Holt said, setting his things on the counter. "She's kind of a mess and I don't know what she's gotten into under that porch, so I figured we should probably give her a bath right away. I don't reckon she'll like it, but I think she'll feel better once we get her cleaned up and cut out some of that matted fur."

"I agree," Lainey said.

He was right. The dog was not thrilled with the bath idea, but between the two of them, they got her shampooed and scrubbed and then used Holt's beard trimmer to cut out the worst of the mats. After her bath, they rubbed at her with a couple of towels to dry her fur.

"Would you look at that?" Holt said as the dog broke away from them to shake the water from her body. "I thought she was a brown dog, but apparently that must've been all dirt because she looks white to me now."

"Me too."

They followed her back into the living room where she shook herself again, then padded over to the box Holt had fixed up for her. She sniffed at the blanket, then pawed at it to reshape it to her liking, then circled around inside it before finally settling into its folds. She let out the smallest sigh as she laid her head on her paws and then closed her eyes.

"Aww," Lainey said. "Sweet puppy. She doesn't look like she's going anywhere for the night."

Holt frowned at the thick flakes of snow swirling outside the window. "No, and I don't think we are either. The snow hasn't stopped, and it was already pretty slick out when I went to the barn earlier."

She offered him a seductive smile, or at least that was the kind of smile he hoped it was. "Are you inviting me for a sleepover?"

A nervous flutter quivered in his belly. *Dang.* He hadn't been nervous around a woman in years. But none of the women he'd been around had been Lainey. He offered her what he hoped was a flirty grin in return and not just a dorky smile from a guy who'd been in love with her for over half his life. "Yeah, I guess I am."

She raised her shoulders in an innocent shrug. "I didn't bring any pajamas."

"You won't need any." He grabbed her waist and pulled her to him, then grimaced at the cool feel of their soaked clothes between them. "I think we may have gotten just as wet as the dog did."

Lainey pulled her damp shirt away from her skin and wrinkled her nose. "And we smell like wet dog too. I think I need a bath now as well."

"You're free to use my shower," he told her. "I've got soap and shampoo. I can't say how fancy it is, but I'm pretty sure it's better than the dog's stuff."

"I think I'll take you up on that offer, since I'm spending the night and all." She was still wearing just his flannel shirt, and she worked the buttons free as she started to walk toward the bathroom. She dropped the shirt to floor, leaving her in only a tiny pair of thong panties, and looked at him over her shoulder. "You want to join me?"

"Yes, I do," he said, already tugging his shirt over his head.

———

The next morning, Holt woke up but felt like he was still dreaming. He couldn't quite believe that Lainey was in his bed, her naked body spooned into his. Her hair spread over his pillows, and he wanted to bury his face in it.

She groaned and squirmed around to face him as her eyes blinked slowly open. She offered him a shy smile, one that felt like they shared a secret. "Good morning, cowboy," she said, her voice still husky from sleep.

"That it is," he said, unable to keep the grin from practically busting his face in two or his body from responding to her squirming. "How'd you sleep?"

"What little we did of it felt amazing." She ran her fingernail down his chest. "Actually, *everything* we did last night felt amazing."

He chuckled. "You know, we got a whole lot of snow last night. I'm not sure I'll be able to even get my truck out. And we've got the ranch to ourselves, and no one even knows we're here. So we *could* just spend the whole day in bed."

"I think that's an idea I can get behind."

He wiggled his eyebrows as he grinned down at her. "I've got another idea of something I can get behind."

Her eyes widened, then she barked out a bawdy laugh. "You, sir, have a dirty mind." She playfully batted her eyelashes. "But I kind of like it."

"Oh, I know you're gonna like it," he said, pulling her toward him, then leaning down to nuzzle a kiss against her neck.

"Promises, promises." She giggled as she rolled over onto her stomach. Pulling her hair over one shoulder, she looked back at him with a naughty grin that sent his pulse racing and a surge of heat through his veins.

He lowered his lips to her shoulder and laid a hot trail of kisses down her spine and into the curve of her waist. All traces of giggles were gone as she squirmed under him and let out a soft, kittenish sigh. He pulled back the blankets and groaned at the sight of her naked and willing body. He leaned down to press another kiss to the smooth skin at the small of her back, already imagining ways to turn those small sighs into moans of pleasure.

He raised his head and growled at the sound of an

engine coming down the driveway. And it was an engine he recognized.

Lainey rolled over, already reaching for the blanket to cover herself. "I thought you said we had the ranch to ourselves."

"We do. Or we did," Holt said, trying to get the words out while all he could think about was how disappointed he was that she'd just covered that luscious body back up. He was going to kill his brother. "Nobody *is* supposed to be around today. I thought the snow would keep people away." He got out of bed to look through the window.

He knew it. That engine *was* his brother's truck. Cade had bought a snowplow for the front of his pickup earlier that fall and been picking up extra money by plowing roads and driveways. But he couldn't have had worst timing by plowing down Bryn's this morning.

"Who is it?" Lainey asked, clutching the sheets to her chest.

"It's no one important. I'll get rid of them," he told her, already pulling on a pair of jeans. "Stay here. I mean stay *exactly* like you are. And don't forget where we were." He flashed her an impish grin as he leaned down to press a quick kiss to her lips. "Keep that last thought in mind especially."

The dog was still asleep, curled up in the folds of the blanket and tucked down in the box. But she woke up as he strode into the room, grumbling as he shoved his arms into a flannel shirt. She raced over to him as he was wrenching his boots on and followed at his heels as he flung open the door and stepped out onto the porch. The dog ran off the porch and out into the snow to take care of business.

Cade pulled up to the bunkhouse and cut the engine. He waved as he got out of the truck and headed toward him. "Mornin', Brother."

"What the hell are you doing here?" Holt asked as Cade bounded up the porch steps.

He jerked his head back. "Is that any way to greet the guy who just risked life and limb to plow your driveway so you could get out of the ranch today?"

"Who says I *wanted* to get out of the ranch today?"

Cade's reply was cut off by the squeal of delight coming from Allie, his thirteen-year-old daughter, as she climbed out of the passenger side of his truck.

"Oh my gosh. Uncle Holt, when did you get a dog?" She knelt down and called the scruffy stray to her. "Here, girl."

The little dog hesitated, cautiously stretching her nose out to sniff at the girl's hand, then with her little furry butt wiggling, she came close enough for Allie to pet her head and ruffle her neck.

"She's not *my* dog," Holt said. "She's a stray I found hiding under the porch."

His niece laughed as the dog licked her chin and nuzzled into her neck. "She's so cute."

"So is that what's got the bee up your butt? A stray dog?" Cade asked as he pushed past his brother and into the bunkhouse. "I mean you've been pretty crabby lately, Brother, but right now you look like you could kill someone."

"I could kill you," Holt muttered under his breath. "I just wasn't expecting visitors."

"We're not visitors," Allie said, scooping the dog up into

her arms and following her father into the house. "We're family. Or at least that's what you tell me when you're trying to get me to load the dishwasher after we have supper at your house."

She had a point.

"Dude, what is going on? You don't even have any coffee made," Cade said, holding up the empty pot from his coffee maker. "Were you still in bed? You never sleep this late." He took a step back. "Are you sick?"

"No, I'm not sick. But yeah, I was still in bed." He lowered his tone. "I just wasn't sleeping."

Cade looked over his shoulder, and a dawning expression followed by a goofy smile lit his face as he must have taken in the array of clothing spread across the living room. "You sly dog."

Holt groaned. He might have been able to come up with a reason for the pair of women's snow boots to be sitting next to the sofa, but there was no other explanation for the black lacy bra flung across the coffee table. "It's not what you think," he sputtered, then cursed himself for the way his eyes cut to the hallway leading to the bedrooms.

Cade's eyes widened as he jerked a thumb in that direction. "Is she still here?"

Holt leveled him with a stare. "Do you think she would leave without her...?" He tilted his head toward her scattered bits of clothing.

"Allie, we'd better get going," Cade said to his daughter, who was on the floor cuddling with the dog.

"We can't leave yet. We still have to talk to Uncle Holt about Sarah," she said.

"Yeah, but your uncle is a little busy right now."

Unfortunately, he *wasn't* busy right now. He'd been *about* to get busy…until they'd arrived. "Who's Sarah?"

"You know, I'm not a little kid anymore, Dad," Allie said, rolling her eyes at Cade. "I know Uncle Holt has a woman in the bedroom. Unless that bra is his," she said pointing to the lacy brassiere. "And if it is, that's okay. You be you. But I'm pretty sure the reason he's acting all grumpy is because we interrupted them."

It was Cade's turn to groan. "Quit growing up so fast."

"She's right though," Lainey said as she walked into the living room, wearing what obviously had to be Holt's clothes. She had on a pair of baggy gray sweats that she'd cinched up with the drawstring and a black T-shirt bearing the logo of some rodeo he'd been in.

Cade's mouth dropped open as he stared at her. He shook his head in disbelief. "Lainey?"

CHAPTER 11

HOLT SIGHED. SO MUCH FOR KEEPING LAINEY ALL TO himself.

She offered his brother a warm smile. "Hi, Cade."

"Lainey," he said again, then strode across the room to enfold her in a hug. "What are you doing here? *How* are you here? Where have you been?"

Even though they'd agreed the night before to leave the past in the past, Holt was still interested in hearing the answers to those questions.

"I'm in town helping my grandpa with the winter festival at Mountainside," she explained.

Cade turned to him. "Did you know she was back? I mean, of course you know she's back, but have you guys been in touch?"

Holt shook his head. "No, I was just as surprised as you when I ran into her at the ranch a few days ago."

The dog leapt out of Allie's lap and ran over to Lainey, jumping up against her legs and whining as if she wanted to be picked up. Lainey reached down to pick up the dog and cuddle it to her chest. "Good morning, sweet dog." She smiled at the teenager, then glanced back at Cade. "This can't be Allie. She was just a baby the last time I saw her."

"She's still a baby to me," Cade said.

"Oh, Dad." Allie rolled her eyes. "Yes, I'm Allie. How do you know my dad?"

"We grew up together." Lainey gestured to both brothers. "We all did. My grandparents own Mountainside, the neighboring ranch to this one."

"We used to all hang out together, Bryn and Bucky too, whenever we were all staying at our grandparents'," Cade explained. "Summers and holidays, mostly. But we met when we were just kids. In fact, I was about your age when this one came riding up to our ranch on a big black horse."

Lainey offered the girl a warm smile. "It's nice to see you again. I didn't know your mom very well, but I'd met her a few times. My grandpa told me what happened. I'm so sorry."

The teenager shrugged and muttered a quiet "Thanks" as if she still wasn't quite sure how to handle comments about the accident that took her mother's life earlier that year.

Lainey set the dog down, and it ran back over to Allie, who pulled it into her lap and laughed as it tried to lick her chin.

"She's beautiful, Cade." Lainey rested a hand on Cade's arm. "You doing okay?"

Cade nodded. "Yeah. I'm doing good."

"I heard you bought Larson's old farm. And that you met someone."

"Yes to both charges. Her name is Nora, and you're going to love her. We moved out to the farm last summer and have spent the majority of our time since then fixing it up. We all love it, but it's a ton of work."

"You still rodeo?"

He shook his head. "Nope. My bull-riding days are behind me. I'm just a boring old family man now."

Allie laughed. "Yeah, right. You love it."

Cade grinned. "I do. And Nora is awesome. I can't wait for you to meet her."

"I can't wait to meet her either. I'm sure I'll see you all at the winter festival. You're coming to the festival, right?"

"Oh yeah, of course. Bryn's got us roped into helping with a bunch of the festivities, so you can count on us for whatever you need."

"That's so nice of you," Lainey said, sneaking a quick smile at Holt. "I'd forgotten how wonderful this small town is. Everyone is so willing to pitch in and help."

Cade moved back into the kitchen and took out the coffee. He dumped heaping teaspoons into the filter, then turned on the water to fill the pot. "The winter festival means a lot to this community."

"It does to me too. I'm really excited to be a part of it and to be able to help my grandpa."

"How's he doing? I heard that he busted up his hip. It must be killing him not to be at the ranch," Cade said, pouring the water into the machine and then hitting the brew button.

"It is. He's anxious to come home, but he's hanging in there," she said. "Holt and I took a Christmas tree over to the assisted-living center where he's staying. We set it up in the common area and got it all decorated, and I know he and the other residents appreciated the effort."

Cade glanced his way, a surprised expression on his face. "Holt decorated a Christmas tree, huh? How'd you talk Mr. Scrooge into doing that?"

Lainey laughed, but it was not lost on Holt how she'd completely ignored and deflected Cade's questions about where she had been and what she'd been doing for the last decade. "I bribed him with sugar cookies. But he's not a total Scrooge." She pointed to the tree in the living room. "He's even got his own decorated tree now."

"I wouldn't really call that decorated," Allie said, wrinkling her nose at the sparsely adorned tree.

"I wouldn't either," Holt said. "And I want it noted that I put up that tree under duress."

"It's true," Lainey said. "But I just keep flinging the spirit of Christmas at him like handfuls of glitter and hoping some of it sticks."

"I hate glitter," Holt grumbled.

"I love it," Allie said.

"Well, good luck with that," Cade said. "You've got your work cut out for you with this grinchy guy."

Lainey shrugged and winked at Holt. "Oh, I don't know. I think he's coming around."

He didn't say anything. He was too busy trying to keep his lips from pulling up in a grin at the way she'd winked at him. Dang, he had it bad.

"Well, we should probably go," Cade said, taking one of his travel mugs from the cupboard and filling it with coffee. "Let you two get back to your…Christmas decorating or whatever you were doing."

"Dad, we can't leave yet," Allie said. "We haven't talked to Uncle Holt about Sarah."

"Who's Sarah?" Holt asked again, thankful to have the conversation switch to anything other than him and Lainey and what they were going to get back to.

"Sarah Gardner. She's a girl I know from school," Allie explained. "She's a year younger than me, but she's really sweet and we like a lot of the same books, and we usually sit together at lunch. But the past few weeks, Sarah hasn't been bringing her lunch. She kept saying she forgot it, but I didn't believe her, and she finally admitted to me that her family is going through a rough time. Her dad lost his job, and they're struggling to pay their bills and buy groceries."

"That's tough," Holt said, not sure what any of this had to do with him.

"It is. But that's not the worst part. Well, I mean, that's bad that the family can't buy food, but they also can't buy food for Copper, her horse. And they want Bryn to come and get it and find a new home for it."

"Oh no," Lainey said, pressing her hand to her chest.

"I know, it's awful. Sarah's been crying about it for days. She loves that horse. He was her first 4-H project, but now she's had him for five years and he's her best friend," Allie said. "So I was thinking maybe you could just go get it and keep it here, then give it back once her dad gets another job."

Holt frowned. "That's not really how the rescue ranch works."

"Why not? It's still rescuing a horse. Couldn't you just stall on trying to find a new home for him?"

"I don't know, kiddo." Holt scrubbed a hand across the back of his neck. "And Bryn's not even here. She's out of town for a few weeks."

"Then it has to be you."

"Why don't we just wait until she gets back. Surely they can hold on for a few weeks."

Allie shook her head. "They can't. Her parents want to either get rid of the horse or sell it and use the money for bills. It was my idea for Bryn to go rescue it. But we have to do it now."

Holt frowned. "Look, I know I'm a grinch about the holidays, but I'm not an asshole. I can't just go take this little girl's best friend away right before Christmas."

"I know. I hate it too. But if they can't buy groceries for their kids, who knows if they're even feeding the horse. It could be starving."

"Damn, kid." Holt rubbed at his chest. "You're killing me here."

"It's a tough situation all the way around," Cade said.

"Let me think on it a bit, okay?" he asked his niece.

She nodded. "Okay. But don't think too long."

"I hear you."

"All right, honey. We've bent your uncle's ear long enough," Cade said. "And we need to get going anyway. Those roads aren't gonna plow themselves."

Allie gave the dog one last cuddle, then set it down and stood up. She crossed the room to give Holt a hug. "Thanks, Uncle Holt."

He hugged her back. "No promises."

"Good to see you, Lainey," Cade said.

"Nice to meet you," Allie said, waving as she followed her dad to the door.

Lainey waved back as she came to stand next to Holt. "Wow, I can't believe how grown-up she is."

"Yeah, she's pretty great."

She nudged his shoulder, teasing him. "So it's not just animals that you're a pushover for, huh?"

He couldn't hide his smile. "Nah. I love that kid. I don't want to speak ill of her mom, but Amber kept her away from Cade and our family for a long time. It's been a tough year for her, but she and Cade have been figuring it out. And she loves Nora. We all do."

"I can't wait to meet her."

He looked around the kitchen. "You want some coffee?"

"Sure," she said. "Since your brother was nice enough to brew it."

He poured them each a cup, then pulled the bottle of fancy creamer he'd picked up at the store earlier out of the fridge and passed it to her.

Her lips broke into a wide grin. "Since when do you have creamer in your refrigerator?"

He gave a casual shrug but was happy that he'd pleased her. "Since you told me you liked it, I guess. It's no big deal." He focused on his own coffee but still watched her over the rim of the mug as he took a drink.

"It is to me. And French vanilla is my favorite." She poured some in her cup, stirred it around, then took a satisfied sip. "Mmm. That's delicious."

He couldn't help but grin, proud of himself for getting her favorite kind and then thinking of other ways to get her to wear that satisfied smile. "Glad you like it. You hungry? You want me to make some bacon and eggs or something?"

She took another sip of coffee, then set her cup down and sidled up to him. "I am hungry. But not for bacon and eggs." She pushed up on her tiptoes and pressed a kiss to his neck.

He groaned before reaching his hand under her T-shirt and brushing his fingers across her waist. "I sure enjoy seeing you in my clothes, but I'd much prefer to see you out of them."

"I think that could be arranged," she said, pulling his shirt over her head and dropping it to the floor. She flashed him a coy grin. "As long as I get to see *you* out of your clothes too."

Later that afternoon, Holt was loading bales of hay into the back of a horse trailer when he looked up to see the now-familiar SUV coming down the driveway. He was surprised because he'd only dropped Lainey off at Mountainside about an hour ago. Why was she back already?

Not that he was complaining. His lips were already curving into a smile as she got out of the car and hurried toward him. She must have had enough time to take a shower because her hair was curly and still damp on the ends and the scent of her shampoo and perfume wafted around him as she got closer.

"Hey, long time, no see," he said, then chastised himself for such a stupid comment.

She paused, the excited expression on her face faltering. "I hope that's okay. I mean, that I just came over. I know that we were just together, but I had this idea and wanted to tell you about it."

"It's absolutely okay. You can stop by anytime." He pulled her against him and gave her a kiss that he hoped told her just how okay he was with seeing her again so soon. "Now what's this idea you wanted to tell me about?" he asked after letting her go.

"Idea?" she muttered, a dazed look on her face.

He grinned down at her, loving the idea that he had as much of an effect on muddling her thoughts as she did on him.

She blinked, then nodded her head. "Idea, yes. I had this idea about how to help with Sarah and her horse situation."

"I'm listening." Actually, he was only half listening because he was distracted by how dazzling her smile was and how pretty she looked with the slight flush to her cheeks. And how ridiculous it was that his stomach was doing flips over being this near to her when he'd spent the night and most of the morning naked and in bed with her.

"I was thinking what if instead of *taking away* her horse, we found a way for her to keep it? At least through the holidays."

"What did you have in mind?"

"Allie was worried that the horse wasn't eating or that they didn't have enough money to buy food for it, so what if we dropped off some hay bales and a few bags of sweet feed? Then the horse could stay with Sarah, and the family wouldn't have to worry about the expense of its upkeep. I'd be willing to chip in some money to help."

He didn't say anything, just grinned down at her.

She wrinkled her brow. "What? Do you think that's a dumb idea?"

He shook his head, then took her hand and pulled her around the trailer to show her where he'd already loaded close to a dozen bales of hay and a fifty-pound bag of sweet feed. "I think it's a great idea. In fact, I was thinking the same thing. This should be enough to get them through the holidays."

Lainey laughed, then threw her arms around him in a hug. "When are you taking it out to them?"

"I was getting ready to head out there now. You want to come with me?"

"You bet I do."

He opened the truck door for her, and she laughed again as a blur of white darted out of the barn and jumped into the truck ahead of her. The little dog propped her paws on the dashboard and let out a happy bark as Lainey slid into the seat next to her. "Looks like someone wants to go for a ride."

He shook his head. "I let her outside after I got home from dropping you off, and the dang thing's been following me all over the ranch ever since. She was shivering as she watched me load all this hay, so I stuck her in the barn, but she must have thought we were gonna leave without her."

"Have you thought of a name for her yet?" Lainey asked

him after he'd gone around the truck, then climbed into the driver's seat.

"I've been calling her Dog," he said as he started the engine and pulled out of the driveway.

"That's not a real name," Lainey told him.

The dog's tail wagged with excitement as she peered out the front windshield, then she settled into the seat, lying down and putting her head on Holt's thigh.

"She doesn't seem to mind it. Besides, if I give her a name, then that would imply that I'm keeping her."

CHAPTER 12

HOLT SPARED A QUICK GLANCE AT LAINEY BEFORE TURN-ing his eyes back to the road. His chest hurt at the thought of it, but he meant what he said. "And just to be clear," he told her, "I'm *not* keeping this dog."

Lainey sucked in a breath as she reached to pet the dog's side. "What do you mean? Why wouldn't you keep her? She's obviously already attached to you."

"She just likes me because I feed her. But look at her. She's too friendly not to be someone's pet." After getting over her initial skittishness of the night before, the dog had been cuddly and affectionate, either following after them if they walked around the bunkhouse or rolling over for belly rubs if she was sitting next to them. "Some family is probably missing her."

"Maybe."

"I need to at least call the Humane Society and the sher-iff's office to see if someone's looking for her."

"Okay, but if no one claims her, then she's for sure your dog. And you should totally name her something Christmas-themed, since this is the time of year when you found her. How about Holly? Or Mistletoe? Or how about Carol?"

He cocked an eyebrow. "What a great idea. Then I can

always be reminded of this holiday I'm such a huge fan of. And also, if I *were* keeping her, there's no way in hell I'd name my dog Carol. Or Mistletoe. Unless you want me to just turn in my man card right now."

Her eyes went dreamy as she stroked a finger along his sizable bicep. "As if. And no, I'm quite partial to your man parts. I mean your manly parts. Wait, I mean your manli*ness*." She dropped her head into her hands. "Pretend I did not say that."

"Too late. You already said you loved my man parts."

"I said partial to...and anyway, we were talking about the dog. And thinking of ideas of what to name her."

"*You* were thinking of what to name her. But I'd rather go back to talking about what you love about my—"

She held up her hand to cut him off. "What about Jingle or Snickerdoodle for a name?"

"For my man parts? I don't think they'd take too kindly to being called Snickerdoodle, but Jingle Balls does have a certain holiday ring to it."

She let out one of her hearty laughs, the kind that came from her belly and snuck out as a surprise. The kind that made his manly heart melt like butter on a hot biscuit. "We are *not* going to start talking about your Christmas balls again," she said, still laughing. "How about Eggnog or Snowy? For the *dog*."

He grimaced. "How about *not*?"

He was acting grumpy, but he was really having fun with her. Too much fun. She was so easy to be with, and not just to be *with*, but to be himself with. He was only this comfortable with a few select people. Although his comfortableness with her was also interspersed with moments of fluttering heart-beats and a racing pulse whenever their hands touched or her shoulder brushed his or if he caught a whiff of her delicious scent. Her nearness could send jittery nerves spiraling through his stomach that made him feel like a love-crazed teenager, which probably shaved several points off that man card they were just discussing.

She tapped her fingers to her lips. "Okay, I'll stop with the too cutesy. But I really still like the idea of a Christmas name. Just give me a second. I know I can think of a good one. Hmm. I suppose Cindy Lou Who is out?"

He shrugged. "Not if I can shorten it and just call her Lou."

She leaned down to the dog's face. "Is your name Lou? Do you like that?" The dog licked her nose, and she laughed. "Okay, Cindy Lou Who it is."

"Glad we got that settled. We're here." He turned into the driveway of the Gardner farm and pulled up in front of a faded red barn. A white two-story farmhouse sat across from it, and a leaning snowman with a stick for a nose and two rocks for eyes stood sentinel in the front yard. Holt peered through the windshield. "Wonder if we should have called first."

Lainey waited in the truck while he went up to the house, then came back a few minutes later. "No one's home."

"Well, then why don't we just leave the hay and food for them to find? Like we're Santa's elves delivering a package."

He thought about it, then shrugged. "That's not a bad

idea. That way, they can't turn down the offer of free food for the horse. I was a little concerned about how they would take to the idea."

"Now we don't have to worry," Lainey said, getting out of the truck. "But do you think it's weird that we're just going into their barn?"

"Yeah, a little. But it's for a good cause. And if they come home and catch us, we'll just explain we're from the horse rescue." He told the dog to stay, then headed toward the barn. "But we should probably check to make sure the horse is actually here before we start unloading."

She followed him into the barn, reaching out to take his hand as they entered the shadowy depths. She shivered against the cold, and he wrapped an arm around her shoulder. "Do you see the horse?" she whispered.

He shook his head. "No, I can't see much of anything." His eyes adjusted to the dark interior of the barn as they walked down the center alley. He'd seen a few head of cattle out in the corral, but most of the stalls inside were empty. Or almost empty, like the one that seemed to be reserved for hay. There were only a few bales left stacked against the side.

A snuffle sounded from the next stall, and they peered inside to see a reddish-toned gelding standing inside. He was thin but didn't appear to be malnourished yet, although he seemed a bit lethargic, and his coat had lost much of its luster. A wooden sign hung from the stall door with the name COPPER etched in the wood.

"Hey, boy," Holt said, holding out his hand. "How are ya, buddy?"

The horse plodded toward him, probably hopeful that he had food. Holt had stuck a few sugar cubes and some apple slices in a baggie in his jacket pocket, and he held the sugar out for the horse. Copper's velvety lips snuffled the cubes off Holt's palm, and the horse nodded his head as if in thanks. Holt held up the baggie to Lainey. "You want to give him some apple?"

She nodded eagerly. "Yes, please." She held the slices out on her flattened palm and scratched the horse's neck as he nibbled the apple from her hand. "You're a sweet boy, aren't you?"

Holt surveyed the barn. "I think we can leave the hay and bag of feed next to his stall. Then there's no question that it's for the horse."

"Good idea."

"Let's get it in here before they come home and find us in their barn."

They worked together, moving quickly as they hauled in the bales and bag of feed. Lainey poured a scoop of the sweet feed into the horse's trough while Holt put a half of a bale of hay into his manger. Copper tucked into the fresh hay, munching it as he surveyed their running back and forth with supplies. When they'd finished, they each gave the horse another neck scratch, and then they hurried back to the truck and got out of there.

Lainey's eyes shone with mischief as she bounced up and down in her seat like a little kid. "That was fun. I feel like Mr. and Mrs. Claus. Who else can we sneak some gifts to?"

Holt chuckled, trying not to think about the fact that

she'd just compared them to an old married couple. "I don't know. And I don't have any other gifts. I'm not sure who else would appreciate a bale of hay or a can of grain."

"True. But that was still fun. Thanks for inviting me along."

"Thanks for wanting to come."

She settled back into the seat with the dog...Lou... He was going to have to get used to that. Although he was still hesitant to call her by any name, sure that she belonged to some family who was probably missing her.

The drive back to the ranch went by way too fast. He tried to think of an excuse to get Lainey to stay longer, but nothing came to mind. Besides, he had work to do at the ranch, and he was sure she had a million things to do too.

"Anything you need help with today?" he asked as he followed her to her car and opened the door for her.

She shook her head. "Not really. I'm snowed under with a bunch of stuff I need to spend time doing on the computer. I've got graphics to make and coloring sheets to design and print out. How are you with creating social media posts?"

He raised an eyebrow. "I'm good at setting *fence* posts."

She laughed. "That's almost the same thing."

He pulled out his cell phone, his palms already starting to sweat at the idea of asking her for her number. They'd been out of contact for over a decade. There was a chance she'd wiggle out of giving it to him. He'd had women ask for his phone and put their numbers into his contacts or had them slide cocktail napkins to him with their numbers written on them, but it had been years since he'd actually asked a woman for her phone number. He cleared his throat, trying to tamp down his nerves. "So I was thinking, maybe we should, um, probably exchange numbers. Just in case you do need my help with something. Or whatever." He held his breath, chastising himself for acting as skittish as that dog had when he'd first met her.

"Good idea," Lainey said, pulling her phone from her pocket. "I was thinking that this morning too when I thought of the idea of taking food to the horse, then realized I had no way to get ahold of you. Which is why I just drove over and barged into your day."

"Well, then maybe we shouldn't exchange numbers because I liked having you barge into my day."

That was a stupid thing to say. What if she decided *not* to give him her number now? Why couldn't he just shut up? Her number might have already been in his phone by now.

She smiled coyly up at him. "Why don't we exchange numbers *and* still be allowed to bust into each other's days if the situation calls for it?"

The tightness in his chest eased, and he smiled back at her. "Deal." He gave her his number and watched as she entered it into her phone, then sent him a smiley face in a text.

"There," she said. "Now we're connected."

He stared at the smiley face text for a beat too long before sliding his phone back into his coat pocket. He let out a breath that felt like he'd been holding for a very long time. Lainey McBride had spent the night in his bed and now he had her number in his phone.

Now we're connected.

Her words echoed in his ears as he pulled her against him and pressed a hard kiss to her lips.

Lainey was back in his life. And this time he wasn't letting her go.

———

Two days later, Holt found himself at Lainey's doorstep holding a take-out French vanilla latte, a pumpkin spice muffin, and a gift bag containing a silver glitter-covered pine cone. It was late morning, and he'd finished his chores at the ranch and had been running errands in town when he got the idea to bring her out a coffee.

He'd been racking his brain the last few days trying to think of an excuse to *barge* into her day. They'd texted a few times, but Lainey had been busy with paperwork and doing the Women's Club brunch the day before, so they hadn't seen each other. Which was fine. It was only a day. But this morning, he'd woke up yearning to see her, to touch her, to make her laugh. If he were being honest, he'd been thinking about doing all those things pretty much the whole time since she'd driven away a few nights ago.

It was probably good for them to have a little space. The time they'd spent together, on the sofa and in his bed, had been pretty intense, and he could use the distance to come back to reality. Because the true reality of the situation was that even though they'd loved each other as teenagers, that didn't mean those feelings were still there all these years later. They were for him, but he didn't really know what Lainey was feeling.

She'd been his best friend growing up, and back then, he would have said he knew her inside and out. But in truth, he knew next to nothing about who Lainey was now. He knew she'd been struggling with finding a job she loved, had moved around a lot, and he was pretty sure she was still living in Montana—at least that's where the plates on her car were from, but he didn't know much beyond that. Although the main thing he did know was that she was only here for a few weeks and then she'd disappear from his life again.

He had a funny way of pushing that thought to the back of his mind.

She was here now, with her sunny smile and her contagious laugh, and even though she kept talking him into doing annoying Christmas things—still not sure how she kept accomplishing that—he just wanted to be around her.

That desire had been what inspired the idea to bring her a latte when he'd walked past Perk Up, the local coffee shop, that morning. As he stood in line, he noticed the display of handcrafted Christmas ornaments next to the counter and couldn't pass up the shiny silver pine cone hanging from a teal-colored satin ribbon.

He'd been so proud of himself on the drive over, but now he just felt like a fool as he stood on her porch and realized she wasn't even home. Although her car *was* in the driveway.

Maybe she'd had a change of heart or a bout of cold feet after their drunken night together and was hiding inside, just waiting for him to go away.

Or maybe she's just in the shower. Or a friend could have picked her up. But who did she know in this town besides her grandfather and the Callahans?

Feeling like an idiot holding the cooling cup of coffee and a ridiculous muffin that was almost as big as his hand, Holt debated just leaving them on her porch step. He couldn't do that at his place because Tiny or Otis would snarf food up within seconds of it being put down, and the last thing he needed was to have that ornery goat hopped up on sugar and caffeine. But Lainey didn't have a nutty goat around or a resident pig.

Before he could decide what to do, the small door of the barn flew open, smacking the wall behind it, the crack of wood thunderous in the hush of the snow-covered farm, and Lainey ran out, sprinting toward him, her eyes wide and a panicked expression on her face.

CHAPTER 13

LAINEY PULLED UP SHORT AT THE SIGHT OF HOLT standing on her doorstep. "Holt. What are you doing here?" she asked, her voice breathless from sprinting across the farmyard.

"Are you okay?" he asked, concern etched on his face. "You were running like your tail was on fire."

"I'm fine," she said, her eyes drawn to the teal take-out cup from her favorite coffee shop, the monstrous muffin, and the small red gift bag he held in his hands. "Are those for me?"

"Yeah, I…um…brought you some coffee…or whatever. But that doesn't matter. What's wrong?"

She melted at the sweet gesture of the gift and the note of worry in his tone. Reaching out to rest an assuring hand on his, she told him, "I'm fine. I've got a small crisis with an event I'm helping with, but it's nothing that can't wait for a second while I swig half that cup of coffee."

His shoulders relaxed as he handed her the cup. "It's a French vanilla latte."

"What? That's my favorite." She grinned as she took a sip, then closed her eyes in contented bliss. "It's perfect. And if that muffin is pumpkin spice, I'm going to kiss you."

She laughed. "Actually, I'm going to kiss you no matter what flavor it is. I can't believe you brought me coffee and a muffin." She pushed open the front door and stepped inside. "Get in here, out of the cold, and I'll split it with you."

He followed her in, and they shed their coats and boots inside the door, then padded sock-footed into the kitchen, where he set the muffin and the gift bag on the center island. "If you're going to kiss me no matter what flavor it is, I think I should get something more than a kiss for bringing your favorite and for remembering how much you love pumpkin *everything*."

"Oh yeah?" She hoisted herself onto the counter in front of him and snatched up the muffin. "First I think I need to see the quality of the product." She tore a chunk off the side and popped it into her mouth, groaning at the delicious burst of pumpkin and cinnamon flavor.

"That sounds like it's pretty damn good," he murmured, keeping his gaze locked on hers as he stepped between her legs and flattened his palm on the counter behind her.

Pretty damn good didn't come close to describing the feeling of having his hips pressing into the inside of her thighs and his gaze dropping to her lips. She shifted to get closer to him, and her leg bumped into the red gift bag. She picked it up, thankful for the distraction from her intense desire to rip off her clothes and climb Holt like a tree. "Is this for me too?"

He shook his head. "No, I got that for Bryn."

"Oh, sorry," she said, heat warming her cheeks as she set it gingerly back down.

He chuckled, the deep timbre of the sound causing

butterflies to take off in her belly as he picked up the bag and placed it back in her hands. "Yes, of course it's for you. You think I would show up at your door with a coffee, a gigantic freaking muffin, and a gift for my cousin?"

She shrugged, excitement at the sweet gesture and anticipation of the gift swelling her chest. "I didn't want to presume. Although I guess I did presume when I picked it up."

"Open it already," he told her. "Although keep your expectations low. It's just something I saw this morning that made me think of you. And if you want the honest truth, I was just gonna hand it to you. The cashier is the one who put it in that fancy bag."

"You didn't have to tell me that," she said, nudging his shoulder. "But I don't care anyway. The fact that you saw something that made you think of me is a gift all in itself. I don't care if it's a paper clip, I love that you got me a Christmas present."

"Now don't get carried away. It's not a *Christmas* present. In fact, it's not really even a present at all. It's just something I picked up."

"Too late. You already said it was," she said, teasing him as she pulled back the layers of tissue paper and peeked inside. A small gasp escaped her lips and tears stung her eyes as she hooked the ribbon and lifted the silver pine cone from the bag. She blinked back the tears as she stared in amazement at the ornament dangling from her fingers. "Oh, Holt," she whispered.

"You said putting a silver pine cone on your mantel at the holidays would bring you good luck all year, so when I saw that ornament this morning, it made me think of you." He looked down as he shrugged off the significance of the gift. "I told you it was nothing."

"No, Holt," she said, lifting his chin so he had to look at her. "It's everything. I love it."

I love you.

She bit back the words, barely stopping them from escaping her lips. But they were true. She'd felt hurt and angry and abandoned by him, but she'd never stopped thinking about or loving this man. They had a painful past and their future was uncertain, but right now, all she cared about was the fact that Holt Callahan was standing in front of her and had just given her the most thoughtful sweet gift she could have imagined.

He looked shy and a little embarrassed, which only made her love him more. "Why don't we go back to talking about that muffin?" he asked.

"What muffin?"

"The one you were tasting earlier to determine what kind of kiss it earned me."

She set the ornament down on the counter and scooted closer to him, pressing her hips against his. "Oh, Holt, forget the muffin. This gift just earned you so much more than a kiss." She pulled her shirt over her head and tossed it toward the kitchen table. It missed and fell to the floor, but she didn't care because Holt's eyes had already gone wide. Then she caught his wolfish grin as his gaze dropped to her cleavage.

A growl sounded at the back of his throat as he hooked his fingers under the straps of her bra, then slowly pulled them down her shoulders. His hands were warm and solid as he pushed the cups down, freeing her breasts as they spilled over the pink lacy fabric.

She arched her back, her body already yearning for his touch, as he leaned down and circled one of her taut nipples with his tongue before drawing it between his lips. He filled his hand with her other breast, cupping the weight of it in his palm as he rolled the other nub between his thumb and forefinger.

"Holt." She breathed out his name and loved the way he kissed her breasts, then her neck before grazing her lips with the softest touch, then deepening the kiss until she couldn't think straight. When he pulled her hips tighter to him, the evidence of his arousal grinding against the most delicious spot, she couldn't think at all. She could only moan and sigh and cry out his name as he kissed and touched and stroked her.

She wasn't sure exactly how he managed it, but he some-how lifted her up and tugged her leggings off in one smooth move. Her hands slapped flat on the counter behind her as he pulled her hips forward, then knelt in front of her.

Her mouth went dry at the feel of his warm breath, hot against the tiny triangle of her silk thong panties. She didn't even care that he was still fully clothed and she was barely wearing her bra and the smallest scrap of underwear. All she cared about was the feeling of his hands on her body and his lips on her thighs. Another cry escaped her lips, and she curled her fingers into fists as he pushed that scrap of silk to the side. The rough scruff of his beard scraped against her thighs, but she barely felt it. All she felt was the heat of his mouth as he kissed her most tender spot and sent waves of desire coursing through her blood.

———

Two hours later, after they'd found her bed and both ended up naked, she lay curled against his side, sated and sleepy as he drew slow circles softly over her back with the edge of his thumb.

He pulled her closer to his side, his voice low and drowsy as he nuzzled his cheek against her hair. "So what was the crisis with your event?"

"Hmm?" she asked, as she started to drift off.

"What was it that had you racing out of the barn and toward the house earlier? You said you had some sort of crisis with an event."

Her eyes popped open, and she shot up in bed, all traces of sleep gone. "Oh shit. I forgot. How could I forget?"

"Forget what?"

"The crisis with my event," she said, crossing to her dresser and yanking out fresh clothes.

"Damn," he said, pushing himself up to lean against the headboard as he watched her wiggle into a bra and undies. "I didn't mean for you to get out of bed."

"No, it's good." She glanced at the clock on her nightstand. "Holy crap, we've been in bed for over two hours."

He patted the sheets next to him. "I've got another two hours in me. Then I'm happy to help with whatever your crisis is."

"No way. I can't. I'm barely going to make it as it is. I'm in charge of the annual town caroling event tonight, and we're expecting a few hundred people to show up at the Methodist church at five."

He shook his head. "Wait a minute. When I offered to help, I didn't know there was singing involved. And I absolutely don't do carols." He flashed her an impish grin. "Well, I did a Carol once, but it was a long time ago, and that's probably bad form to mention considering…" He nodded at the tangle of sheets around him.

She picked up one of the throw pillows they'd carelessly shoved off the bed earlier and threw it at him. "Yes, that is bad form. And now I get why you didn't want to name the dog Carol. And anyway," she said, her voice muffled as she pulled a light-blue Henley over her head. "I don't need you to sing. I need you to bake."

"Bake?"

"Yes, bake. Part of the event tonight is a Christmas cookie raffle, and they're expecting two dozen of eight different kinds of Christmas cookies. The woman who was in charge of making them went into the hospital last night with appendicitis. So now I need to make close to two hundred cookies and have them to the church in less than four hours."

"Oh shit. That is a crisis. But why do you need to *make* them? Why can't you just *buy* them? They have cookies at the store, and buying them would only take twenty minutes."

"I can't. They *have* to be homemade. And there are eight *specific* kinds. It's part of the tradition." She grabbed his pants off the floor and tossed them to him. "If I start right now, I might just barely be able to make it. *If* you help me."

He reached for his pants. "Okay. As long as I don't have to sing, I'm all yours. Just tell me what you need."

I'm all yours.

The words struck Lainey hard in the chest. How she wished that were true.

But she didn't have time to dwell on that now. She had two hundred cookies to make.

Ten minutes later, they stood next to each other in the kitchen looking down at the eight different Christmas cookie recipes Lainey had compiled. Some were handwritten on recipe cards that claimed to be from "Grandma's Kitchen," and some she had just printed off.

Holt picked up one of the handwritten cards. It was for spritz cookies and had a dark drop on the corner that looked like it could have been vanilla. "This one looks like a favorite."

"It is," Lainey said. "And be careful with that card. That recipe was personally written out by my grandmother, so it's special to me."

"Really?" He pulled the card closer to his face. "Her handwriting looks just like yours."

"I know. Isn't that funny?" She plucked the card from his hand and put it back on the counter with the rest of the recipes. "Now forget about the card and focus on our task at hand. Some of these are going to take a little more work, like the sugar cookies, the gingerbread men, the spritz, and the peanut butter blossoms. But luckily, half of them are no-bake and come together pretty quickly like the buckeyes, the pecan snowballs, and the peanut butter bark. And the last one is just a couple of pans of fudge cut into small squares, so that should be super easy."

Holt frowned at her. "I don't know what half of those things are that you just said. What the hell are buckeyes and nut snowballs, and since when is bark a Christmas treat?"

"It's peanut butter bark. And it's made with melted peanut butter and white chocolate. You mix in peanuts, marshmallows, and Rice Krispies and drop it by the spoonful onto a sheet of wax paper, and when it hardens, it's so yum." She rubbed her lips together, already anticipating the crispy treats. "And don't worry, I'll explain the others when we get to them."

"All right. Just tell me what to do."

"First off, I only have about half this stuff here, so we need to go down the lists of ingredients to see what we need to pick up from the grocery store. Then maybe I can start on a couple of the recipes while you run into town and pick up what we need. Or the other way around if you're more comfortable starting the sugar cookies."

"I'm comfortable with making a list, then calling down to Pete at the Price Rite and getting him to deliver them to us."

"Oh, great idea. Do you think he would do that?"

"I'm sure he would. Folks around here love chipping in if they're doing something for the community. Especially when it comes to *Christmas*."

She ignored his exaggerated eye roll and let out a sigh of relief. "I love this town." She passed him a pen and a notebook, and they got to work creating a list of what they would need. By the time they got through the last recipe, she'd set out all the ingredients they had, covering the countertop with flour, sugar, vanilla, sticks of butter, baking soda and powder, cocoa, cinnamon, salt, ginger, powdered sugar, a jar of peanut butter, and two bags of pecans.

Lainey dropped two sticks of butter and a cup of sugar into the KitchenAid mixer and switched it on, creaming them together while Holt pulled out his phone and called the grocery store.

They had the sugar cookies in the oven, two pans of fudge made, and all the pecans chopped when a car sped down the driveway and pulled up to a stop in front of the house. But instead of Pete, the grocer, Aunt Sassy jumped out of the driver's side of the car, and a very pregnant woman climbed out of the other side. The trunk popped open, and both women had their arms filled with bags and were on their way up the steps by the time Holt and Lainey got to the door to hold it open for them.

"What are you guys doing here?" Holt asked, taking a handful of the bags and following them into the kitchen. "What happened to Pete?"

"We were in the store when you called, and he told us you and Lainey were making the cookies for the caroling party tonight, so we offered to bring the groceries out and lend a hand," Aunt Sassy said, already reaching into the pantry and pulling an apron from one of the hooks inside.

He looked at the belly of the other woman. "But you're…"

"I'm pregnant, Holt," she said, laughing as she rubbed her stomach. "That doesn't mean I can't roll a pecan snowball."

He shook his head. "How does everyone know what these snowball things are?"

The woman turned to Lainey, holding out her hand as she offered her a warm smile. "Hi, I'm Elle Brooks Tate. Nice to meet you."

"You as well," Lainey told her, liking her already. "When are you due?"

"Not for another two weeks," Elle said. "But I wouldn't mind if this little Tate-r tot stopped hanging out on my bladder and made an early appearance."

Holt grimaced, then turned his focus to unloading the bags of groceries.

Sassy gave Lainey a quick hug. "Elle is the wife of Brody Tate, one of our local veterinarians. They got married earlier this summer, and you've never seen such a gorgeous wedding. They had it outside at their ranch, and it was just beautiful."

Elle laughed. "It was beautiful, but it was also hot, and my ankles were swollen, and my dress had to be altered at the last minute because I'd gained an extra ten pounds of baby between when I'd ordered it and when it arrived. And don't get me started on the adventures of having a mini-horse and a hyper puppy as part of your wedding party."

Sassy laughed with her. "But Shamus was so cute in that little matching vest and bow tie that Bryn made him."

"Yeah, he *was* cute, until he got away from our daughter, Mandy, and took a huge bite out of the back side of the wedding cake."

"Wow," Lainey said. "That does sound like an adventure."

"Yes, but it was all worth it," Elle said, practically beaming with happiness.

Lainey felt a small pang of jealousy for the happy family life the other woman obviously had. She had thought she'd be married to Holt with a few kids and a dog underfoot by the time she turned thirty, but none of that had happened.

Maybe it wasn't too late for them, a sneaky voice of optimism tried to whisper.

But Lainey was only going to be here a few more weeks, and even though they'd agreed not to dig into their past *for now*, that didn't mean they weren't going to have to face it at some point.

"We're here to help," Aunt Sassy said, pulling Lainey out of her musings. "So put us to work. What can we do?"

Lainey hated asking for help, but in this instance, she hadn't asked, she'd been offered. And she wasn't one to look a gift cookie-baker in the mouth. "Well, Aunt Sassy, if you want, you can start working on the spritz cookies, and Elle, you sound like you know your way around a pecan snowball, so you can work on those. I'll mix up the batter for the peanut butter blossoms, and Holt, you can start unwrapping thirty-six of those Hershey's Kisses." She passed him the bag of chocolates and a small bowl. "You can put them in here."

"Are you sure you still need me?" he asked. "It seems like now that the cavalry is here, I might just be in the way."

Aunt Sassy huffed. "You're not getting out of here that easy. Just because the cavalry's arrived doesn't mean we don't still need a few extra soldiers. Now get to work unwrapping those kisses."

"Yes, ma'am," he said, grinning and sneaking a wink at Lainey.

She wasn't sure if the wink was about Aunt Sassy bossing him around or that he was thinking of all the *actual* kisses they'd shared that afternoon. But now *she* was thinking about all those kisses, especially the ones that were hot enough to melt the white chocolate she was stirring.

Focus on the cookies, she told herself as she dumped a bag of marshmallows into her bowl.

———————

Three hours and fifteen minutes later, they had twenty-four neatly wrapped plates of a dozen cookies each with all eight varieties. And they'd washed all the dishes and cleaned the kitchen to within an inch of its life.

"We did it," Holt said as they all stood back to admire their progress. "Pretty impressive," he told the women standing next to him.

Lainey had found some green and gold curling ribbon, and she and Elle had made snazzy bows to tie around the cellophane-wrapped plates, giving them an extra festive flair.

"They look amazing," Aunt Sassy said. "Good work, everybody."

"We couldn't have done it without you," Lainey said, hugging Sassy and Elle. "Thank you so much."

"No problem. It was fun," Elle said, unwrapping an extra Hershey's Kiss and popping it in her mouth. The smartwatch on her wrist dinged, and she peered down at it while she chewed. "That's Brody letting me know he just left the clinic, so I need to get home and get everyone ready for the festivities tonight."

"Me too," Aunt Sassy said, already collecting their purses and hurrying toward the door. "Doc is meeting me at the house to get ready. I let him be in charge of finding our sweaters for tonight, and I'm nervous about what he picked."

"That's why I got our sweaters weeks ago," Elle said. "I found us some really hilarious ones that have these huge gold bows on them. The real ugly part is going to be if mine no longer fits. My belly keeps expanding, and you can only stretch a sweater so far."

"Oh shoot," Lainey said. "I forgot about the ugly sweaters."

"I could loan you a couple. I've got plenty," Aunt Sassy said. "I've been collecting them for years. Although I have to admit, some of them didn't start out as ugly sweaters. They just sat in my closet longer than their fashion expiration date."

"Thank you, but I'll bet we can find some around here we can wear. My grandma loved that tradition," Lainey told her.

"All right then. We're gonna run," Aunt Sassy said, holding the door for Elle. "But let me know if you change your mind. Otherwise, we'll see you at the church in thirty minutes."

"Thanks again," Lainey called as the two women loaded into Sassy's car. She shut the door and turned back to Holt. "And thank you. Really. Sassy and Elle were a huge help, but I couldn't have done this without you."

"Happy to help," he said, then narrowed his eyes as he leaned against the counter. "But what's all this business about ugly sweaters, and who's this 'we' you're talking about who are going to wear them?"

CHAPTER 14

HOLT HAD A BAD FEELING AS LAINEY offered him an innocent smile. Although he was having a tough time keeping his stare hard when she looked so adorable with her hair a riot of curls around her face and a dusting of flour across her forehead. How did she even *get* flour on her forehead?

She held up her finger and said, "Stay there. I'll be right back," before racing down the hallway and up the attic stairs. Which was not any kind of answer to his question.

It was only a couple of minutes until he heard her running back down the stairs, and she bounded into the living room. "Ta-da," she said, spreading one of her arms wide with a flourish to show off the red-and-green sweater emblazoned with a dancing caricature of Mrs. Claus across her chest.

He raised an eyebrow but had no words.

"What do you think?" she asked. "Oh wait, you haven't seen the best part." She dug around under the side of the sweater, then must have flipped some switch because the lights on the Christmas tree Mrs. Claus was dancing next to flickered to life and blinked in a colorful display.

He shielded his eyes. "That is not an ugly sweater."

Her face fell. "It's not?"

He shook his head. "No. It passed ugly on that last stretch

of blinking lights and is coming around the bend to completely hideous."

She barked out a laugh. "There's more."

He pressed a hand to his chest. "Please no. I don't think I can take any more."

She'd been keeping one hand behind her back, and she drew it forward now and shook out the large red sweater she held. It was a match to the one she wore except it had Santa instead of Mrs. Claus doing an animated jig around the tree. She offered him an impish grin. "This one's for you."

It was his turn to laugh. "Like hell it is."

"Oh, come on," she said. "These are hilarious. They were my grandparents', and they told me they were the hit of every Christmas party they attended."

"Are you sure they didn't say they *got* hit at every party they attended? Because those sweaters are a train wreck. Or maybe they said they were *lit* at every party because I think you'd have to be drunk to wear those."

"No. That's terrible."

"Listen, darlin'," he told her. "I've helped you with driving the sleigh and collecting pine cones. I've baked sugar cookies and rolled buckeyes, and I'll even help you take all these cookies down to the church. But I draw the line at singing carols, and there's not a pecan snowball's chance in hell that you'll talk me into wearing that sweater."

"Fine," she huffed, folding it into a square. "But I'm bringing it in the truck just in case you change your mind."

"Suit yourself, but don't blame me if it *accidentally* falls out on the way into town."

Holt fed the animals at Mountainside while Lainey boxed up all the cookies and secured them in the back seat of his truck. Then they stopped by his ranch on the way into town to take care of the animals there. Lainey let the dog—Holt still wasn't used to calling her Lou—out and got her some food and water while he went out to the barn to feed and water the horses, cows, goat, and pig.

"Cindy Lou Who was very disappointed she didn't get to come with us tonight," Lainey told him as they drove into town.

"I'm sure *Lou* was, but with the number of dog owners in this town, if they all brought them tonight, there would be more dogs howling than people singing."

Lainey laughed. "True. But now you've given me the idea that I need to create some kind of fun Christmas event that is tailored to pet owners."

He shrugged. "Easy. Just have folks bring their pets out to the ranch to get a picture with Santa. Then charge 'em ten bucks a photo. You're already doing that for families with kids, so just block off a certain time that's just for pets."

She grinned and grabbed his hand to squeeze it. "Holt Callahan, you are a genius."

He shrugged. "I don't know about that." Although he was feeling pretty smart that he'd said something that just got her to hold his hand. He turned his palm over and entwined his fingers with hers, ensuring she wouldn't let go. The drive into town was short, but he considered taking the long way to the church just to hold her hand a little longer.

"This is a great idea. We can cater to couples with fur babies *and* make some extra money for the ranch with an activity that we were going to do anyway." She leaned back in the seat, and it made Holt happy to note that she didn't even make an effort to pull her hand away.

"Speaking of Lou, I did call the Humane Society and the sheriff's office yesterday, just to let them know I found her."

"You did? What did they say?"

"Nothing really. They took the information, but neither of them has had any calls or reports of a missing dog that matches her description."

"Then it sounds like she's your dog."

"Let's not get ahead of ourselves," he said, turning into the church parking lot. "We need to give them time to see if they can find her real family."

"Speaking of time," Lainey said, glancing at the clock on the truck's dashboard. "We must be late. Look how many cars are already here."

"Nah. People in this town just always show up early. But it does look like half the town is here." He parked the truck and came around to her side to help with the boxes of cookies.

Lainey pointed to the sweater folded up on the back seat. "There's still time to change your mind about the sweater. Everyone's going to be wearing them."

He growled by way of an answer as he hefted the boxes into his arms. "I told you that I'm just dropping you off and making sure you get these cookies inside, then I'm taking off and letting you enjoy your singing party."

She stopped at the door and turned to look at him. "I

thought you were just kidding when you said that. You're really not staying for the party?"

He shook his head as he shifted the box to one arm so he could hold the door open for her. "Not my thing. You know that. But call me when you're done, and I'll come pick you up. I'm not gonna leave you stranded here."

"Forget it. If you're not staying, I'm not calling you for a ride like you're an Uber. I'll find my own way home," she said with a miffed huff as she pushed past him and headed down the stairs to the church basement.

Between the Christmas music blaring and all the people talking and laughing, the noise in the basement was deafening. Holt cringed as he followed Lainey through the reception hall and into the kitchen, where he set the box of cookies down in an empty space on the counter.

Lainey was right about one thing. Everywhere he looked, in the kitchen and the reception hall, was a sea of ugly red and green Christmas sweaters. He saw glittery pom-poms and antler ears and elf legs protruding from the chests and bellies of the merry revelers. And Lainey's was not the only sweater that blinked and flashed annoying lights.

The amount of Christmas cheer in this basement was enough to choke an elephant. He needed to get these cookies set up and get the heck out of here. "I'll go back and get the last box," he told Lainey.

"Fine," she said, her tone decidedly cooler than when she was holding his hand in the truck and talking about the dog.

"Fine," he grumbled back as he pushed his way through the crowd to get to the stairs. Who needed all this Christmas crap anyway? Not him, that was for sure. Everything was too loud, too flashy, or too cutesy. And everyone seemed to be in way too happy of moods. Although some of that might have to do with the schnapps he just saw Aunt Sassy pouring into the eggnog in the kitchen.

Thinking about schnapps reminded him of the night he and Lainey had spent together and how she'd wrangled him into putting up a tree in his living room. How did she keep getting him to do all this Christmas junk he didn't like anyway?

You used to like it.

Shut up, he growled at that stupid inner voice. Although he *had* liked it. He'd *loved* the holidays and used to get off on all this holiday cheer shit too. He remembered Lainey and him building a snowman by their tree, making green and red food-colored popcorn balls, and going to the Christmas Eve service together one year at this very church. And now that he thought about it, they'd come to this caroling event together too.

It was an annual event that had been going on forever. After the caroling, everyone gathered in the town square for hot chocolate and cider while the Rotary Club built a huge bonfire and then lit the giant Christmas tree on the courthouse lawn. He mainly had remembered hanging out at the bonfire and making s'mores. He'd probably blocked out the singing part, and maybe that's why he hadn't put it together that they had come to this same event all those years ago.

Maybe that's why Lainey was so miffed that he wasn't staying for the party.

By the time he got the last box of cookies from the truck and fielded several conversations from townspeople about how he was doing, where Bryn and Zane were, when they were coming back, and if they'd rescued any new horses lately, Lainey was no longer in the kitchen.

The boxes they'd already brought in were unloaded and displayed on a table set up for the Christmas cookie raffle and silent auction.

"Hi, honey," Aunt Sassy said, appearing from somewhere behind him and taking the box from his hands and setting it on the counter. "We've got this," she said, already unloading it and passing plates to Doc Hunter. They wore matching green-and-red sweaters except Doc's sweater had the word *Nice* knit across the chest while Aunt Sassy's proclaimed the word *Naughty*.

Despite his grinchy musings, Holt had to smile at the pair. And their sweaters were spot-on.

"We got this," Aunt Sassy said, waving him out of the kitchen. "You can go on and enjoy the party."

"Oh, I'm not staying."

She raised an eyebrow at him. "Oh, really? Are you sure that's a good idea?"

He frowned. "What do you mean?"

She offered him a casual shrug that he knew was nowhere near as nonchalant as she was making it seem. "It's just that I overheard Betty Richardson talking about how she'd seen Lainey at the grocery store and how pretty she'd thought she was and how she'd be a perfect match for her grand-son, Lance. Apparently, he's a lawyer and has been living in

New York, but he's just moved back to town to help with his father's law firm."

Holt's frown deepened. "Lainey wouldn't be interested in some big city lawyer."

Sassy shrugged again, her expression the picture of innocence. "I don't know. He's rich and quite a looker too. Oh look, there he is, talking to Lainey." She pointed toward the punch table across the reception hall where Lainey stood talking to a tall, dark-haired man in a green sweater.

Damn. He was good-looking. Even Holt could tell that. And so could half the women in the room who kept sneaking glances at him. The guy looked like freaking Captain America or at least the captain of a football team, with his broad shoulders and blinding, *obviously whitened* teeth. Holt could *see* his teeth because he kept smiling and laughing uproariously at whatever Lainey was saying.

Come on. Lainey was pretty witty, but she wasn't that damn funny. Another growl worked its way up his throat. He swallowed it back. Lainey could talk to whomever she wanted.

The guy had his choice of any number of women to talk to, so why was he so interested in Lainey?

Because look at her. She's gorgeous.

She wore stretchy black leggings that hugged her curves and were tucked into her red cowboy boots. Her hair was pulled up into one tall triangle on top with two high ponytails sticking out of the sides that she'd rigged to look like something out of Whoville, threading glittery tinsel and tiny, colorful Christmas balls through the curls and braids.

He was pretty sure she had a candy cane or two stuck in there too. But even with the kooky hairdo and the obnoxious Christmas sweater she wore, her beauty shone through in her enchanting emerald-green eyes, wide smile, and easy laugh. And those damn adorable freckles that she still had sprinkled across her pert little nose.

Lance was obviously under her spell. He couldn't take his eyes off her. Then he laughed again at something she said and lifted his hand to rest it on her shoulder.

"Lance and Lainey—it has a bit of a ring to it. And they seem to be having fun together," Aunt Sassy said.

But Holt didn't answer. He was already striding across the room toward them. "Hey," he said, probably a little too forcefully as he came up beside them, since his voice made Lainey jump and her hand flew to her chest.

"Geez, you scared me," she said.

"Who's your friend?" he asked, but he was already sticking his hand out toward Captain Awesome. "I don't think we've met. Holt Callahan."

"This is Lance Richardson," Lainey said. "He's helping with the bonfire and lighting the tree tonight."

Of course he was.

And what kind of name was *Lance Richardson*? He even *sounded* like a lawyer. Or a douchy politician who was running for Congress.

"Good to meet ya," Lance said, assessing him as he reached to shake his hand and gripping it a little too firmly.

Holt gripped his back, squeezing just hard enough for the guy to get the message to back off from his girl.

But she wasn't *his* girl. And she hadn't been for a very long time.

He let go of Lance's hand and turned to Lainey, stepping another territorial inch closer as he did. "I brought the rest of the stuff in from the truck," he told her, hoping his statement gave Lance the impression they were involved.

"Thanks," she said stiffly. "Lance was just telling me a funny story about a Christmas party he attended with his grandma. He just *loves* doing holiday stuff."

He knew she was trying to needle him. And dammit, it was working. "I can tell," he said, looking at Lance's bright-red sweater with a goofy smiling reindeer on the front of it. "Nice sweater."

"Isn't it hilarious?" Lance asked, then laughed a little too heartily. Was this guy for real? "I have five of these. They crack me up." He glanced down at Holt's plain blue T-shirt. "Hey, where's your ugly sweater?"

"Oh, Holt's not staying for the party," Lainey said, dismissing him with her hand. "He's not a fan of all this Christmas business."

Lance pulled his head back and looked at Holt as if she'd just said he hated Santa. "Who doesn't like Christmas?"

Holt stuffed his hands in his pockets. This guy was really starting to bug him.

"The caroling is supposed to start in about ten minutes," Lainey told him. "So you'd better take off before someone mistakes you for a caroler and puts a songbook in your hands."

"Oh man, I hope they've got 'The Little Drummer Boy'

in there. That's one of my favorites," Lance said, then in a deep baritone belted out, "'Pa-rum pum pum pum.'"

Who was this guy?

"All right, yeah," Holt said. "I'll see you later."

"See ya." Lainey gave him the slightest wave as she joined in singing with Lance. "'I am a poor boy too. Pa-rum pum pum pum.'"

Forget it. Holt turned on his bootheels and strode across the reception hall and up the stairs. He stomped back to his truck and slammed the door. The stupid Santa sweater lay on the back seat as if mocking him. He turned the key in the ignition.

Screw all this. Lainey could have her stupid Christmas party, and he hoped she and Sir Lancelot of the Whitened Teeth had a great night together. As for him—he couldn't get out of here fast enough.

CHAPTER 15

LAINEY TOOK ONE OF THE SONGBOOKS FROM THE STACK they were passing out, then handed one to Lance. She was feeling kind of bad that she'd been a little snotty to Holt. He just made her so mad. He was so adamant about sticking to his grinchy guns that he didn't even *try* to let himself have any fun.

She also might have been waiting for him to mention something about the time they'd gone to this event together and had the best night. And the fact that he hadn't—and had even seemed to be poking fun at the event—hurt her feelings. Yeah, he'd said he wanted to leave their past behind them, but how could he not remember them at sixteen, desperately kissing by the bonfire, their mouths sweet and sticky from eating roasted marshmallows, knowing they weren't going to see each other again until summer?

He'd bought her this adorable little wooden snowman from one of the craft booths set up on Main Street. It wore a top hat and a purple vest—her favorite color at the time— and she still had it.

"You want some punch or a cookie before we head out?" Lance asked, rousing her from the memories.

"No, I'm fine," she said, forcing a smile. She'd thought

needling him a little might convince Holt to stay for the party, but he'd really left. And now she was stuck hanging out with this douche nugget who was driving her crazy with his stupid New York office stories that sounded like they would have been much funnier, or even semi-amusing, if she'd been there. Or if she cared even one tiddlywink.

"You sure?" Lance asked. "The punch is pretty good."

"I'll take it from here," a deep voice said from behind them.

A voice that had butterflies taking off in Lainey's belly. She turned to see Holt squeezing between them, pushing Lance aside with his broad shoulders. He held two cups of water, and he passed one to Lainey.

She automatically took it but couldn't stop staring at Holt, who had not only come back inside but was holding his chin high and wearing a bright-red sweater with a dancing Santa on it.

"Uh…I thought you weren't staying for the party," Lance said, disappointment written all over his face.

Holt shrugged and slipped an arm around Lainey's shoulder. "Oh, Lainey was just kidding about that. I love caroling. Wouldn't miss it. I just had to go back to the truck and get my favorite sweater. I always get told it's such a hit at Christmas parties."

She pressed her lips together to keep from laughing.

"Huh," Lance said, then looked down as if studying his songbook.

Lainey was still in shock that Holt had come back *and* was wearing the sweater, but then he stunned her even more when he waved a pretty blond toward them.

"Hey, Julie," he said to the woman who was smiling a little too warmly up at him.

"Hey, Holt."

The green-eyed monster punched Lainey squarely in the stomach, and she suddenly felt even worse for trying to use Lance to make Holt a little jealous.

But apparently, Holt was a better person than she was because he hadn't called Julie over to talk to *him*.

"Julie, have you met Lance Richardson? He just moved back to town to help with his dad's law firm," Holt said.

"Nice to meet you, Lance," Julie said, cutting her eyes from Holt to Lance as she stuck out a perfectly manicured hand, her long fingernails painted to look like red-and-white-striped candy canes.

Lance took her hand, and then his face broke into a grin as he glanced down at the blinking Christmas tree on her chest that read, "Let's Get Lit." "Nice to meet you, Julie. Fun sweater."

"Thanks. Holt says you're a lawyer." She left her hand in his and batted her eyelashes as she smiled coyly at him. "Any chance you're looking for a *Mrs. Clause*?"

He chuckled. "Dang girl, you should call me Rudolph instead of Lance because you just sleighed me."

Julie giggled. "How about we get some punch?" she asked, turning back to mouth "Thank you" to Holt before leading Lance into the crowd.

Lainey looked up at Holt, who wore a smug grin on his face. "All right, who are you, and what have you done with Holt 'The Grinch' Callahan?"

"Oh, he's still around." He leaned down to speak closer into her ear and sent a delicious shiver down her spine. "And just so you know, I may be wearing this sweater, but I refuse to turn the blinking lights on."

"Who cares about the lights?" She batted her eyelashes like Julie had just done. "Just so *you* know, having you show back up to the party *and* in this sweater turns *me* on."

He chuckled softly, then pressed a quick kiss to her cheek.

She turned, hoping he'd plant his next kiss on her lips, but they were interrupted by a familiar voice.

"Holy crap, Brother. I never thought I'd see the day," Cade said, slugging Holt in the shoulder. "Nice sweater."

Holt glared at his older brother. "You say one more thing, and I *will* punch you in the throat."

"Hey, I'm not saying a word," Cade said, laughing as he opened the front of his Carhartt jacket to reveal a bright-blue sweater with a snowman on the front.

Allie burst out of the crowd, pulling a woman by the hand as they made their way to Holt and Lainey. Both of them wore blue snowman sweaters that matched Cade's.

Holt looked from the women to his brother. "*Dude.*"

Cade laughed again. "I told you. Not saying *a* word."

"Dad, Nora was trying to outbid Sheriff Rayburn on that basket of peanut butter blossoms, and he told her he was going to arrest her if she didn't let him win." Allie's face shone with excitement as she crushed into Cade's side.

"You don't need to get yourself arrested for those cookies, Nora," Holt told the woman. "I can whip you up a batch all of your own."

She looked up at him. "*You're* going to bake me some peanut butter blossoms?"

"Heck yeah, I'm not just a pretty face, ya know. Lainey and I made all those cookies this afternoon."

Nora's eyes widened as she looked from Holt down to Lainey. "Hi, I'm Nora. Did you really make all those cookies?"

"Nice to meet you. I'm Lainey. And yes, we did. Although Holt's big contribution to the peanut butter blossoms was unwrapping the Kisses and trying not to eat them all before putting them in the center of the warm cookies. But he did make a batch of that fudge all on his own."

"And cut out a bunch of gingerbread and rolled about eighty buckeyes," he reminded her.

Lainey grinned. "More like thirty-six, but you still get the credit for those too."

"It felt like eighty," he muttered.

They were interrupted by a loud whistle coming from the front of the hall. Lainey looked over to see Aunt Sassy standing on a piano bench and waving a handful of songbooks.

"Everyone grab your coats and hats and make sure you get a songbook. Just like last year, we'll start by going down the middle of Main Street, then follow the parade route, turning up Fourth, then looping around the park and coming back to the town square where we'll light the bonfire and the Creedence Christmas tree."

A cheer went up in the crowd as the group started collecting coats and making their way up the stairs.

Holt kept his arm around Lainey's side as he leaned down and told her, "I hope we get to sing 'The Little Drummer Boy.' It's my favorite carol."

She laughed as she nudged him in the rib with her elbow. "I expect to hear you singing it the loudest then."

"Try to stop me."

Forget the caroling. Try to stop my heart from falling more in love with you.

━━━━━━

Lainey and Holt stuck mainly with Cade, Nora, and Allie as they wandered down the middle of the street singing carols from the songbook. Well, singing might be an overstatement. The girls tried to sing while the two brothers tried to best each other by either singing in funny accents or seeing who could caterwaul the loudest. Lainey couldn't remember a time lately when she'd laughed so hard.

Aunt Sassy and Doc had donned matching Santa hats, and he was driving them up and down the group of carolers in a red golf cart decorated to look like Santa's sleigh.

Between the folks Lainey had met through her grandparents and the whole Callahan bunch, she and Holt knew just about everyone they ran into. Lainey found out that Nora was a physical therapist and had built quite a practice for herself in town, and several kids waved and shouted greetings to Allie. Holt had told Lainey what a hard time Allie had had earlier that year, adjusting to her mother's death and moving in with her estranged father, so Lainey was glad to see the teenager looking so happy.

Elle found them by the bonfire and introduced Lainey to her husband, Brody, and his ten-year-old daughter, Mandy.

The worry over her sweater had been a valid one as the knit stretched tautly across Elle's belly, the giant gold bow sitting on top as if declaring Baby Tate as a Christmas gift.

By the way they hugged and laughed with each other, it was obvious Elle and Nora were friends, and they introduced Lainey to the Bennett sisters, Jillian and Carley, who, along with Bryn, were the other women in their tight-knit friend group.

"We usually meet at Bryn's on Tuesdays for tacos and margaritas," Carley told her. "You should join us as soon as Bryn gets back."

"That would be great," Lainey said, already liking all the women in the group.

"Just don't let Aunt Sassy be in charge of the margaritas," Jillian, the wife of the peanut-blossom-loving sheriff, warned. "Or your head will be spinning, and you'll be drunkenly spilling all your deep dark secrets to the group." She pointed to the top of her head. "I say this from experience."

It had been so long since Lainey had been part of a group of friends. She and her mom had moved around so much, she'd never again found the kind of friendship and camaraderie that she'd had when she'd run around with the Callahan kids. And that had only been during the summers and holidays.

She found herself yearning to be part of this fun group of women who seemed to laugh at and with each other as they shared inside jokes and sarcastic remarks. Holt seemed to be part of this group, so remarkably the women just accepted her too.

Similar to at a tailgating bash at a football game, the group had created their own party spot by the bonfire by parking a truck on either side of a small camper and stringing colorful Christmas lights on its awning. They'd set up a portable fire-pit in the center of a semicircle of folding chairs facing the bonfire and had stacks of blankets available and a table laden with long skewers and bags of various sizes of marshmallows and the rest of the makings for s'mores.

Lainey had just finished chatting with one of the ladies she'd met at the Women's Club brunch when Holt came over and offered her a perfectly toasted marshmallow dangling from the end of a skewer.

"Just how you like it," he said. "Light brown on the outside, gooey on the inside, no burnt edges."

She beamed up at him as she pulled the warm marshmallow from the end of the skewer and popped it in her mouth. She'd barely finished chewing it when he leaned down to capture her mouth in a sticky kiss. He pulled back, using his tongue to lick marshmallow from his top lip. "Just how *I* like it," he said, grinning down at her.

Maybe he *did* remember.

She pushed up on her toes to kiss him again. He wrapped his arms around her, pulling her to him, but something hard jabbed into her hip. She pulled back. "Is that a candy cane in your pocket or are you just happy to see me?"

He let out a low rumbling laugh, the kind that told her his mind just went to the same dirty place hers had. "Darlin', I'm always happy to see you. But we could go back to my place, and I'll show you just *how* happy."

A warm heat coiled inside her just imagining the things he would show her. "We can't. They haven't even lit the Christmas tree yet." She pointed to the giant tree on the courthouse lawn behind him.

"All right. But if they don't light that thing in the next five minutes, I'm taking you home and we're going to make this a Not-So-Silent Night."

She giggled and let him kiss her again. He tasted like a s'more, chocolaty with a sweet flavor of marshmallow. He pulled her to him again, but she winced and pulled away as she got poked by the thing in his pocket again. "Okay, seriously, what is in your pocket?"

He ducked his head, looking suddenly shy as he stuck his hand in his pocket. "It's nothing, really. Just something I picked up for you at one of the craft booths while I was helping with the bonfire."

"For me? What is it?"

He pulled his hand free and held it out to her. On his palm was a wooden snowman, almost exactly like the one he'd bought her all those years ago, except this one was wearing a top hat and a teal vest.

She picked it up and held it to her chest, blinking back tears that she was going to blame on the smoke from the fire. Swallowing at the emotion burning her throat, she peered up at him. "You *do* remember that night."

His lips curved into a sentimental smile. "Of course I do. I remember everything."

She grabbed the lapel of his collar and pulled him down to kiss him hard on the mouth. His arms wrapped around her, and this time when he pulled her close, there was nothing between them. Fireworks exploded inside her, an eruption of too many feelings and emotions. She opened her eyes, and the giant Christmas tree in the square lit up behind Holt's head, the brilliance and magic of the colorful lights sparkling off the glass balls equivalent to the feelings radiating through her.

Holy strands of tinsel. She was in trouble here. The emotions she was having for this man were too much. Her heart was becoming too invested. He'd broken her heart before—shattered it into a million pieces that she thought would never be able to be put back together again. But over the last week, he'd been slowly mending it, making her believe in love again.

But the last time, he hadn't just broken her heart, he'd broken her.

———

Lainey and Holt said their goodbyes and left the party not long after the tree had been lit. They held hands as they walked back to the truck, waving and calling out "good night" to people they passed.

She loved the way he picked up her hand again as soon as he started driving, loved the feel of his thumb as he rubbed it over her knuckle and drew circles on the back of her hand.

Everything about this night had been so fun, and things were going so great with her and Holt. She held back a sigh. Maybe *too great.* In her life, good things didn't last for long.

Just when she started to settle in and think things were going well was the exact time that the rug got ripped out from under her.

Was that about to happen again? Should she rein things in before they got even more carried away?

She shivered, suddenly cold, and put her free hand in her coat pocket. The little wooden snowman was there, and she pulled it out and held it in her lap. Peering down at it, she felt like it represented so much. She and Holt had so much history together. At one time, she'd loved him more than air— had felt like she couldn't breathe when they weren't together.

Then her mom had ripped her from the only place she'd ever truly thought of as her home and dragged her halfway across the country and back, never staying in one place too long for fear that Randy would find them. She'd thought her running days were over when she'd turned eighteen, that she and Holt would finally build the life they'd always planned.

But he didn't show up. He'd abandoned her with no explanation, no excuse. And when she'd asked if he'd gotten her letter asking him to meet her, he'd claimed they were just stupid kids. And they probably were. Stupid kids with teenage dreams.

But they weren't kids now. And her heart was too fragile to take a chance on it getting broken again.

The memories of her eighteenth birthday swirled through her mind, the anticipation of seeing Holt again, the excitement of them starting a new life together, then the bone-deep sorrow when he didn't show up. She'd waited for days, but he never came.

Remembering that time was making her stomach hurt, and she swallowed at the dryness in her throat. This was different, she told herself as he pulled to a stop in front of her house. She looked at Holt, his face as familiar as her own. Even in this new grown-up face, she still saw the boy she'd fallen in love with when she was ten years old.

This *wasn't* different. It was just the same. As much as she tried to tell herself that none of the other stuff mattered—their history, his abandonment, the fact that she was only going to be here for a few more weeks—and that she should just enjoy their time together, she knew she was already in too deep. And this time, he could truly destroy her.

"I can't do this," she whispered.

"What?" Holt asked, killing the engine and turning toward her in the seat.

She pulled her hand from his. Taking a deep breath, she repeated the words. "I said…I can't do this."

He looked bewildered. "Do what?"

"This." She pointed from his chest to hers. "This thing we're doing. It's all happening so fast. It's scaring me to death."

"Okay, take it easy. I get that." He gently touched her shoulder as if the weight of his hand might break her.

But it wasn't the weight of his hand, it was the weight of her heart.

She shook her head, the emotion of her conviction burning her throat. "I know we said we weren't going to talk about the past, but tonight felt like we were reliving those days again. It was all so perfect—the bonfire, the tree lighting, the marshmallow kisses. And suddenly, I'm right back where I was then, falling in love with the cute boy who bought me a snowman and completely oblivious to the fact my heart is about to be ripped out."

"Lainey—"

She cut him off before he could say anything more. "I just need to take a beat," she told him. "When I'm with you, I forget everything else—to eat, to sleep, to breathe. And I *need* to be doing all those things. Especially now with so many people counting on me." She opened the truck door and climbed out before she could change her mind. "I'm sorry, Holt. I need some time. Alone. To catch my breath."

She didn't give him a chance to answer, to try to talk her into staying with him, or to agree with her and tell her none of this mattered to him anyway. The latter would have devastated her.

Although from the pained look in his eyes, she might have been destroying him.

But right now, she had to protect herself, her heart.

"Thank you. For everything. I'll call you," she said, her words coming out in disjointed phrases. Then, before she could change her mind, she slammed the truck door and ran up the porch steps and into the house.

CHAPTER 16

I NEED SOME TIME. ALONE. TO CATCH MY BREATH.

What the hell did that even mean?

Holt lugged a hay bale out into the corral and tossed it into the trough for the horses, ignoring Otis, who ran over and snatched the first mouthful.

Holt had been trying not to think about Lainey for the last two days, trying not to check his phone or get excited when it rang with a call or dinged with a text, hoping it was her. He didn't actually get very many calls or texts, so that one shouldn't have been a concern, but it seemed like his phone had been going crazy the last two days. He'd heard from Bryn and his brother, and Allie had texted him with some cat video to watch. He'd almost thrown his phone out the window once when he'd gotten a junk text.

But he hadn't gotten a single text or call from Lainey.

He'd played her words over and over again in his mind. Not that she'd said a lot, but a few things really stood out. Like the part where she'd said she was falling in love with him again.

In the past ten years, if a woman had told him she was falling for him, that was his cue to hit the road, Jack. He didn't do relationships, didn't say the *l*-word. He'd been burned by that one before. Nope. If things with a woman ever started feeling too serious, he got the heck out of Dodge. Until Talia. Things with her had happened so fast, and he'd convinced himself that since it had been over a decade, he needed to stop pining for Lainey and try to make a go of it with someone new.

Fat lot of good that did him. All that convincing netted him a nonrefundable weekend at a resort in Aspen and a renewed grudge against Christmas. *And* love.

Which should have made him glad that Lainey wanted some time apart or, in her words, to "take a beat." Whatever the hell that meant.

But he *wasn't* glad. He didn't *want* time apart. He knew that was going to happen eventually. Once the holidays were over, she was going to go back to her "real" life, and he'd be left behind again. He didn't want to think about that right now. He was putting that thought into a little box and setting it aside to think about later. For now, he just wanted to be with Lainey in the time they did have.

She was worried about her heart getting ripped out. He hadn't even been sure that he still *had* a heart—not until he saw her walk out onto her porch last week. Then his heart suddenly exploded in his chest, and for the first time in years, it felt like it started beating again.

Hopefully he *wasn't* going to need it anymore because when she left in a few weeks, she was surely going to take it with her. Not that it would do her any good. Her leaving was going to obliterate his heart again, so she'd only be walking away with a wrecked organ that would most likely never work again.

Damn, he was getting sappy.

He stomped back into the barn, grabbed a pitchfork, and set to work mucking out the stalls—a fitting job for his current mood. But at least he was moving, doing something to burn off his frustration.

Bryn was going to be happy when she got home. He'd spent the last two days doing every labor-intensive task he could think of. He'd fixed fences, repaired a stall door, restocked the feed bags, and brushed, groomed, and farriered every horse. He'd saddled Bristol and ridden out to the pasture to check cattle, galloping the horse hard across the field. He'd changed the oil in the ranch truck, repaired the loader implement for the tractor, and chopped enough firewood to last three winters. But no matter how hard he worked, it wasn't enough to push Lainey from his mind.

He still wasn't sure what had happened. One minute, they were laughing and practically making out at the tree lighting; the next she was jumping out of his truck like a scared rabbit who'd almost gotten caught in a trap or a spooked stallion who'd almost stepped on a rattlesnake.

He sighed. Did that analogy make him the snake? Or the trap?

He couldn't see himself as either because the real truth was that he was just as scared as she was.

━━━━━━

That night, Lainey rolled over and punched her pillow into a different shape, then sighed as she laid her head down again.

She glanced at the clock. Almost eleven. She'd been tossing and turning for over an hour, unable to sleep as she replayed the things she'd said to Holt after the bonfire over and over in her head.

What was wrong with her? Why did she have to get all emotional and dramatic about them being together again? If she hadn't said anything, they would have gone into the house, and Holt would have lit her up like that Christmas tree in the town square, and then they probably would have spent the last two days in bed together.

Thinking about that had her cheeks heating, and suddenly the room felt too warm. She threw off her blankets, but that wasn't enough to cool her down. Getting out of bed, she opened a window and let the wintry air cool her cheeks.

She peered down at the barn and was surprised to see a light shining inside. Had she left the light on? She'd been so scattered the past few days, she'd walked into the kitchen, then forgotten why she'd gone in there, had left the water running in the bathroom after she'd brushed her teeth, and had found her car keys in the freezer when she'd opened it to get an ice cream carton to drown her sorrows in.

So she easily could have left the light on in the barn when she'd gone out there to feed the animals that evening. But if she'd forgotten to turn out the light, what else had she forgotten to do? Feed all the animals? Lock all the gates to their stalls?

She distinctly remembered filling a rubber feed tub with water and putting it in Merry's stall, but she couldn't recall if she'd even closed, let alone latched, the gate. Surely she had.

Well, now she for sure couldn't sleep. Not until she'd checked on the horse. And made sure the gate to the corral was secure. That was all she needed, to lose her grandparents' whole herd because she was too busy thinking about monkey sex with the hot cowboy from the farm next door.

She grabbed a pair of socks and hurried down the stairs to the front door, where she pulled on the socks and her snow boots. Finding her coat, she put it on over her thin T-shirt and pajama shorts, considering for a moment going back upstairs to find some flannel pajama pants, then deciding against it. She was hot anyway, and she was only running out to the barn to make sure the gates were shut and turn out the light.

Her scarf was hanging by the front door, and she grabbed it and wrapped it around her neck as she hurried down the porch steps and toward the barn. The moon was full and glistened off the remains of the last snow they'd had, making it light enough to easily see by. The night was quiet, the only sound a whinny coming from inside the barn, as if Merry knew Lainey was coming her way.

Inside the barn, she was thankful to see the gate to the corral securely locked but surprised to see the door to Merry's stall not quite shut. Oh geez, what would have happened if the big black horse had gotten out and run away?

"Hey, girl," she said, holding up her hands as she approached the horse. "It's okay."

Although something didn't feel okay. Something just felt a little off. A sliver of fear skittered down her spine, like the whispery legs of a spider, and she shivered in her jacket as she looked around the barn wondering if maybe a wild animal, like a coyote or a bobcat, had gotten in and spooked the horse.

But the light in the barn couldn't have been turned on by a bobcat, which meant either that she'd left it on or, the more frightening scenario, that another person had been out here and turned it on. She shivered again, praying that wasn't the case and that if it was, the person still wasn't here.

Holy crap. Now she was scaring herself.

She needed to shut the gate, hit the lights, and get back to the house and the safety of her bed. Although now she *really* wasn't going to be able to sleep.

The black mare seemed a little wild-eyed as she got closer to the gate. She let out another whinny, then stamped at the door of the stall, slamming it open. Lainey jumped back as the heavy wooden door swung toward her and the horse raced out.

Oh shit. Not again.

She grabbed a halter and ran after the horse, praying she would stay on the farm. But this was not the night her prayers would be answered as she caught sight of the horse racing across the field. She had to catch her. Especially if it was an animal that had spooked her. She couldn't leave the horse out here to fend for herself against a coyote. Merry was big enough that one coyote probably wouldn't mess with her, but those jerks often ran in packs, and several of them could take the mare on.

Plus, Merry had been her grandmother's horse, so there was no way she was taking a chance on losing her. Which was why she was sprinting across the pasture, praying she didn't step into a hole and bust her ankle.

"Merry, come back," she called to the horse, knowing the mare wasn't the same as a dog and most likely wouldn't just come when she was called, but it was worth a try.

She patted her coat pockets, finding only her gloves as she realized she'd left her phone and its nifty flashlight app on her nightstand. But with the bright moonlight, she could still see all the way across the field to where the horse had just splashed through the stream and passed by her and Colt's tree as it galloped onto the Callahan property.

Great, she thought as she picked up the pace. When she'd been by here before, she'd seen that the bridge was broken, *their* bridge, the one Holt had made for them and where he'd carved their initials—LM + HC = 4Ever—into the top step. Seeing how the bridge had fallen apart from weather and decay had felt like a symbol of what had happened to their relationship, and she wasn't looking forward to seeing the reminder of that again. Or of splashing through the creek in her ankle-high sheepskin UGG boots.

But she came to a full stop when she reached the creek, and her heart swelled as she saw that the bridge had been repaired. Slowly approaching the new structure, she blinked back tears as she took in the fresh lumber forming the new steps leading over the rushing water and the cedar railings worn smooth from recently being sanded. Holt had to have fixed it, but when?

She slowly walked up the first step, then the next, then she sank to her knees, the tears coming freely as she ran her hand over the smooth top step where their initials were supposed to be.

If the bridge symbolized their relationship, then what did it mean that Holt had repaired it? A fresh new start for them? But then what did it mean that he hadn't recarved their initials?

Oblivious to the cold, she leaned down and pressed her tear-soaked cheek against the smooth wood. She brushed her fingers over the wood as if it might hold the answers, then caught her pinkie on a small dip in the plane. Sitting up, she saw that someone *had* carved something into the side of the step. It was about three inches tall and oval-shaped. Peering closer, she caught her breath as she realized what it was and knew Holt was the one who had made the steps.

Their initials weren't there, but the sign of renewal, of starting over, was. And who else but Holt would have known that symbol was a pine cone?

A faint whinny rent through the air, and Lainey clamored over the stairsteps, brushing the tears from her face as she ran toward the sound. She was sure Merry was heading for the Heaven Can Wait ranch. She could see the mare's black form as it galloped into the farmyard.

Damn. She needed to get to the horse and get her out of there before Merry woke Holt up.

Too late. She heard the dog bark and saw the bunkhouse lights turn on at the same time she realized she was running up to Holt's house in the middle of the freaking night in UGG mini boots and skimpy pajamas. *And* she wasn't wearing a bra.

CHAPTER 17

HOLT SHOT UPRIGHT IN BED, SURE HE'D HEARD THE SOUND of jingle bells, then a horse's whinny, right before Lou went crazy barking her fool head off. The dog had taken to sleeping on the end of his bed and was now jumping around the mattress and yipping at the window.

"What the devil is going on out there?" he asked, more to himself than to the dog as he climbed out of bed and reached for his pants. Even though it was late, he hadn't been asleep. His mind had been racing with thoughts of Lainey and all the things that had happened and been said over the last week. What else was new? It seemed his mind was always full of thoughts of her.

"All right, chill out. I'm checking on it," he told the dog as he crossed the room to peer through the blinds.

A familiar black horse was galloping around the farmyard. He blinked and drew closer to the window. He couldn't believe it—it was like his thoughts had manifested her—but Lainey was outside too, racing around the yard trying to catch the runaway horse.

Holt grabbed a shirt and ran for the front door, stopping to pull on his boots and jacket, then telling the dog to stay before yanking the door open. "Lainey? What are you doing out here?" he called as he hurried down the steps of the porch.

"Trying to catch this d-dang horse. And f-freezing my ass off." Her teeth were chattering, and she had her arms wrapped around herself.

"Pass me that halter, then go on inside," he told her, slowly approaching the horse. "I got this."

She shifted from one foot to the other as if trying to decide if she should pass him the halter or continue trying to catch the horse herself. Her frozen tush must have won out because she handed him the halter, then hurried past him toward the bunkhouse. He heard Lou's excited barks as she went inside.

"It's okay, girl." Holt held out his free hand and spoke softly to the horse, gently reassuring her as he took a few steps closer. The mare bucked her head up a few times and let out one more whinny before settling down and letting Holt approach her. "That's it," he crooned, giving her neck a scratch before holding the halter out and gently sliding it over her nose, then pulling the strap over her head and buckling it behind her ear.

He continued to talk quietly as he walked her into the barn and secured her in an empty stall. "You're a good horse, aren't you? Although maybe not that good because you somehow escaped the barn and dragged Lainey across the pasture in the middle of the night. But I've been missing her, so in my estimation, getting her over here, whether it's in the middle of the night or the middle of the day, in her Sunday best or what looked like her pajamas, I'm just glad you brought her here."

Once the mare was secure in the stall, he removed her

halter and gave the horse a sugar cube. "Good night, Merry. I'll either see you in a bit to take you home, or if all goes well in the next few minutes, you and Lainey will be sleeping over, and I won't see you until morning."

The horse raised her head and let out a neigh that Holt hoped meant "Good luck" and not "You don't stand a chance in hell, sucker."

Lainey was huddled under a blanket in the corner of the couch when Holt walked back into the bunkhouse. Lou was curled against her leg, as if offering her all the warmth her small body had to give. The dog looked up when he came inside but then put her head back down in Lainey's lap.

"I put Merry in the barn," Holt said, crossing the room to sit on the edge of the coffee table in front of her. He picked up her foot and rubbed it between his palms. "You must be freezing. What happened?"

"I don't know exactly," she said. "I couldn't sleep, and I saw the barn light was on, so I went out to check on the animals and turn it off. I just thought I'd run out and back inside, but when I got out there, Merry was acting all skittish and her stall door was open."

He frowned. "How did that happen?"

She shrugged but wouldn't look at him. "I don't know. My mind has been a little preoccupied lately, and I may not have latched it."

"That's understandable. You've got a lot going on with the festival."

She rolled her eyes, then gave him a piercing look. "The festival is *not* what I've been preoccupied with."

"Oh" was all he said. He was sorry she was having a hard time, but a little part of him was happy to hear that she'd been having as much trouble concentrating as he had.

"Although that's what I *should* have been focused on," she said. "I spent the entire weekend working on things for it, but I still feel like I'm running behind."

"I'm still willing to help. Just say the word. I'll do whatever, and I can totally stay out of your way. You can just text me a list of what you need done, and you won't even have to see me."

She sighed. "I don't think my idea of us taking a break from each other is going so well."

His heart leapt in his chest, but he didn't want to seem too enthused, like a golden retriever running around begging for her attention. "No?"

"No. And it seems like there's a higher power at work since I somehow ended up on your sofa in the middle of the night."

He raised an eyebrow and offered her a grin. "And in your pajamas."

"That too. I can guarantee I was *not* planning to leave my phone on my nightstand and run all the way over here in the snow. I'm sorry I got you out of bed."

He wasn't. Especially if she ended up back in it with him. He picked up her other foot and rubbed it. "Don't worry about it. I've been a little preoccupied too, so I wasn't asleep. Although maybe I *had* drifted off because I swear I heard sleigh bells ring right before I heard Merry whinny. Just like the last time she was here. That first day I brought her back to Mountainside. But when I put her in the barn, she wasn't wearing any bells."

"That's funny. I didn't hear any bells, and you're right, she wasn't wearing any when she escaped the barn." Her lips quirked up in a grin. "Are you sure it wasn't Santa's sleigh you heard?"

"I doubt it. There's no reason for him to stop here. I can't imagine I'm on the 'nice' list."

Her grin widened. "Are you saying you've been naughty?"

"Not as much as I'd like to be." His lips curved, and he slid his hand higher up her leg, grazing his fingertips along the back of her knee, then up the outside of her thigh.

A shiver shook her shoulders, but he hoped it wasn't from the cold. "In one way, everything feels so easy with you, like we're right back where we used to be. Like the other night at the bonfire."

"I feel the same way. But I don't get why that's a bad thing."

"It's not exactly a bad thing. It's just…you know…a lot. Like these feelings are so intense and everything with us has happened so fast. I don't usually jump into bed that quickly with someone."

"You didn't jump. I carried you."

She let out a small laugh. "True. But what I'm trying to say is that I'm not usually like that. I haven't been with a lot of men, probably because you're so hard to measure up to, and I've certainly never… I mean, the other day I was practically *naked*…on the kitchen counter…and I didn't even care… because you were doing that thing…with your tongue… and…" She buried her face in her hands. "I can't believe I'm even talking about it."

Holt couldn't stop the grin crossing his face. He loved the way she got embarrassed and loved that he was the only man who'd "done that thing with his tongue" to her on the kitchen counter. "There is so much to think about in what you just said, like, I'm kind of stuck on the part about me being hard to measure up to, although I'll admit I heard that in a dirty way, but then you said 'naked' and 'kitchen counter,' and I couldn't really focus on anything other than that image after that."

She laughed and nudged him with her foot. "I know. Now I'm thinking about it too."

He nodded toward his kitchen. "I've got plenty of counter space."

She laughed as she shook her head. "See, this is what I mean. I have so much fun with you. And I can talk to you like I can't talk to anyone else."

"That seems like a good thing."

"It's a scary-as-hell thing. Especially because we aren't talking about the fact that I'm only here for a few weeks."

His smile fell. The reminder of her leaving was like she'd just doused him with a bucket of cold water. "Yeah, I know. I saw your half-full suitcase sitting out in your bedroom the other day."

"I don't know if I can take getting hurt again. That's why I said I wanted to take a step back. I'm trying to protect myself."

"I get that. I hear everything you're saying, and I've had all the same thoughts, but I don't care. I've dreamed of seeing you again, holding you again, for so many years. And now here you are, in my life and in my bed, and I can't get enough of you. I'm terrified that I'm going to blink, and you'll disappear again, but I'm more scared of wasting the time we do have together."

He reached for her and pulled her onto his lap, then nuzzled his lips against her neck. "I don't want to think about what happened in the past, and I don't want to worry about what's going to happen in the future. We can cross that bridge when we come to it. For now, I just want to take advantage of the time we have and be together. And I don't just mean in the bedroom, although I'm certainly all for that too, but I also just want to spend time with you. Whether we're collecting pine cones or baking cookies or making better use of the counter in the kitchen, I just want to be with you."

He watched her swallow, and then she raised her hands to cup his cheeks. "I just want to be with you too."

Her hands were cold, and he turned his face to press a kiss into the center of one of her palms. Then he looked into her eyes, trying to convey all the feelings he had for her, how she meant so much to him. His voice was soft as he whispered, "Stay with me tonight?"

And every night.

Her smile was slow and easy, and the flirt was back in her tone as she lifted one shoulder in a shrug. "I guess I might as well, since I'm here and already wearing my pajamas."

"Oh, darlin'," he said, sliding his hand under her shirt. "Give me ten seconds and you won't be wearing those pajamas at all."

CHAPTER 18

THE NEXT MORNING, HOLT WOKE UP SLOWLY, BLINKING his eyes and relishing the feel of the warm, lush body curled against his. He still couldn't believe that Lainey was here, in his bed, the scent of her on his pillow.

But for how long?

Having her here was just like the holiday he loathed—so exciting and wonderful and perfect leading up to it, then as soon as it was over, all he'd be left with were an empty wallet, a stomachache, and a bunch of regret over how much he'd let himself indulge in the *magic* of the last few weeks. Or in this case, he'd be dealing not just with pain in his stomach but heartache too.

He peered down at her long eyelashes, her perfect mouth, the mess of curls spread over his pillow, and his chest tightened with the intensity of the love he felt for her.

Love?

He tenderly touched her cheek with the back of his fingers. Her skin was so soft. Everything about her was soft. Including the small sigh of contentment she'd just breathed out as she snuggled closer. Yeah, it was love.

Been here before. Didn't work out so great. Remember?

No. He couldn't go there. Wouldn't. He couldn't let

himself think beyond the next few days. She was here now, and that was all that mattered.

Well, her and the farm full of animals who were waiting to be fed. He pressed a soft kiss to the side of her forehead, then eased out of bed. The dog, who had been curled at their feet, lifted her head to watch him as he collected clean clothes and slipped out of the room.

He let Lainey sleep as he put on the coffee, let the dog out, and took a quick shower. He'd fed Lou but needed to get to his other chores. Two more sips of coffee, then he set his cup on the counter and peered down at the dog sitting by his feet. "I'm going out to the barn. Do you want to come with me or go back to bed with Lainey?" He pointed at the door first, then toward the bedroom as he offered her the choices.

Lou looked up at him, tilting her head one way, then the other, then she ran down the hall and back into the bedroom. He heard the tapping of her toenails stop and the quiet landing of her body on the bed.

"Good choice," he muttered. If he didn't have a farmyard full of animals to feed and water, he'd be jumping back into bed with her too. But probably not to sleep.

It took him close to an hour to take care of the animals and handle the farm needs. Lainey was up and standing in the kitchen when he came back into the bunkhouse, a small carton full of fresh eggs in his hands. The dog was at her feet, and she wagged her tail as she ran to him.

Lainey laughed at the dog, then flashed him that smile she reserved just for him. "Good morning, cowboy," she said, her voice still husky with sleep.

"Mornin'." He swallowed at the sudden emotion burning his throat. She was wearing his sweats and T-shirt again, and her hair was sticking out in a bedhead mess, but she was still just so damn beautiful.

They stood there for a few seconds, just smiling at each other. Then the dog jumped up on his legs, trying to sniff at the box he was holding. He held it up. "The chickens have been busy. You feel like bacon and eggs for breakfast?"

She nodded, then lifted her cup. "Coffee first. Then shower. Then breakfast. Then words."

He chuckled. "Got it." He set the eggs on the counter and picked up his cup. "Did you leave enough for me?"

"Barely," she said, grabbing the pot and filling his cup. "I considered foregoing the cup and just using a straw in the pot."

"Sorry, between me and the horse, we didn't let you get a lot of sleep last night."

She shrugged and offered him one of her flirty grins. "It was worth losing the sleep. You, not the horse."

He pulled her to him, leaning in to press a kiss to her neck. It didn't matter that they'd been together hours before; he wanted her again. But as much as he wanted her, he also wanted answers. They'd been sidestepping the most important conversation, the one where they talked about what happened all those years ago.

He took a step back, leaning his hip against the counter, and let out a sigh. There wasn't enough coffee in the world to make this conversation any easier. "Listen, Lainey, as much as I want to drag you right back to bed, and I do, I think we need to talk."

She looked down into her cup, her expression sobering as she nodded. "Yeah, we probably do."

"I'm so happy to be here with you again. It feels like I finally have my best friend back in my life."

"Me too."

"I don't want to mess that up, but I need to understand what happened back then, why you left like you did."

"I have questions too. Like how you could just let us go."

He jerked his head back. "Me? I wasn't given a choice. You're the one who—" He was interrupted by the sound of retching, and he turned to see Lou standing by the door, her small body convulsing. He raced over and pulled open the door, hoping she could make it outside, but instead she heaved a giant glob of half-digested dog food onto his boot.

"Oh no. Poor baby," Lainey said, hurrying toward the dog.

"What the heck did she get into?" he asked, peering down at the red and green bits of tinfoil mixed in with the dog food. "It looks like the wrappers off some chocolate Kisses."

Lainey picked up the dog and held her to her chest, oblivious to the fact that she might throw up again. She carried her into the living room and stopped in front of her overturned purse. Reaching down, she picked up the remains of a plastic bag that had a dog-mouth-sized hole chewed through it. "That's *exactly* what used to be in this bag. She must have smelled them in my purse."

He nodded, reaching for a paper towel to clean the mess off his boot. "Sounds about right."

She peered down at the dog with a concerned expression.

"I want to scold her, but I think barfing them back up probably taught her more of a lesson."

He shook his head with a huff. "You must not have spent
enough time around dogs. They don't have the best memory
when it comes to food. If you offered her a whole bag of
chocolate Kisses right now, I'd bet my last dollar she'd scarf
every last one up."

"But isn't chocolate supposed to be deadly to dogs?"

"Yes, but not in that small of a quantity. And she barfed
most of it back up, so I can't imagine it was too dangerous."

"We should call the vet anyway."

Thirty minutes later, after cleaning everything up, including the dog, and verifying with Brody that a few chocolate
Kisses weren't going to kill her, Lou was sleeping peacefully
on a throw blanket in the corner of the couch.

"I need a shower," Lainey said, pulling at the front of her shirt.

"Want some company?" He'd already showered but suddenly felt the need to take another. A burning need.

"I was just thinking I could use someone to wash my
back." She batted her eyelashes and offered him a coy grin.
"And my front."

He grinned back, all traces of their earlier conversation
pushed aside as he envisioned her slick, wet naked body.
"Pass me the soap."

It was midmorning before they made it back into the
kitchen, but Holt couldn't remember a time when bacon
and eggs had ever tasted so good. He loved having her in
his kitchen with him, buttering the toast and making fresh
coffee as he fried the eggs.

They sat on the sofa together to eat, her legs across his lap. The dog curled against his hip, her gaze trained on their plates in hopes of seeing a crumb fall.

"So what's on your to-do list for today?" Holt asked as he passed his last bite of toast to Lou, then set their empty plates on the coffee table in front of them.

"Mainly paperwork-type stuff. I'm feeling pretty on top of things," she said.

"I like it when you're on top of…things," he said, unable to stop the impish grin from creasing his face, then couldn't stop the laugh that broke out of him.

She shook her head but laughed with him as she sat up and straddled his lap. "Yes, you made that quite clear."

"Are you sure? Because I was thinking you might need a little more convincing." He wrapped his hands around her waist and pulled her closer.

She leaned down to kiss him but was interrupted by a sharp knock on the door.

"Who the devil could that be?" Holt grumbled as Lainey climbed off his lap.

He opened the door to a middle-aged dark-haired man holding a yellow sheet of paper and wearing a scowl. "You the Callahan that runs this horse rescue outfit?"

Holt nodded. "One of 'em, I guess." He didn't know the man, but he did recognize the paper he held as one of the flyers for the horse rescue Bryn had posted around town. "Something I can help you with?"

"Seems you already did. Without my permission."

"I'm not following."

"I'm Stan Gardner. Sarah's my daughter, and it seems that instead of coming out and taking that horse of hers off our hands like we thought you were going to, you just brought out some hay instead. Which nobody asked you to do."

Ah. He was caught up now. "Listen, Stan...Mr. Gardner, we didn't mean any disrespect. We were just trying to help."

"By giving my daughter false hope? We told her we couldn't afford to keep the horse, and now you've only prolonged the inevitable."

Lainey came to stand beside him. "Hi, Mr. Gardner, I'm Lainey McBride. My grandparents run Mountainside Ranch, and I helped Holt bring the hay and feed out to your farm. And like he said, we were just trying to help."

Holt nodded. "I just couldn't see my way to taking that little girl's horse away right before Christmas."

"So what? You think you're some kind of Santa and Mrs. Claus? Like you bestowed some miracle on us? Two weeks from now we'll be in the same boat and the horse will still have to go. In the meantime, you've made me look even worse in the eyes of my child, that I can't make enough money to feed her dang animal."

"I'm sorry if you took it that way," Holt told him. "Like I said, that was not our intention. I know what it's like to fall on hard times, and the pressure of the holidays only seems to make it worse." *Another reason to hate Christmas.* "But I'm sure you'll find another job, and we're trying to come up with some ways to help you keep the horse until you do."

His scowl deepened. "I'm no charity case."

"It's not charity," Lainey said, her tone soft and caring.

"It's community. The people of Creedence take care of each other. If your neighbor was in trouble and you had the means to help him, wouldn't you lend a hand?"

"'Course I would."

"That's all we're doing. Just trying to lend a hand," Holt said. "Our job is to rescue horses, but that doesn't mean we have to take them away from good homes. We can also help by offering hay and feed until you get back on your feet. Nobody is trying to make you the bad guy."

"In fact," Lainey added. "You have the chance to be the hero here by letting Sarah keep her horse. And no one has to even know we're helping." She chewed on her bottom lip. "Although I was tossing around a few ideas for a fundraiser for Copper that we could do at the winter festival, but maybe we could change it up a little and give Sarah and Copper a way to make their own money for feed and supplies?"

Stan eyed her suspiciously. "Like what kind of way?"

She tapped her fingertips against her lips, and Holt prayed she would come up with something quick. "What if Sarah brought Copper to the festival and they had their own booth? She could outfit him with tinsel and twinkle lights and charge folks to take a picture with Copper the Christmas Horse. Or maybe she could offer rides to kids for a small fee, and she could lead them around in the corral."

Stan scratched his head. "I don't know about any of that."

Holt could see he was considering it though. They just needed to close the deal. Then once Sarah was at the festival, they could figure out how to get her booth to rake in some cash. "I think these are great ideas. And I'll bet she could make enough to cover hay and feed for several months." Especially if the horse rescue made a large *anonymous* donation to her and Copper.

"And maybe you could come and help Sarah with Copper and the booth," Lainey said. "I'm sure she'd love that, getting to spend time with her horse *and* her dad."

"Maybe." Stan narrowed his eyes. "But what's in it for you? You planning to take a cut of the profits?"

Lainey jerked her head back. "No, absolutely not. Whatever she makes is hers to keep. I..." She paused and pointed to herself and Holt. "*We* just want to help a little girl and her family hold on to their horse. No strings. I swear."

He kept his eyes narrowed, but Holt could see him softening. "Let me talk to my wife. And Sarah."

"Sure, of course," Lainey said. "We can set up a space for you right next to the barn. I could put you next to the hot chocolate station and maybe even pay Sarah for running that booth for a few hours too." She put her hand on his arm. "I promise you, Mr. Gardner, we just want to help."

"Call me Stan," he said.

Yeah, he was softening all right. Another victim falling under Lainey's spell of kindness.

"All right, Stan. We hope to see you on Friday. You and Sarah and Copper. Heck, bring the whole family. The festivities start at ten and go all day, so if you want to come out around nine, you should have plenty of time to get set up. We'll have a space ready for you, and if you think of anything else you need, just call out to Mountainside and let me know."

"I will," he said, then raised his hand in a small wave. "See you then."

"See ya then," Holt said, before closing the door.

Through the kitchen window, they could see him walk to his car and get in.

"He looks kind of dazed," Holt said. "Like he's not quite sure what just happened."

Lainey laughed. "You mean because he came here to give you a piece of his mind and walked away after agreeing to do a fundraising booth with his daughter and her horse at the winter festival?"

He laughed with her. "Yeah, that's exactly what I mean. Poor guy."

"Poor guy? He's going to turn out to be a hero in his daughter's eyes."

Lainey ended up sticking around for lunch and into midafternoon. She and Holt had made sandwiches and talked through their plans for the festival and how the events of the schedule would go. They'd spend the better part of the day on Thursday making sure everything was set up for the big day on Friday when all the festivities happened. Thankfully, Holt agreed to do sleigh rides again on Friday, although this time she wouldn't be able to ride along. Then Saturday night was the Holiday Ho-Ho-Hoedown. The band had been booked months in advance, and they'd already set up the stage and moved the hay bales in preparation for the dance.

"I've made lists for everything we need to do for each day and what to prep the night before," Lainey told him. "And I've got a bunch of volunteers lined up to help."

"If you've got so many volunteers, are you sure you need me?"

"Yes, of course I need you. You'll be the only other one who knows how everything is supposed to be running. I hope you'll be there for *all* of it." She emphasized "all" because she was still being careful how she was talking about the dance on Saturday night with him. They both knew it was a touchy subject, and it felt intentional that neither of them was talking too much about it.

All those years ago, when she and her mom had fled from her stepdad, it had been the night before the annual Ho-Ho-Hoedown. She and Holt had planned to go together, just like they had every year since they'd met. But that year had been different. That year they would have gone as a real couple instead of with the whole group. But she never made it.

Her grandma told her later that Holt had shown up that night to pick her up for the dance and had been crestfallen when she'd told him that Lainey had left. She knew he had to have been so mad and confused. She just prayed it hadn't taken him long to find the letter she'd left him in their tree.

Had her standing him up that night been part of the reason he'd stood *her* up on her eighteenth birthday? He'd never been big on retaliation. In fact, he had always been more forgiving than her. That's why she thought he'd be able to let her deserting him go and find his way back to her. But it hadn't happened that way.

Should she invite him to go to the dance with her this weekend? Or would that just bring up old wounds that they were working so hard to ignore? They'd tried to talk about what happened back then when they were in the kitchen that morning, but then they got interrupted by the dog. Maybe now was the chance to try again.

"So…um…about the dance," she said, testing the waters to see if he would tense up or shut down.

But she didn't have a chance to see anything because his phone buzzed in his pocket. He pulled it out, then frowned at the screen. "Sorry, I'd better take this. It's the sheriff."

CHAPTER 19

The sheriff? Lainey leaned forward. Why would the sheriff be calling Holt?

He tapped the screen, then held the phone to his ear. "Callahan here."

She watched his face, trying to decipher what kind of information the sheriff was telling him by his expressions. Whatever the news was, it wasn't good.

Holt's frown deepened. "Yeah, sure. I can saddle up a horse and ride up there now. See if I can find her. Text me the coordinates of where she was last seen. I'll let you know what I find." He tapped the screen again and pushed the phone back in his pocket.

"What's happening?" Lainey asked, her heart racing. "Who are you going to go look for? Please tell me it's not a lost child."

"No, thankfully. It's not a person," he told her. "It's an injured horse. Couple of hunters were in the mountains just west of our property, and they spotted a horse in the trees. Thank goodness neither of them shot it. But they said it was cut up pretty badly and they could see a lot of blood on its flank. They said it was pretty worked up, so they didn't get too close to it, but it looked to be well groomed, so they figured it belonged to someone, which is why they let the sheriff know."

"Did they say how it got hurt?"

Holt shook his head. "Could have gotten caught in some barbed-wire fencing or could have been attacked by a mountain lion or coyotes. I'm familiar with the general area where she was spotted. It's up past our hunting cabin, but it's weird that a lone horse would be up there."

"Poor thing."

"I'm going to put together a pack of medical supplies, and I'll ride up to see if I can find her." He pulled a thermos from the cupboard and poured the rest of the coffee into it, then grabbed a bag of beef jerky from the pantry and tossed it on the counter next to the thermos.

"Could you use another set of eyes?" Lainey asked, already deciding she wanted to go with him. "You know I can ride, and I'd like to help if I can."

Holt paused and looked at her, as if trying to gauge how serious she was. Then he nodded. "Sure. If you'd like. You can ride Beauty, Bryn's horse. But you're gonna need warmer gear." He glanced down at his sweats and T-shirt she was wearing, then pulled his keys from his pocket and tossed them to her. "Why don't you take my truck back to your place and get changed while I tack up the horses? The sun's out now, but once we get up in the trees, it'll get cold, so you're gonna need a warm jacket and a hat and gloves. I've got some thermal socks you can borrow, but I'd trade those slipper boots you wore over here for the Sorels you had on the other day."

"Got it. I've got a CamelBak I can fill with water, and I've got some protein bars too. Anything else I can bring?" she asked as she shrugged into her coat.

"I don't think so."

"I can be back in twenty minutes. Maybe fifteen."

"Twenty's fine. It'll take me that long to put together the medical gear we'll need and to get the horses ready." He narrowed his eyes. "It's gonna be a hard ride up the mountain, and it's gonna get cold. You sure you want to go along?"

She gave him a hard nod. "I'm sure. And don't worry about me. I'll be fine." She had plenty of cold-weather gear, but she *was* a little nervous about the ride. It had been years since she'd been on a horse, but her main concern was finding and rescuing the injured mare. "I'll be back as fast as I can."

He nodded back, and then she was out the door and hurrying toward his truck, secretly pleased that he had so readily tossed her his keys and entrusted her with his pickup. But she didn't take too much time to think about it as she sped out of the driveway and raced toward her grandparents' ranch.

Eighteen minutes later, she pulled back into the driveway and parked in front of the barn. She'd changed into her winter gear and twisted her hair into braids, then pulled a wool beanie over her head. She'd filled two CamelBaks with water and stuffed some protein bars into the pockets of her jacket, along with a couple of apples from a basket on her counter.

Both horses were tacked and ready, and Holt was buckling the saddlebags on Bristol when she walked into the barn. "I brought us some water and protein bars," she said, passing him one of the CamelBaks. "And I grabbed a couple of apples thinking maybe we could use them to get the horse to trust us."

"Good thinking," Holt said, patting his front coat pocket. "I stuck in a handful of sugar cubes and some sweet feed for the same reason."

"Anything else I can do to help?"

"Nope. You made good time. I'm impressed." He unwound the reins from the saddle horn of a gorgeous brown quarter horse and passed them to her. "This is Beauty. She was Bryn and Zane's first rescue, and she's a real sweetheart."

Lainey took the reins, then patted the horse's neck. "Nice to meet you, Beauty. I appreciate you taking me up the mountain."

The horse let out a low snuffle and stamped one foot, as if to say, "Nice to meet you too." Lainey led the horse from the barn, then pulled herself up into the saddle and gave Beauty's neck another affectionate pat before falling in step next to Holt and his horse.

They rode side by side through the pastures, and then she fell in behind him when they started up the steep trail that zigzagged up the side of the mountain.

It had been years since she'd been on horseback, but she remembered how much she loved it as she settled into the saddle and fell into the rhythm of moving with the horse. Beauty was sure-footed and confident as she climbed the rocky trail. Lainey figured Bryn probably took her on this trail frequently since it led toward the lake and the Callahans' hunting cabin.

They rode mostly in a comfortable silence, Lainey

sensing Holt's need to keep his focus sharp as she looked for signs of the horse. Following the sheriff's coordinates of where the hunters had seen the mare, they topped one ridge, then rode north and up another.

The sun had been shining brightly when they left, and they'd both had their coats unzipped and open, but as they climbed higher into the mountains and the trees blocked the warmth of the sun, they zipped their coats, and Lainey pulled her beanie lower over her ears.

They'd been riding for close to an hour when Holt stopped and pointed to the ground. "I think this is her. I can make out horse tracks plus there's blood in the snow. It looks like she headed up through those trees. We should be able to follow her tracks."

Holt led them through the trees, pointing out broken branches and spots of blood. Lainey followed, keeping a sharp eye out for any signs of the horse. They wound through a rocky area and had just ridden around an outcropping of boulders when they spotted her.

"Look. There. I think I see her." Lainey pointed to some evergreens about fifty feet ahead of them.

Holt pushed his horse forward, then slowed as they got closer. "I think she's trapped in those trees." He slid off his horse and wound Bristol's reins around a branch. Then he slowly approached the trees.

As Lainey got closer, she could see the small clearing where the horse stood. It looked like lightning had struck one of the larger trees and it had fallen across the opening to the clearing, trapping the horse inside.

Lainey caught her breath. *Poor baby.* She followed Holt's lead and dismounted from her horse, tying Beauty up next to Bristol. She hung back a bit, waiting for Holt to let her know how she could help.

"It's okay, baby," he crooned to the horse as he carefully climbed over the fallen tree. "We're gonna get you out of here."

The mare was a dark golden color, except for a patch of white on her forehead and one white sock, but her coat was dusty now and streaked with mud. Her eyes were wild as she stamped her feet and galloped back and forth across the small clearing. Her right flank was crusted with dried blood, and Lainey could see a six-inch gash running across it.

Holt stopped about five feet from her and pulled a few of the sugar cubes from his pocket. He held them out on his flattened palm and waited for the horse to come to him. She took a few steps forward, then reared back, then stamped her feet again.

Lainey held her breath, fascinated as she watched Holt standing perfectly calm, his shoulders loose and relaxed, his tone soothing as he murmured softly to the horse, patiently waiting as he let the horse come to him.

She stamped once more, then stood still, her breath huffing out little clouds as she eyed Holt. Finally, after what seemed like another full five minutes, she shook her head, then plodded slowly toward him. When she got close enough, she tentatively drew her head toward his outstretched hand, then pulled back slightly, then lowered her head again as she carefully nibbled the sugar cubes from his palm.

He pulled a handful of grain from his pocket and held that out, then gently brushed his fingers across the side of her head as she ate the feed from his hand. Taking his time, continuing to talk to her in soothing tones, he eased the halter he'd brought from inside his jacket and calmly drew it up over her nose then pulled it over her head and buckled it behind her ear.

Lainey let out her breath. *He did it.*

"Easy now," Holt told the horse as he ran his hand along her back and over her rump. "I'm just gonna take a look at your leg." She stamped her back leg as his hand slid down her flank, but she didn't walk or run away. "There're several cuts and scrapes here, but none of them look deep enough for stitches. And most of the blood has dried. My bet is that she scraped herself up on a fence or some branches as she was tearing through the trees. What the hell she's doing up here is still a mystery though."

"Can I do anything to help?"

"Yeah, I put a lead rope in that saddle bag closest to you. Can you get it out and carefully ease it over to me? You can hand it to me over the branches."

Moving slowly, she retrieved the rope and grabbed the first aid kit too. Keeping calm, she walked toward the branches and handed them both to Holt. The horse watched them but didn't flinch as Holt stepped closer and hooked the lead to her halter. He tied the end of the rope around a branch, then set to work cleaning the wound the best he could with the supplies they'd brought.

"We're gonna need to move these branches to get her out

of here," he told Lainey after he'd done what he could for the horse's leg. "I'll see if I can't break some of these big limbs off so it will be easier to move." He passed her the first aid kit, and she returned it to the saddlebags, then pulled on her gloves and set to helping him clear the path.

Working together, they were able to move enough branches and pull the tree far enough out of the way to make a path for Holt to lead the horse through. He brought her over to Bristol and gave them a minute to get to know each other before he swung himself into the saddle and they started back down the mountain, him leading the injured horse behind them.

Lainey left a good space between them as she followed behind, impressed with Holt's skills as a horseman as he maneuvered his horse through the trees while keeping the horse on the lead calm as well.

The ride back down to the ranch took longer than the way up, and by the time they reached the barn, Lainey's fingers and toes were frozen. But she was still glad she'd gone along and could assist in the rescue.

She held the horse's halter as Holt prepared a stall, laying in fresh water and straw and filling the trough with hay before leading the horse inside. Once she was settled and had started eating, he could spend more time and thoroughly clean and bandage the wound.

"There's not much more I can do other than clean it and goop it up with antibiotic ointment," Holt told her after he'd finished. "I put a couple of butterfly bandages on the worst cut, but like I said, the others don't look deep enough for stitches."

"I think she'll feel better just having them cleaned and knowing she's in a warm safe place. And it looks like she's made a friend." They hadn't put the other horses away yet, and she pointed to where Bristol was leaning his head over the stall gate as if checking on the new mare.

"Good, that'll help keep her calm too. Hopefully she can get some rest now that she's back in a stall. Just looking at the way her mane is cut and the condition of her coat, I think she did belong to someone. I'll let the sheriff know we found her."

"Wouldn't he know if someone's been looking for her?"

"Not necessarily. She could be from another county. Or more than likely, someone couldn't afford to keep her anymore, so they just let her loose."

"No. Who would do that?"

"You'd be surprised. All of Bryn's rescues have different stories, some involving terrible treatment and abuse, but most of them had been abandoned or the owners couldn't afford to keep them anymore. At least if they let them go, they have a chance of surviving on winter grass, but it's the ones they leave tied up in the barn that get me. When I first got here this summer, Carley and her fiancé, Knox—you met them the other night at the bonfire—had just rescued a mare and a dog that had been left behind in a dilapidated old barn. The dog had been digging through a trash pile and bringing the horse scraps of food to keep it alive."

Lainey covered her mouth. "Oh my gosh. That's terrible."

"We see a lot of terrible stuff in these rescues. But we've also seen a lot of good people come together to help these horses."

She shivered, both from the thought of anyone hurting an animal and from the cold.

"Hey, you must be freezing. We should get you inside," he said. "And Lou's probably ready to be let out."

They headed back to the bunkhouse and were greeted with yips and licks from the little dog before she ran outside to take care of business.

"I should probably be getting back to the ranch," Lainey said, although part of her just wanted to curl back up on the sofa with Holt.

"You probably haven't been able to check anything off that massive to-do list today."

"No, but it helped to talk through the schedule for the weekend with you earlier. It just solidified the timetable and reminded me of a few other things I haven't taken care of." Although she was tempted to leave them there in hopes of another invitation for a sleepover, she collected her pajamas from the night before and stuffed them into her coat pocket.

"We've still got plenty of sunshine if you want to walk back," Holt said. "And that might be an easier way to take Merry home than to trailer her for such a short ride."

"Oh geez. I almost forgot about Merry." The horse was the whole reason she was there. Well, the horse and the hot cowboy she couldn't seem to stay away from. "Yeah, sure. A walk sounds good."

The dog whined at the word "walk" and lifted her paws in the air.

Holt shook his head. "You can't tell me that dog doesn't

belong to someone. I don't think a stray would get that excited by just hearing the word 'walk.'"

Lainey frowned. "This is so hard. I mean, I don't want a family to be missing their dog, but I've already fallen in love with this sweet girl, and I can't imagine her leaving."

"I know the feeling," Holt muttered.

At least that's what Lainey thought he muttered. He'd turned away and was already shrugging into his coat, so she couldn't be sure. Maybe she just wanted him to have said that.

Holt opened the door and gave a little whistle for the dog. "Let's go then."

Lou ran in an excited circle around Lainey's legs, then raced out the door. And ran smack into the large pig sunning herself on Holt's porch.

"Watch out for Tiny," Holt told her, reaching down to give the pig an affectionate scratch on the neck. "How's my best girl?"

"Hey," Lainey cried, nudging Holt with her elbow. "What does that make me?"

He shrugged as he offered her a mischievous grin. "You're okay too, but Tiny brings a lot to the table."

"Tiny looks like she could *eat* the table. No offense," she told the pig. Tiny gave a snort, then smiled as Lainey scratched her under the chin before laying her head back down on the porch and closing her eyes. "Apparently lounging in the sun is pretty strenuous work for a pig."

Holt chuckled with her. "Somebody's gotta do it."

They retrieved Merry from the barn, then set out across

the pasture with Lou racing ahead of them. Holt held the horse's lead rope in one hand and Lainey's in the other. The sun was warm on their faces as they walked, and she felt good, happy.

Until they walked up to their tree and she remembered the bridge.

CHAPTER 20

WALKING HAND IN HAND ACROSS THE PASTURE FELT LIKE old times for Holt. But he needed to be careful. This was a feeling he could get used to.

And a feeling that could just as easily be ripped out from under him like a magician's tablecloth. He was all too familiar with how easily this could all disappear.

He felt Lainey's body tense as they neared *their* spot.

"You fixed the bridge," she whispered, then looked up at him with what looked a lot like love in her eyes.

He lifted one arm in a shrug, suddenly overcome with emotion. The bridge meant a lot to him, but it meant something more to know that she still shared the sentiment.

"I saw it the other night when I followed Merry to your place," she said. "I liked the pine cones."

If she saw the pine cones, then she must have also seen that he didn't carve their initials in the new step. "I wasn't sure what to put on the top step. I wanted to restore it to the way it was but then wasn't sure. But I liked the whole fresh-start symbolism with the pine cones, so…"

She squeezed his hand. "I thought it was perfect."

He let out his breath. He wasn't sure what else to say, so he didn't say anything. But he held on to her hand as they crossed the creek and walked through the fields back to Mountainside. He returned Merry to her stall, and together, they fed the animals for the night. It was a little early, but he wasn't sure how long she'd want him to stay, and he wanted to help before he went home.

He followed her up to the house, waiting to take his cue from her, assuming she'd turn around at the top step to tell him good night. But instead, she walked right into the house, leaving the door open behind her.

Lou ran in before he could stop her, and the little dog raced all around the house, sniffing everything in her path, then sprinting to the next thing. As soon as she'd smelled the sofa and recliner, she raced down the hallway and into Lainey's bedroom.

"Sorry," he told Lainey, as he hurried after the dog. She'd never had an accident in the bunkhouse, but all the smells here were new, and he didn't want her to have her first in Lainey's bedroom.

"She's fine," Lainey said, following right behind him. "She can't hurt anything."

Holt heard her start to bark right before they rounded the door to the bedroom, but he was surprised at the offensive object causing her to get upset. The dog was standing in front of Lainey's suitcase and growling at her luggage.

"What is that crazy dog doing?" Lainey asked, hurrying over to where the suitcase was sitting open on her hope chest. "There's nothing in here but some jeans, a few sweaters, and some wool socks." She picked up the top sweater and held it down for the dog to sniff.

"Maybe she just doesn't like the idea of you packing up your things and leaving," Holt said. *The dog wasn't the only one.*

"That's silly. How could the dog know if I was leaving or not?"

"Are you?" he asked softly.

But she must not have heard him because the dog had bitten into her sweater and was playing tug-of-war with it. Lainey let it go, presumably so it wouldn't get damaged, and the dog took off with it, running back down the hall and into the living room, dragging the sweater behind her.

It took them almost five minutes to catch her, but Holt finally picked her up after Lainey had backed her into a corner of the living room. He held open her jaw and lifted the knitted sweater from her teeth, then held it out to Lainey. "It's probably a little slobbery, but at least she didn't rip it."

"You silly mutt. This is one of my favorite sweaters," she told the dog before folding the sweater and setting it on the kitchen counter, well out of the dog's reach. She looked at Holt. "Now that we got that sorted out, you want to stay for supper? I've got some hamburger or some chicken. Or I can whip up a couple of omelets."

He shook his head. "Nah. I think I'll just head on home." Seeing her suitcase, with clothes in it, was a harsh reminder that this thing with Lainey was temporary. She *was* leaving eventually. And she'd break his dang heart in the process.

"Okay." She seemed surprised and a little taken aback. "If you're sure."

"I'm sure. I've got chores to do, and I know you've got things to do for the festival too." He kept telling her that he didn't want to think about her leaving and that he just wanted to take advantage of the time they had together, so he should be wanting to stay. But that suitcase, sitting open and ready to be filled with her things, was just too much for him, and he needed to get out of there. "I'll call you tomorrow."

He knew he should kiss her goodbye, but if he did, he'd never be able to leave. So instead, he whistled for the dog and headed out the door before he could change his mind.

The next afternoon was sunny and clear, and Holt was down to his shirtsleeves as he mucked out stalls and groomed the horses. The new mare was doing well. He'd changed the bandages on her leg, and she'd let him brush her.

The warm Colorado sun was thawing the latest snow, and he could hear its steady dripping as it melted from the barn roof and the tractor sitting outside the barn door. That was one thing he loved about the state. They could get a big snow one day, then the bright sun would come out the next and melt it all away.

Tiny had stayed in her sty most of the day, enjoying the sunshine and wallowing in the mud the snowmelt was creating. But Shamus, the mini-horse, and Lou had been keeping Holt company as they followed him around. Otis had wandered into the barn a few times to check on things, and by *things*, he was really just checking to see if Holt had anything to eat. He and Tiny had both made an appearance thirty minutes ago when he'd cut into an apple for his midafternoon snack. Good thing he'd brought out two since he ended up giving more slices to the animals than he got to eat himself.

He hadn't talked to Lainey yet today, other than a quick exchange of texts to say good morning, so he was surprised to see her SUV turning into the driveway when he walked out of the barn.

"Hey. What are you doing here?" he asked as she got out of her car and headed toward him.

She arched an eyebrow. "Geez, grumpy pants. What kind of greeting is that?"

He drew in a breath, then let it out slowly. "Sorry. What I meant to say was 'Good morning, Lainey. How are you?'"

"I'm fine. Thank you. How are you?"

"I'm fine too." He tilted his head as he stared at her. "Was that enough awkward casual pleasantries for you?"

She wrinkled her nose. "Yeah, that was kind of lame."

"So. What are you doing here?"

"Oh yeah, right. I, um, came to borrow an extension cord."

It was his turn to raise an eyebrow. "Really?"

"Yeah, really. I need an extra cord to plug in the glue guns at the card-making station."

He shrugged. "Okay, sure. Hold on a sec." He ducked into the barn and crossed to the workbench where several extension cords were wound up and hung from pegs. He grabbed a green twenty-five-foot one and took it back out to her.

"Thanks," she said, taking the cord and tossing it into the back seat of her car.

"Anything else?"

"Hold on. I'm thinking."

Their attention was drawn to a new car that had turned into the driveway and came to a stop in front of them. It was also a compact SUV, but this one was a Maserati and loaded, way more high-end than the kind they normally saw around town. A man and woman got out, both in their mid- to late twenties. Holt was no expert when it came to designer anything, but he recognized that they were wearing expensive clothing and pricey ski jackets.

"Can I help you with something?" he asked. "You lost? Need directions?"

The man shook his head. "I don't think so. We saw the sign, and our navigation brought us right here. This is the Heaven Can Wait Horse Rescue, isn't it?"

"It is." Holt eyed their vehicle but couldn't see anything through the dark tinted glass. "You all have a horse in there you need rescuing?"

"Not a horse," the woman said. "But we do need to drop off an animal."

He cringed. He hated it when people acted like they could just "drop off" an animal, like it was their dry cleaning and they had no responsibility for it.

The man raised his hand in a wave. "I'm Maxton Chadwick, and this is my girlfriend, Raine Fitzgerald."

The girlfriend smiled. "It's Raine—with an E."

"Nice to meet you," Lainey said. "I'm Lainey, and this is Holt."

"With an O," Holt muttered, but they all heard it. "So what kind of animal do you have?" They'd seen all kinds at the ranch: rabbits, parakeets, ferrets, and even a tortoise. He prayed they weren't going to hand him a snake. He could handle them, but they still gave him the willies.

"Have you ever seen those videos of the fainting goats?" Maxton asked.

"You know, the ones where someone makes a noise and the goat goes stiff and then just falls over," Raine said. "They're hilarious."

"Can't say I've had the pleasure," Holt said, still not sure what they were after.

"Well, they're hilarious, until you actually own one," Maxton said. "They cracked us up so much, we thought it would be fun to get one."

"Maxi actually bought it for me for my birthday," she said. "He flew it in from Tennessee just in time for my party. Oh my gosh, you should have seen my face. And it was so funny at the party. It fainted like eighty times. You can check out the reels on my Insta or TikTok. We made so many that night. It's under LetItRaine, with an—"

Holt cut her off, his patience with this couple wearing a little thin. "Yeah, with an E, you said." He didn't know what the hell they were talking about. They'd lost him at the words *Insta or TikTok*. But it didn't sound like the goat was enjoying itself quite as much at the party. He didn't appreciate anyone making an animal miserable just for sport.

"It was funny at the party," the guy continued. "But then when we brought it home, it got scared of everything."

"That's why they faint," Raine explained. "Because they get startled. But they don't really faint. They just stiffen up, then they fall over."

"But everything at our place startled it—the coffee maker, the television, even the video instructor calling out directions when I'm riding the Peloton."

Raine wrinkled her nose. "And I don't know if you know this, but goats don't smell very good."

Well, gee, we only run a ranch with a half a dozen different farm animals on it. How could we possibly know how they smell?

"Yes, we've been around a goat or two." Or eight, counting the baby pygmy goats they'd rescued earlier that summer. Oh, and also the ornery one who ate anything in sight and was often responsible for the hijinks he and Shamus got into. Holt frowned at their vehicle. "So you've got a goat in that car?"

He was surprised that it fit *and* that it hadn't been raising holy heck to get out.

"Oh yeah," Raine said, as Maxton opened the hatchback. "She's only the size of small dog, so she fits in a crate."

Holt and Lainey walked around to the back of the car. An adorable little gray and white goat blinked up at them from inside a black mesh crate. She was cuddled in a pink blanket but stood up as Maxton opened the door of the crate. He reached in, lifted her out, and set her on the ground.

Holt crouched down and held out his hand to let her sniff it, and she started toward him. Then Lou came running toward her to say hello, and she let out a tiny bleat as her legs went stiff and she fell over.

"Oh my gosh," Lainey said, crouching down next to her as if to help.

But neither Maxton nor Raine seemed worried about the goat as they both cracked up laughing.

"Isn't that hysterical?" Raine said. "It's still funny. Even after you've seen it a million times. And don't worry, it doesn't hurt her. See, she gets right back up."

The goat did seem unfazed as it pushed back up on its feet and practically launched itself into Lainey's lap with excitement. She was about the same size as Lou, and like a dog, she was sniffing Lainey and trying to lick at her face and neck.

"Her name's Esme," Raine said. "And she's super cuddly. Like she wants your attention and your pets *all the time*. She was the runt of the litter, so she was the last one sold and spent a lot of time with the breeder's kids. They even house-trained her. For real, like, she's never had an accident in our house."

"She's a real sweet goat," Maxton said as he unloaded the crate and a clear tub of what looked like dog toys and two pink food dishes. "And she totally made us laugh, but we just can't handle her anymore."

"We heard about you from one of my mom's friends. I guess she brought her show dog out here to get a haircut last summer. Are you the one who styled her?" Raine asked Lainey.

"No, that was our friend Carley," Holt answered, after Lainey looked at him in confusion. He'd heard the story of the wealthy woman who'd paid Carley a mint to give her dog a fashionable haircut.

"Well, she did a really great job and said this place was nice." Raine looked around the ranch, and her eye caught on Shamus, standing just inside the barn. "Oh my gosh, what a cute little horse. Maxi, look at that little horse. I've got to take a pic with it." She started toward Shamus, then turned back to Holt, who thought she was going to ask if it was okay. "Is it tame? Like, can I pet it? Or will it bite?"

"His name is Shamus, and he hasn't bitten anyone yet," Holt said. Was it wrong that he secretly hoped Raine with an E might be the horse's first chomp?

But no, Shamus ate up the attention as Raine posed and snapped pictures with him. Holt swore the horse might have even smiled. Which was unusual for the mini-horse, who normally reminded Holt of a grumpy old man.

"He's soooo cute. My followers are going to die when they see these pics," Raine said, tapping at her phone. She looked up at Holt. "Is he for sale?"

Not for a million dollars. And no way in hell would Holt send Shamus home with this couple in their fancy car.

"No. Sorry. He's part of the family around here."

Maxton let out a huff as Raine pouted. "Babe. We're *not* buying that horse," he said as if he hadn't just heard Holt say Shamus wasn't for sale. "We're here to get *rid* of a pain-in-the-ass animal, not take on another."

"Fine. You're right. But he is cute."

"Not when you have to pick up his poop," Holt said, holding his hands up and about a foot apart to illustrate the size of a typical pile of manure. He tried to keep from laughing at the look of horror on Raine's face. He couldn't help himself. He just had to keep going. "He may look small, but he poops eight to ten times a day and can clear a room with his gas. And that horse is definitely *not* housebroken."

He looked down at Lainey, who was pressing her lips

together as she tried not to laugh. She was now sitting cross-legged on the ground, and the goat was curled in her lap.

Maxton grimaced, then tapped the top of the car. "We should probably get going, Babe." He pulled an envelope out of his coat pocket and handed it to Holt. "My parents make me pick a place every Christmas to give a donation to—apparently it's a tax thing—so I figured I'd choose this place. I just need a receipt to prove that I did it and for them to give to the accountant."

"Last year he was drunk and donated to the Society of Naked Clowns and his parents were so pissed," Raine explained. "Donating to you guys might help him redeem himself."

Holt frowned, but then his eyes widened as he peeked into the envelope and saw a check made out to the Heaven Can Wait Horse Rescue ranch for ten *thousand* dollars.

CHAPTER 21

HOLT COULDN'T WAIT TO TELL BRYN ABOUT THIS. SHE was going to flip. As annoying as this couple was, they'd just handed the horse rescue a very merry Christmas.

"Well, this is mighty generous of you there, Maxton." Holt gestured toward the house where he knew Bryn kept a receipt book in her office. "Let me just go write out a receipt and get you folks on your way."

"Thanks, man. And you're keeping the goat, right?"

Holt nodded, glancing down to where the goat was blissfully enjoying a chin scratch from Lainey. *Just try to take that goat back.* "Yes, we're keeping the goat."

Maxton let out a relieved sigh.

Holt hurried up to the house to write out a receipt before they changed their mind and took back their check. But they were already in the car by the time he made it back outside. The little goat was standing next to Lainey as she stood by the car. He passed them the receipt, they waved, and then they sped off out the driveway and down the highway.

"Dang. Did they even tell the goat goodbye?" Holt asked.

"No, but since they were looking for places to donate, I told them about the situation with Sarah and Copper and how we were trying to help keep this little girl's horse at home. I swear, Raine got teary-eyed, then started pulling hundred-dollar bills out of her designer wallet and handing them to me. She told Maxton to give me some too. And before I knew it, I was holding *eight hundred* dollars."

"Eight hundred? You're kidding me?"

Lainey laughed and flashed him a wad of bills. "I'm not. She said that this was less than their bar tab at the club last weekend."

"Damn. How many people were on their tab, and what the hell were they drinking?"

"I don't know. But they didn't ask me for a receipt, so I'm assuming the check he wrote you was for more than eight hundred dollars."

He huffed out an incredulous laugh. "It was for ten *thousand*."

Lainey's jaw dropped open. "Dollars?"

"Yep. And you can damn sure bet I'm taking that check to the bank today before they have a chance to change their minds. And speaking of minds, Bryn is going to lose hers when I tell her about this."

Lainey shook her head, still looking a little dazed. "Were they for real? Or did they just make up those crazy posh names because they felt so guilty for ditching their pet and didn't want us to know their real identities?"

"The check seems real. And that was the name on the top of it," he said. "And that goat that's trying to eat your scarf is sure real."

"Oh shoot," Lainey said, pulling the end of her scarf out of the goat's mouth. But she must have said it too harshly because the goat stiffened up and fell over. She barked out a laugh, then covered her mouth and peered up at Holt. "It is kind of funny." The goat wiggled on the ground, then popped up and bounced to Lainey for another cuddle. "I was googling this breed while you were talking to them, and Raine is right. They aren't actually fainting. They've got a genetic condition called myotonia congenita that causes their muscles to stiffen when they get startled. They never lose consciousness, and apparently it doesn't hurt them when they fall over other than making them nervous that they can't run away from whatever scared them."

"That's so weird. But she is a cute little bugger." He held his hand out to scratch her head, and she leaned into him.

"I guess they can faint when they get excited too. I read that they can fall over just on their way to their food bowl."

Lou had been hanging back, but now that the car was gone, she was slowly getting closer to Lainey and the newcomer.

"It's okay," Holt told her, calling the dog to him. "This is Esme. She won't hurt you."

The dog came closer, and she and the goat sniffed each other. Her tail was wagging a hundred miles an hour, and she went into play mode, flattening her paws on the ground and wiggling her butt. Esme seemed excited to play too. Until Lou let out a yip, and then the goat's legs went stiff, and she fell over again.

This time Holt and Lainey both laughed. The goat was too dang funny.

"I was going to head back to the ranch," Lainey said, "but

now I'm dying to stick around to see you introduce her to the rest of the animals."

Holt chuckled again. "Just wait until she meets Otis. That ornery old cuss startles me all the time."

―――――――――

By the next afternoon, the little goat was getting used to the ranch and its residents and wasn't getting startled as often as when she'd first arrived. Lainey had stayed the rest of the afternoon and into the evening the night before, watching the goat while Holt ran to the bank and picked up some takeout for them for supper. Esme hadn't left Lainey's side, following her everywhere she went, even into the bunkhouse.

"I don't care if they did say she was housebroken," Holt had told her when he caught her yawning. "That goat is not sleeping in my bed."

"It's just as well," Lainey had said. "I've got an early morning meeting, so I'm going to head home and get some sleep."

He'd kissed her good night and thought she'd almost changed her mind, but she'd finally pulled away and headed home. He'd spent the rest of the night and most of the day thinking about her and what could have happened if she would have stayed.

The day before, he'd had Shamus and Lou following him around. Today, Tiny and the new goat joined the audience. Every once in a while, Otis would wander into the barn, just long enough to startle Esme into toppling over, then he'd give her a sniff and run off. Holt wasn't sure if the old goat was flirting or just being his ornery self.

It was a little after four, and Holt was just thinking maybe he'd call Lainey and see if she wanted to grab a pizza when his phone buzzed in his pocket. He smiled when he saw the call was from her and hoped she was going to invite him out as he tapped the screen and held the phone to his ear. "Hey, beautiful."

"Oh, I'm so glad I got you," she said, her voice sounding panicked and out of breath. "I need your help. It's an emergency."

"What kind of emergency?" he asked, already heading toward his truck. "I'm on my way. I'll be there in two minutes. What do you need? Are you hurt? Should I call an ambulance? Or the police?"

"No, I'm fine. I mean, I'm not hurt. It's not that kind of an emergency. It's a Christmas emergency."

He stopped in his tracks. "What the hell is a Christmas emergency?"

"I just got a call from the church. And the whole Caldwell family all just came down with the flu."

"Well, I feel awful bad for the Caldwell family, but I'm not sure how that affects me or constitutes an emergency in my book. Christmas or otherwise."

"The Caldwell family was in charge of the live Nativity scene that's supposed to happen tonight in front of the church. The family is huge, so they were filling the majority of the roles, and now all we have left is one wise man. They heard I've been playing pinch hitter for some events in town, so they called me and asked me to take it over."

"And you said no, of course, since you've got so much going on with trying to run your own." He held back a groan because he already knew she'd agreed to do it.

"No, I said yes, of course, because who's going to say no to the church? And besides that, it's just for a few hours tonight, and how hard can it be?"

"Famous last words. So what do you need from me?"

"Besides their whole family playing the parts, they were also supplying all the animals. I think they've still got the camel, but now I need an entire Nativity cast and as many barnyard animals as we can muster. Which is where you come in."

"I can help rustle up some animals, but I sure as hell hope you're not planning on me to fill in as one of the other wise men."

"No, I've got them covered. I need you to be Joseph."

———

Two hours later, Holt was standing in a plywood crèche with a towel wrapped around his head and wearing what he was pretty sure was someone's old bathrobe. He'd drawn the line at the fake beard, claiming he had enough stubble of his own to make do.

At least he wasn't the only sucker Lainey had roped in to help. His brother was dressed similarly to him but stood back and to the side. He held a shepherd's hook in one hand and the leashes of two woolly sheep in the other. Holt wasn't sure how he got collars on those sheep.

Elle Brooks was playing the part of Mary, although with her large swollen belly, she looked as if she were ready to *give* birth rather than that she just had the baby lying in the manger between them. Thankfully, they'd given Elle a camp-stool to sit on instead of making her stand the whole time or sit on the ground.

"How'd she talk you into this?" Holt asked Elle as they waited for the event to start.

"She just asked us, and we were glad to fill in," Elle said. "Brody's on call. Otherwise I'm sure he would have agreed to be Joseph. Sorry." She offered Holt an apologetic shrug. "But Mandy and I love all this Christmas stuff, and we thought it would be fun. Doesn't she make the cutest shepherd?"

He looked over and grinned at Mandy, who was standing next to Shamus. She waved and grinned back, her excited smile lighting up her face. They hadn't been able to find a donkey, so he'd brought Shamus and they'd fashioned big ears out of cardboard and somehow managed to make them stick up behind his real ears. He'd also brought Lou, Esme, Tiny, and an old docile cow, one who he knew would be happy to lie down in the grass and eat hay for two hours and wouldn't be bothered a bit by hundreds of people driving by their makeshift barn scene.

Oh, please don't let it be hundreds. Although the church normally got quite a crowd. Cars would line up to drive through a series of sets, from a winter wonderland to Santa's workshop. They didn't charge, but there were a couple of volunteers holding red stockings at the beginning, just in case anyone wanted to donate. The route started in the block prior, went through the alley, then ended in front of the church with the grand finale of the live Nativity.

The wise men were ushered in, and Holt wasn't surprised to see Sam from the Creedence Country Feed & Supply shop or Doc Hunter, but he was a little shocked to see Aunt Sassy bringing up the rear, a long white beard glued to her face.

Elle busted out laughing. "Of course Aunt Sassy is one of the wise men."

"Lainey must have been desperate to fill the role."

"Sassy probably volunteered. She does consider herself pretty wise. Or at least she dispenses a lot of advice. Whether you ask for it or not."

"According to Lainey, she's had a heck of a time finding people who were free to fill in for the cast. Which is the only reason she was able to talk me into dressing up like an idiot and subbing for Joseph."

Elle smirked. "Yeah, I'm sure that's the *only* reason." She set her hand on his arm. "You do look happy though. I didn't realize you even knew *how* to laugh."

He gave her a grudging shrug and a half smile, knowing she was just teasing him. But he *had* felt happier. Even if he knew it was only going to last a few more weeks.

Elle reached out her hand to pet Esme, who was standing so close to him, she was practically on his feet. "Who's this little cutie?"

"This is Esme. She's our newest rescue. But she's already attached and practically scrambled into the truck with the dog in an effort not to be left behind. I hope I don't regret bringing her."

"Why would you regret it? She's adorable."

He huffed. "You'll see."

"Places, everyone," Lainey called as she walked around to stand in front of them. "We've got just a few minutes until showtime, and I wanted to thank everyone for coming out on such short notice and pitching in to make this Nativity scene possible. Especially Elle and Mandy Tate, who not only freely volunteered but brought two sheep as well, and big thanks to Holt, who supplied most of the other animals. They may not be the exact representation of the animals in the barn in Bethlehem that night." She grinned down at the scruffy dog sitting next to the goat at Holt's feet. "But they're the best we've got. Does anyone have any questions before I proceed up to my perch?"

Lainey was dressed in a white gown and had silvery wings attached to her back. She was playing the part of the angel, and the plan was for her to appear as though she were float-ing above the barnyard scene. The volunteer fire department had brought one of their trucks out, and once Lainey was positioned on the end of the extension ladder, they would push it out over the scene. She was supposed to lie on top of it to appear as if she were flying.

Yeah, nothing could go wrong with that idea.

Holt kept an eye on her as she climbed up onto the ladder, ready to lend a hand if she needed help. Or to catch her if she fell. After trying several positions, she must have decided it was just easier to sit on the end of the ladder, instead of trying to lie across it, and her legs dangled above them as the firemen cranked the ladder out.

"It's six o'clock. Get ready, everyone," Lainey called from above them. "Here comes the first car."

The church bells chimed to signal the start of the event. Esme's body tensed up, and she fell into the cradle and knocked the baby Jesus out.

"Oh, shit. I mean shoot." Holt grabbed the doll and stuffed it back into the manger as Esme shook herself and got back to her feet.

Elle's shoulder shook as she cracked up. "What in the heck just happened to your goat?"

"She fainted."

Before he had a chance to explain, the cars started driving through. He pushed the manger closer to Elle and pulled Esme closer to him. Which was a good idea because the second car in line honked its horn and down she went again.

He heard Aunt Sassy snort and looked up to see her and Doc Hunter holding their sides as they tried not to double over with laughter. "You're not making a very demure wise man," he whispered at her.

"Honey, I haven't been demure a day in my life," Sassy whispered back, then let out another snort as another car honked, and Esme went down again. "Oh shoot, there she goes again."

As the next hour progressed, he found that if he petted the goat while cuddling her against him, she got less startled. Either that, or she was getting used to the cars. But the church bells were a different story. Every time they chimed, she stiffened and fell over. Which sent Aunt Sassy, Elle, and Mandy into another fit of giggles.

They weren't the most serious group. He saw Mandy break character to wave and smile to her friends from school, and the camel was mostly either trying to steal the hay from the cow or goosing Sam. At least he figured that was what was happening every time he heard Sam give a little yelp, then shoo the camel away from his backside. Where the heck had they found a camel anyway?

For the next hour and fifteen minutes, they had a steady line of cars and several people just walking down Main Street and gawking at their scene. There was a lot of pointing and laughing. They acted like they'd never seen a dog, a fainting goat, or a bearded old lady in a Nativity scene before.

"We've just got to endure this for another fifteen minutes," Holt said to Elle through gritted teeth.

"Uh-oh," Elle said, her face going pale. "I don't think I'm going to make it that long." She looked down to where water was dripping into a puddle under her chair.

"Aww, hell. Please tell me you just spilled your water bottle."

She shrugged. "Sorry. Looks like Mary isn't the only one giving birth tonight."

CHAPTER 22

Holt blinked at the woman struggling to get up from the sodden camp chair, not quite believing what had just happened. Then his shock broke, and he leapt forward to take her arm and help her stand.

"What are you doing?" Lainey whispered down from her perch above them. "We've got fifteen more minutes."

He looked up at her, then nodded to the soaked ground. "Elle's water just broke. We need to get her to the hospital."

"Oh no, there's a ton of cars blocking the roads," Aunt Sassy said. She pushed Doc Hunter forward, and he almost tripped into the manger. "You're up, Wise Man. Looks like you're going to have to deliver this baby."

"I don't think it's coming right *now*," Elle said. "And I'd certainly prefer to have it in the hospital rather than in some dirty hay in front of a parade." She frowned at the steady stream of cars. "But the traffic does seem to be a problem."

"How can traffic be a problem in Creedence? We only have one stoplight." But Holt could see cars, both parked and moving, obstructing the road for several blocks.

"Do you want to ride Shamus?" Mandy offered, pulling the mini-horse forward. Her face had gone white, and her hands shook as she held out the horse's lead rope. "He's not a real donkey, but he's a good horse, and he'd get you to the hospital."

"That's okay, honey," Elle told her, pulling the girl in to hug her against her side. "I'm sure we can figure out a ride."

"If we can get it out of the parking lot, I've got my truck," Cade said.

"I do too," Holt told him. "Dang. Except the trailer's hooked to mine."

"Could someone get me down?" Lainey called to the firemen.

The Nativity scene fell apart as they all scrambled to try to help. Holt looked around at the pandemonium. The wise men *and woman* started directing traffic away from the church. Sam was trying to corral the camel and the cow, who had chosen this moment to stand up and try to head for the trailer. Lou was racing around the cow, yipping at her heels as if she were trying to herd her back into her place.

Holt shook his head as if to clear it. He couldn't think about any of that right now. His main priority was the woman at his side who was clenching his hand in a death grip as a contraction seized through her.

"*Somebody get me off this ladder*," Lainey yelled, which startled Esme, and she fell over again.

"What can I do?" Cade asked, taking Elle's other arm. He looked down at her with concern and assurance. "You're going to be okay, darlin'. We got you."

"I appreciate that." Elle sucked a pained breath in through gritted teeth. "But right now, can you just *get* me to the hospital?"

Creedence was a small town. Its population was barely twelve hundred and that was if you counted a few of the dogs—but it *did* have a hospital. And a good one. Now, if they could just get to it.

"We're only five blocks from the hospital," Holt assured her. "I'll carry you there if I have to."

"And I'll help," Cade said.

"Me too," a different bearded woman said, hurrying up behind Cade and taking Elle's free hand.

"Nora?" Holt asked. "Why do you have a beard?"

"I was filling in as one of the shepherds," she explained, as if that were the most logical thing in the world. "Why are we just standing here?"

Elle let out another pained groan and doubled over, squeezing Holt's hand like a vise as she did.

"Enough of this," he said, reaching down to pick Elle up. Cradling her in his arms, he yelled, "Somebody get me a vehicle. Now."

"Holt! Over here!"

He heard Lainey's voice and looked around to see her coming toward them in Doc's North Pole–decorated golf cart. She jumped a curb, and a tinsel-covered wreath fell off the front bumper as she pulled to a stop in front of them.

"Get her in here," she told Holt, then jumped out to grab Mandy, who must have shrunk back in the excitement. She was clutching Shamus's neck, a frightened and bewildered look on her face. Lainey pulled the girl into her arms and gave her a quick hug. "It's okay, honey. Elle's going to be fine. You come with us." As she led Mandy back to the golf cart, she called over to Cade. "Can you round up all these animals and get them back to the ranch?"

"Yeah, sure. Whatever I can do," he said.

"Make sure you get the dog and the little goat. And somebody needs to call Brody."

"I already did," Aunt Sassy said, coming up to the golf cart and giving Elle's arm a squeeze. "He's on his way to the hospital. He'll meet you there."

"Hold on, everybody," Lainey said as she cranked the wheel and put her foot on the gas. "Get out of the way," she yelled again and again as she barreled down the bike lane of the road. "Pregnant woman coming through."

Elle punctuated her commands with another groan accompanied by a cramp of pain, and Holt was glad to see people and cars rushing to make a path.

They drove up to the hospital just as Brody was pulling in. Leaving his truck in the middle of the driveway, he jumped out and ran toward Elle, tossing his keys to Holt as he did.

Wrapping his daughter and his wife in his arms, he gave them both a hug, then pushed Elle's damp bangs from her forehead as he peered lovingly down at her. "Honey, I know you were taking your part as Mary in the Nativity pretty seriously, but actually *having* a baby seems a little extreme."

———————

Two hours later, it looked like it had been a bad night in Bethlehem as the waiting room was full of the Nativity cast, sprawled in chairs and sofas, costumes in disarray.

Cade and Nora had taken all the animals back to the ranch and gotten them fed and watered for the night. They'd called Brody's hired man and arranged for him to take care of their animals that evening and in the morning as well.

Nora and Aunt Sassy had taken off their beards and Lainey had lost her wings, but otherwise, everyone else was still mostly dressed in their Bethlehem garb. Someone must've called Jillian and Carley because the sisters had shown up not long after they'd arrived and had kept Mandy pretty much sandwiched between them the whole time Elle had been in labor.

Sam, the third wise man, and his wife had shown up with hot drinks, bottled waters, and Christmas cookies to pass around.

"Thanks for the grub," Holt said to Sam as he sank into the chair next to him.

"Thank the wife. It was her idea," he said.

Holt checked his watch, surprised to see it was already after ten, then scrubbed a hand over his face. "It's getting late. Especially for you. Don't you have to open the feed store early tomorrow?"

"Yeah, but I've got some time. And I'd really like to wait around to offer my congratulations. Elle and Brody are good people. They always try to buy local and support the shop, so I want to be here to support them as well."

Holt understood the sentiment. The couple had been good to him too, treating him as a friend from the moment he'd arrived in Creedence. "You've been running that shop for as long as I can remember, Sam. I figured you'd be retired by now."

"My wife's been bugging me to retire for years, but I haven't found someone I trust to take over running the shop. Seems everyone wants to work either down in Denver or from their sofa in their pajamas. And I don't trust leaving my shop with just anyone. I need someone with management experience who can handle inventory and sales and still cares about customer service and treating people right. The way I would myself."

The door of the waiting room swung open then, and Brody strode in, a smile beaming from his face. "We had a baby. I mean, Elle had a baby. I just stood there, helplessly wishing I could do something for her."

Mandy pushed off the chair and ran to her dad. He crouched down and pulled her into his arms, hugging her tightly to him. Tears shone in his eyes as he pulled away to look at her. "Guess what, big sister? You've got a new baby brother."

Her face broke into a grin, and she hugged him again as he looked up at everyone else. "Oh yeah," he called out to the room. "I forgot to say…it's a boy!"

The next morning, Holt stood in the barn scratching his head as he surveyed the animals in the stalls. Some of them were not his.

He called Lainey, who sounded a little breathless as she picked up and said hello. "Good morning, gorgeous," he said, the sound of her voice causing a little something in his chest to do a cartwheel.

"It is a good morning," she said, and he could hear the happiness in her voice. "What's up with you?"

"I'm just standing in my barn wondering why there's a camel in here."

CHAPTER 23

LAINEY LAUGHED OUT LOUD. "SO THAT'S WHERE THE camel ended up. Thank goodness. We've been wondering all morning."

"Who's we?" Holt asked.

"Me and the guy who owns the camel," she said. "I've been down at the church helping clean up for most of the morning, and the camel's owner arrived about half an hour ago, asking if anyone had seen it."

"Oh dang. The guy must be worried sick. It's not every day you lose a camel."

"He doesn't seem too worried about it. I was just over at the coffee shop, and he was in there with a couple of his buddies having a latte and a scone. He said he has a lot of faith in his neighbors and figured somebody took care of it and that it would eventually show up. It's not like someone else in town could suddenly claim they'd recently acquired a camel."

"It doesn't seem too bothered about being here. It's sitting down or lying down, or whatever it's called when camels are on the ground, and calmly eating a half a bale of hay."

"I'll head across the street to let Sherm know and try to send him out your way to pick Murray up."

"Who's Sherm?"

"The guy who owns the camel. Sherman Hess."

"And who's Murray?"

"The camel."

"Ahh. Good to know. I think I'm caught up now."

"I'll text you after I talk to him."

"Sounds good," he said, then paused for a second. "Hey, Lainey?"

"Yeah."

"Any chance you know who these sheep belong to?"

―――――――

Sherman was glad to hear Lainey had found Murray and told her he had his trailer and would head out to the horse rescue as soon as he finished his coffee.

She texted Holt that Sherm was coming his way, then was heading out the door when a distinguished older gentleman stopped her. "Pardon me, but aren't you Lainey McBride?"

"I am."

He held out his hand. "Mayor Hightower. I've known your grandpa for years."

"Nice to meet you, Mayor," she said, shaking his hand.

"I've heard some really great things about you the past few weeks. Sounds like you've made quite an impression on our little town with the way you've stepped in and turned what could have been disasters into triumphs."

"I don't know about that."

"My wife, Lyda, is on the board of the Women's Club,

and she said the brunch you threw was the best they'd had in years. I'll warn you, they're hoping to recruit you as a new member."

"Gosh, that's nice." And would be fun except for the fact that she didn't actually live here.

"Lyda was also on the committee for the drive-by Christmas event last night, and she said they asked you to help at the last minute and you still managed to pull off a success. It isn't an easy feat to round up wise men, shepherds, and barnyard animals."

"Oh, that wasn't too hard. You can barely throw a rock in this town without hitting a cow. Although the camel *was* quite a coup. But Murray had already been arranged before I took over."

The mayor chuckled. "I like you, Lainey. And so does my wife. I've got a position available as a special events coordinator that I think you'd be perfect for. A job with the county comes with some pretty great benefits—health, dental, vision, plus an office on the third floor of the courthouse that has one of the most spectacular views of the mountains in town."

Lainey's mouth had gone dry. Was the mayor of Creedence really offering her a job? "I don't know what to say."

"Don't say anything now. But call me tomorrow, and we'll arrange for you to come down to the courthouse to discuss it further." He handed her a business card. "I've got money in the budget to offer you a competitive salary, and our town could use someone like you, new blood who has fresh ideas, a positive outlook, and the organizational skills to pull together great events on a moment's notice. I can't wait to see what you can do with some planning and a dedicated budget."

"Thank you so much," she said, tucking his card into her pocket. "I'll call you tomorrow."

"Tell your grandfather I said hello and I hope he's feeling better."

"I will. And he's doing better every day. Thanks for thinking of him." She'd stopped by to see him that morning before she'd headed downtown, and he'd told her he'd been working with using a walker and that his hip was practically healed. She figured they'd let a doctor determine that, but she was glad to see him in good spirits and feeling hopeful.

She pushed through the door of the coffee shop, and her steps were light as she headed across the street and went back to cleaning up. She couldn't believe the mayor—the *mayor* of Creedence—had just walked up to her and offered her a job.

The rest of the morning flew by as she worked alongside other people from the town, and she was surprised by how many folks she already knew. Some were people she remembered from spending time here as a teenager, like Sam from the Feed & Supply store, several parishioners from the church, and other kids she'd met who were now adults with kids of their own. But she'd also met a lot of new people.

She and her mom had moved so many times that they'd never let themselves get involved in a community, but she was starting to feel like she might have a place here, and that thought excited and scared her to death.

A familiar truck pulled up in front of the church, and a tall, sexy-as-sin cowboy got out and looked around. Speaking of things that scared her to death. Just seeing Holt had her heart pounding against her chest as if it were competing with the little drummer boy. He spotted her, and the smile that crossed his face, a smile just for her, made her chest tighten and flutters race through her stomach.

She waved, and he sauntered toward her. The fluttering turned to surges of heat. Damn, but that man could saunter.

"Hey, beautiful," he said, pulling her into a hug. "You're the best thing I've seen all day."

"Well, considering your morning has consisted of seeing cows, horses, goats, and Murray the camel, I'm not sure I should be too flattered."

"I also saw one somewhat grizzled old man," he said, teasing her. "But I was glad to meet Sherm and thankful to have him take Murray off my hands. I talked to my brother, and apparently the sheep belong to Mandy. Nora was going to text Elle and tell her the sheep could stay at the ranch until they had time to come get them. Or I figured you'd probably want to see the baby, so I thought we could drop them off at their place in a couple of days and sneak a peek at the little guy."

"I love that idea." And she loved that he'd thought of it as something she'd like and that they would do together. It was amazing how easy it was to start to feel like a couple again.

"I was hoping I could talk you into letting me buy you lunch," Holt told her.

"That sounds like an offer I can't refuse." She dumped the trash bag she'd been using to collect errant flyers and candy cane wrappers into the designated pile on the curb. "I was just finishing up here, so your timing is perfect."

They ran into Doc and Aunt Sassy as they headed toward Holt's truck and stopped to say hello.

"Thanks again, Lainey, for all your help with the event last night," Aunt Sassy told her. "I've had so many people tell me what a great job they thought you did."

"Thank you, but I didn't really do that much. And our Nativity scene went *pregnant belly* up fifteen minutes early. I still feel bad for the people at the end of that line of cars who thought they were going to get to see Mary and Joseph and instead witnessed some wise men and a couple of bearded women rounding up a bunch of animals."

Doc chuckled. "That sounds like it would be worth the price of admission."

"The event was free," Aunt Sassy reminded him.

"That's what I meant." Doc grinned and waggled his bushy gray eyebrows, and they all laughed together.

"Hey, Doc," Lainey said. "I didn't get a chance to tell you last night, but thanks for letting me abscond with your golf cart. It really saved the day."

"Happy to help. But maybe that had more to do with Christmas magic and Santa Claus than it did with me," Doc said.

Holt huffed. "Or maybe it had to do with the fact you walked off and left the keys in the thing."

"Doc takes this Santa business pretty seriously," Aunt Sassy said. "And there's something about him that just feels like he's got a little Christmas magic in him."

"Maybe it's his reindeer-scented aftershave," Holt muttered, then let out an *oomph* as Lainey nudged an elbow into his gut.

"You can laugh, but I'm serious. And I'm not the only one who thinks so. Even though he wasn't in the Santa costume last night or today, I swear every time he sits down, a little kid climbs up on his lap and starts to tell him what they want for Christmas."

Lainey pressed her hand to her chest. "Oh my gosh, that's adorable."

Aunt Sassy turned to smile warmly at Doc. "It's adorable the way he so patiently listens and passes out hugs like they're candy. He's a darn good man."

Doc shrugged, and Lainey was pretty sure he blushed under his white beard. She loved hearing the stories of little kids sharing their Christmas wishes with Doc. She sucked in a breath as she suddenly remembered a story he had told them the week before when they'd been on the sleigh ride. "Hey, Doc, do you recall telling us about a little girl who'd asked Santa to bring back her lost horse?"

"Of course I do. I just saw her ten minutes ago. And she asked me about it again."

"Is she still here?"

He looked around the spattering of people left, then pointed to a couple in their midtwenties who were coming out of the coffee shop. The mom was holding a little girl's hand while the dad was trying to juggle three take-out cups and the door. "That's them. I think their name's Wilson. And the little girl's name is Winnie. I remember because she wanted her horse back for Christmas and a 'Winnie' is the sound a horse makes."

"Smart," Holt said.

"Yeah, he's practically a genius," Aunt Sassy said, nudging Doc in the shoulder. "Except for last night when he dropped his dentures into my ginger ale."

"I already said I was sorry about that. I told you, I thought it was my Efferdent. It was clear and bubbly. Anyone could make the mistake."

Lainey ignored the older couple's bickering. "Who cares about the dentures? Do you remember how she described her horse?"

"Hmm, maybe, let me think." Doc scratched at his beard, then his eyes brightened as he snapped his fingers. "I do remember. She said it had a white star on its forehead and a single white sock on its leg. She said the mare's name was Goldie and she called her a *palminio*—so stinkin' cute that one."

Lainey was tapping Holt's arm as Doc relayed the description. "We just *rescued* an injured mare. And it's a palminio...I mean, a palomino." She looked up at Holt. "I think we found that little girl's horse."

Holt frowned. "She does meet the description—white patch on her forehead and one white sock."

Lainey wasn't listening anymore. She was already dragging him across the street and toward the couple. She waved as she called out, "Hello, Mr. and Mrs. Wilson?"

The couple turned at their name but looked a little startled at Lainey and Holt barreling toward them. "Can we help you with something?" Mrs. Wilson asked.

"I think *we* can help *you*," Lainey said. "We found a—"

"*Something*." Holt cut her off with a raise of his hand as he nodded to the cutest little girl staring up at them. "Look, my name is Holt Callahan, and this is Lainey, and we found something a couple of days ago that we thought you all might want to know about. Now, we don't want to get you folks' hopes up or a little girl's hopes up, but I think it's worth a trip out to our ranch to check out this yellow H-O-R-S-E we just rescued."

"It's Goldie," the little girl cried, jumping up and down. "They found Goldie."

"*How*?" Holt asked, looking bewildered, after he'd tried so hard to speak in code.

The little girl planted a tiny fist on her jutted-out hip. "I can spell 'horse,' ya know." Then she grabbed for the hem of her dad's coat and yanked it up and down. "Come on, Daddy. We have to go. They found Goldie. I just know it."

Mr. Wilson stared at them, a skeptical expression on his face, as if he was trying to decide if they were legit or if they were serial killers who were trying to lure his family out to an abandoned farm to murder them.

"It's okay," Aunt Sassy said, huffing up behind them with Doc in tow. "We know them. Holt and his family run the Heaven Can Wait Horse Rescue ranch just outside of town."

"Santa," the little girl cried, throwing her arms around Doc's legs. "You did it. You found Goldie."

"Well, I…," Doc stammered.

"Winnie, honey, we don't know for sure that the horse they found is Goldie. There are plenty of other yellow horses out there," her mom told her.

Winnie peered up at Holt, her blond curls bouncing as she tipped her head back. "Does the horse you found have a white sock on her foot?"

"Yes," Holt said.

"And a white star on her head?"

"She's got a white *patch* on her forehead."

Winnie turned back to her parents. "See, it's her. I know it. We gotta go get her."

The dad looked just as bewildered as Holt had, but the mom picked her daughter up and nodded at Holt. "Can we come now?"

"Sure," he said, pointing back toward his truck. "That blue pickup is mine. You can follow us out. Our ranch is about two miles up the highway once you pass the diner. There's a sign." Bless his heart for trying one more time. "But again, I don't want you all to get your hopes up."

"Let's go," Winnie's mom said, already heading toward a white minivan parked across the street.

Holt looked down at Lainey. "You comin' with us?"

"Try to stop me," she said, practically jogging toward his truck. "I don't even care about my car. We'll come back and get it later. Come on."

The drive to the ranch, which normally felt fairly short, seemed to take forever as Holt kept his speed down so as not to lose the white minivan. Lainey prayed the whole way there that the horse they'd rescued was Goldie.

They pulled up in front of the barn, and the minivan pulled in behind them. The mom was out her door and yanking the back door open the second the van stopped.

"She seemed to be doing better, so I put the mare in the corral with the other horses this morning," Holt told her, as they got out of the truck.

But the corral looked empty.

"They must be around behind the barn," Holt told them as the mom set the little girl down next to her and turned to him. "I need to warn you. The horse had been hurt when we rescued her, so she's got a bandage on her flank, but she's okay."

"I understand your concerns," Mrs. Wilson said. "But can you just show us the mare? She's been *my* horse since I was sixteen, but Winnie claimed her as hers the first moment they met. They have a special bond, but she's really *my* horse. I'll know if it's her."

"All right. I hear ya," Holt said. "I'm just trying to keep you from being disappointed."

"Goldie!"

They all turned at the sound.

Lainey and Holt had been standing next to her parents, and none of them had noticed the preschooler, who must have run over to the corral and climbed through the fence.

Winnie was standing at least twenty feet inside the paddock when she yelled for the horse. Only a second later, the sound of thundering hooves rent through the air.

Then the yellow horse came galloping around the back of the barn at full speed, running straight toward the little girl.

CHAPTER 24

LAINEY STARED IN HORROR AT THE HUGE HORSE BARREL-
ing down on the tiny girl. It felt like they were all moving in
slow motion as they took off sprinting toward the corral.

Holt got there first and practically vaulted himself over
the fence.

But it was too late.

The horse pulled to a hard stop right as she made it to
Winnie. Then she leaned her white-starred head down and
gently touched her nose to the small girl's cheek.

Winnie threw her small arms around the big horse's head
and hugged it tight. "Goldie," she cried. "I knew it would be you."

Holt scooped the little girl up into his arms just as her dad
made it to them. He passed Mr. Wilson his daughter.

Lainey grabbed Holt's arm as she doubled over, trying
to catch her breath. She and Mrs. Wilson had both scrambled over the gate and made it to Winnie just seconds after
the men had. She could feel Holt shaking. He reached for
the horse's halter with one hand, and she grabbed his other,
holding it as tightly as he gripped the halter.

"I think it's safe to assume this is your horse," Holt said, as
the palomino turned her head to nuzzle against Mrs. Wilson's
shoulder.

"Yes, this is her." After she'd hugged Winnie, she put her arms around the horse's neck and hugged her too. "And yeah, that was terrifying for a second, but she never would have hurt Winnie."

"How about we go on up to the house and fill out the paperwork? Then we can get you all and your horse home." Holt gestured toward the farmhouse.

"I can make us some coffee," Lainey offered.

"Make mine a double," Holt muttered. "And add a shot of whiskey. That about gave me a heart attack."

"Can my wife do the paperwork while I head home and get my truck and trailer?" the man asked. "We just live up the road a few miles. We bought the old Zimmerman ranch last summer."

Holt nodded. "I know the place. Kind of a fixer upper."

Mr. Wilson laughed. "That's putting it mildly. But the price was right, and we wanted to get out of the city and find a place in the country that was in a good community."

"It feels like we found it," his wife said. "We're Stef and Logan, by the way. And you obviously know Winnie."

"Good to meet you," Holt told them. "Welcome to the neighborhood."

"Thanks," Logan said. "I'm a software guy and I work from home, so we've been fixing things up on the weekends and have mainly been focusing on the house. I thought the barn and the pasture fences were secure, but Goldie must have found a place to get out."

"Don't beat yourself up. Your fence might have been secure, then the snow or an animal could have damaged it.

That big storm we had a couple of weeks ago might have downed a tree on a section of it, or there could have been a big enough drift that she just walked over it. I've got some time in the morning if you want me to come over and run the fence with you."

"That would be great. I think. I'm not sure exactly what that means, but I'll take any help I can get."

Holt chuckled. "Yeah, we just walk, or ride, depending on how much acreage you've got, the perimeter of your fence and check it for damaged places. I'll bring my tools and help you fix up any bad places we find."

"That'd be great. And I've got a couple of four-wheelers we can use." He nodded to his wife and daughter. "I know Stef and Win aren't gonna want to leave Goldie's side, so I'll be back as quick as I can with the trailer so we can take her home. Thanks again." He jogged to the minivan as the rest of them headed toward Bryn's.

Winnie bounced in her mother's arms all the way to the farmhouse. When Stef set her down on the porch, she ran to Holt and hugged his legs. Her blue eyes were big and round as she peered up at him. "Are you one of Santa's elves?"

Lainey pressed her lips together to keep from laughing. She wanted to pull out her phone and take a picture of this adorable moment but thought that might be weird, so she captured a mental image instead.

"No," Holt said firmly. "I'm *not* one of Santa's elves."

"Well, I told Santa the only thing I wanted for Christmas was to bring Goldie home. But *you* gave her back to me instead of him. Maybe you have to keep it secret, and you just can't tell me cuz I'm a kid," she said, nodding her head in a knowing manner that seemed way too mature for a four-year-old child. "But I *know* you're one of Santa's elves. Or maybe his son." Her curls bounced as she whipped her head toward her mother. "Momma, does Santa have kids?"

Her mom shook her head. "I don't think so, honey."

Winnie shrugged her small shoulders as she looked back up at Holt. "Then you *must* be an elf."

It took another hour for them to do the paperwork and to load up the horse once Logan got back with the trailer. Lainey took Stef and Winnie to meet Lou, Esme, Tiny, and Shamus, and she was completely enamored with the adorable little girl by the time they were through.

Unfortunately for her parents, Winnie had decided that now that Goldie was home, she had a few days before Christmas to change her request and now was hoping for a mini-horse under the tree.

Lainey and Holt waved as the couple pulled away.

"That was so fun," Lainey said. "I loved getting to return that horse."

"Yeah, this was a good ending. Most horse rescues don't turn out that way."

They were starting to go back into the bunkhouse when they heard the sound of an engine, and both turned back to see the county sheriff's SUV pulling into the driveway.

Holt grimaced. "And our day had been going so well.

Nothing ever good comes from the sheriff showing up at your place."

No, having the sheriff show up never meant anything good in her life either. For Lainey, that usually meant her stepdad had gotten too drunk and the neighbors had called the police because they either heard him yelling or caught him hitting her mother. The worst time had been when her mom had just gotten out of the shower and was still in her towel, and Randy had chased her into the front yard and had started hitting her with a spatula because she hadn't made his lunch before she'd gotten into the shower. Lainey had been the one to call that time. Her mom was half-naked and covered in red squares from the spatula when the police showed up. They took him in, but he was back home again within a week.

Lainey could remember thinking the only way they were going to keep him in jail was if he actually killed her mother. She was right in a way. He *had* beaten a woman to death, but thank God it hadn't been her mom. She rubbed at the panic building in her chest.

Just breathe. It's okay.

Randy was in prison. And her mom was safe. They'd gotten away in time. After more than a decade of moving around, her mom had finally settled in one place and met a good man, who just happened to be a police officer. For the first time, Lainey felt like she could breathe, knowing her mother was happy and with someone who could protect her with his body and with the law.

"Hey, you okay?" Holt asked as he touched her arm. "You just got a little shaky on me there."

She forced a smile and nodded up at him. "I'm fine."

Sheriff Ethan Rayburn exited the truck and waved a hand as he walked up to them. "Hey there." Lainey recognized him as Jillian's husband from when they'd met at the bonfire and tree lighting.

"Ethan," Holt said, reaching out to shake the man's hand. "Good to see you. You remember Lainey McBride? She's staying over at Mountainside, her grandparents' ranch."

"Of course," Ethan said, nodding at Lainey. "Nice to see you."

Holt glanced at the county vehicle, then back at the sheriff. "So what brings you out this way?"

Ethan looked down at Lou, who was sitting at Lainey's feet. "I'm actually here about the dog."

CHAPTER 25

LAINEY GASPED. "OH NO," SHE WHISPERED, REACHING down to pick up the dog and cuddle her to her chest. Lou stretched out her neck to lick Lainey's ear.

"Now, darlin', we knew this would probably happen," Holt said. "We talked about how she was too sweet of a dog not to be someone's pet." He rubbed a comforting hand over her shoulder. "And now we get to return another beloved pet to some family who's been missing her. Think what a great Christmas gift that'll be for them."

"Actually," Ethan said, nodding to the dog. "I think you all are the ones who are going to get a dog for Christmas. If you want to keep her, that is."

"What do mean?" Lainey was afraid to get her hopes up.

Holt frowned. "I figured you were coming out to pick her up because someone had seen our flyer or the notice about her on your website."

"Someone did," Ethan said. "Do you know the Riveras? Young couple, Ruben and Camila? They live in that big white house by the grade school."

Holt nodded. "Yeah, I've met them a couple of times. They go to our church."

"Well, they were heading down to visit their family in

Arizona a few weeks ago, and as they were heading out of town, they saw an old beat-up truck pull over to the side of the highway and pitch that dog out, then drive off."

Lainey gasped again and cuddled Lou closer.

"Where were they?" Holt asked.

The sheriff pointed out toward the highway. "Right down the road from here. Ruben said he remembers just passing your sign when he saw the guy swerving on the highway, so he slowed down behind him. Something just felt odd about it to him, especially when the guy suddenly pulled over to the side of the road, so he slowed down even more and that's when they saw the dog go flying." He dipped his chin toward Lainey. "Sorry, his words, not mine."

"How do they know it was *this* dog?" Holt asked, gesturing toward Lou.

"Camila had her phone out, and she grabbed pictures and a video of the whole thing. I won't show you the video, but she got a couple of good photos of the dog," Ethan said, pulling his phone from his pocket. He scrolled to the correct spot, then held the phone up to show a clear picture of a small terrier-mix dog that looked exactly like Lou. "They said the guy peeled out and went flying down the road, so they took off after him to get a good shot of his license plate, then turned around to come back for the dog, but it must have run off. They searched but couldn't find it, so they headed out of town, meaning to call the information in that afternoon and to have someone get ahold of Bryn to tell her to be on the lookout for it. But then Camila got a call from her family saying that her dad had had a heart attack. He's okay now—I guess it was a mild one—but understandably, the thing with the dog got pushed to the back burner. They just got back to town yesterday, and Camila brought this information in to me this morning."

"I hope you got the bastard who threw his dog away," Holt said.

"We're working on it," Ethan said. "But there's no way in hell we're giving the dog back. So you all can either keep her, or I can take her in to the Humane Society."

"We're keeping her," Lainey and Holt said at the same time.

Ethan grinned. "I figured that's what you'd say. She's yours then." He looked from Holt to Lainey, then back to Holt again. "I'll leave it to you all to decide which one of you she ends up with. Take care now." He waved as he headed back to his truck.

Holt shook his head as the sheriff drove away. "What kind of person just throws a dog out of their car like she's a piece of trash?"

"I know," Lainey said. "It's probably a good thing he didn't show us the video of the truck or the license plate. I might be tempted to find the guy and throw *him* in a ditch."

"After I punched him in the throat."

She held Lou out to him. "I spoke up pretty fast for keeping her, but I know that she's really *your* dog."

He wrapped an arm around Lainey and pulled her to him, cradling the little dog between them. "I never planned on getting a dog, always too busy and spent too much time on the road to be able to take care of one. And if I ever did think about getting one, I sure wouldn't have picked a little scruffy pip-squeak. But this one has kind of grown on me."

"She obviously loves you," Lainey said, peering up at him. She knew the feeling.

"The thing is, I think she loves both of us. How about for as long as you're here, we just agree to share her?"

"That's sounds good, but what about at night? She loves sleeping in the bed. Should we just take turns on who gets to keep her overnight?"

"Hmm. That *is* a conundrum." He pulled her closer as his lips curved into a roguish grin. "It seems a shame to make her miss out on one of us every night. I guess we'll just have to start sleeping together."

"We're already sleeping together. Ohhh…you mean actually *sleeping*?" She laughed as she teased him.

"I'm not exactly clear on the difference. Maybe we better go on inside and you can show me." He leaned down to kiss her.

Lou yipped and tried to get her face between them as she licked at each of their cheeks.

"Ugh," Lainey said, laughing again as she pulled back and wiped her cheek on the corner of her scarf. "I have to tell you, you're a much better kisser than the dog."

"Best compliment I've had all day," Holt said, setting the dog on the ground between them, then taking her hand.

Lou ran ahead of them up the steps of the bunkhouse. As she followed Holt inside, Lainey couldn't help but think about the events of the day.

It seemed like maybe everyone was finding their forever home today.

They had perfect weather for the festival on Friday, with the sun shining brightly and the temperature a balmy sixty degrees. Lainey and Holt had spent the entire day before prepping for the festival—setting out all the supplies for the craft stations, filling the sleigh with warm blankets, calling all the volunteers, printing out judge's sheets for the Christmas tree decorating contest, creating multiple photo booths and stocking them with holiday props, and chopping peppermints, malted milk balls, and toffee bites for the hot cocoa bar. They'd prepped everything they could for the Ho-Ho-Hoedown the following night and even tried out the Christmas tree maze.

They'd fallen into bed exhausted, but it had been worth it.

Lainey checked her watch—quarter till twelve—fifteen minutes before the festival was supposed to start, and already cars were lining up down the highway to be expertly directed where to park in the far pasture by her parking volunteers.

Christmas music was playing softly through speakers strategically placed around the ranch, and every twinkle light she had was on and sparkling, even though it was light outside. She was excited that Sarah and Stan had shown up with a festively decorated Copper an hour before and had been working steadily ever since on setting up their booth with him.

Several local food vendors were parked around the perimeter of the festival, and she could smell BBQ, fried potatoes, and the stomach-rumbling scent of fresh kettle corn. She'd have to make sure she got a big bag and set it aside for later, when she'd have a spare minute to eat. Holt had made coffee and breakfast burritos that morning and insisted she eat one before starting the day. Which was a good thing, since they'd already suffered a couple of setbacks.

She'd had two volunteers call to cancel that morning, realized she'd forgotten to make the signs directing people to the parking lot, and discovered a raccoon had gotten into Santa's workshop overnight and taken off with a bag of chocolate Kisses, several handfuls of candy canes, and a Santa hat.

But she'd made a few calls and found a couple of replacement volunteers and had quickly made signs and had Holt post them in the pasture when he'd left earlier to go take care of the animals on his ranch. It had only taken a quick call to Aunt Sassy, who had assured her that Doc had an extra Santa hat and that they would stop at the store on their way out for more chocolate and candy canes.

Lainey took a deep breath and let it out slowly.

Today was going to be perfect. It had to be.

The first family was out of their car and heading toward the craft stations in the barn. It was *go* time. She checked her watch again. *Where is Holt?*

He'd left two hours ago to take care of the chores on his ranch, but she'd expected him to be back before the festival started. She'd sent him a quick text asking where he was twenty minutes ago, but she hadn't gotten a message in return.

Another ten minutes passed. She checked her phone in between greeting festivalgoers. No calls. No messages. She was starting to get miffed. She'd wait about ten more minutes, and then she'd really start worrying.

She was directing a family with the most adorable three little girls to the cookie-decorating tables when she heard a horn honk and looked up to see Holt's pickup slowly driving up the path they'd left to get to the house. *It's about time he got here.*

Now that she knew he wasn't lying in a ditch somewhere after being in a horrible accident, her frustration at him being gone so long bubbled to the surface and she stomped toward him.

He didn't even notice her annoyance because he was so focused on something in his truck. Running around to the passenger side, he opened the door with a flourish, and she stopped in her exasperated tracks.

Tears filled her eyes, and she pressed her fingers to her lips as she saw her grandfather beaming at her from inside the truck.

"Merry Christmas, Granddaughter," he called, and she ran the last few steps to him and threw her arms around him in a hug.

"Gramps, what are you doing here?"

"I couldn't miss the festival."

"Yeah, but I didn't think you were able to leave the assisted-living center."

Walt jerked a thumb at Holt, who was unfolding the wheelchair he'd just hauled out of the bed of the truck. "This guy showed up this morning and sweet-talked the nurses into giving me a day pass."

"I had to promise we'd have him back by five," Holt said, getting a hand under Walt's arm and practically lifting him into the chair. "And he swore he would stay in this chair the whole time he's here."

Walt raised two fingers. "Scout's honor."

"Oh, I'm just so happy you're here," Lainey said, hugging him again, then sweeping her arms open toward the ranch. "What do you think? How does it look?"

Her grandfather's eyes beamed with pride. "It looks wonderful. I can't wait for you to show me around."

"Wait. Hold on one minute before you start the tour," Holt said, then reached into the back seat of the truck and pulled out a fuzzy Santa hat and a red-and-green throw blanket. He maneuvered the hat onto Walt's head and then spread the blanket across his lap.

Lainey laughed out loud as she peered down at the three Christmas gnomes and the words *Just Chillin' with my Gnomies* embroidered on the blanket.

Holt shrugged. "It was the only one I could find at the mercantile this morning."

She threw her arms around him, then kissed him hard on the mouth. "I can't believe you did this. I was so mad that you were late, and then you show up with my gramps. I'm still stunned." She nudged her elbow into his side. "And you call yourself a grinch."

He grinned down at her as he shrugged again. "Some of your damn Christmas spirit must be rubbing off on me. Plus, I'd do just about anything to see that smile of yours."

She kissed him once more. "I think maybe you *are* an elf."

"All right," Walt called. "Enough smooching. I want the full tour. I already see some new things we've never had before. I like the 'Get Your Pet's Picture with Santa' idea, but what the blazes is a selfie booth?"

———————

Holt probably should have been wearing sneakers instead of his cowboy boots because he felt like he hadn't stopped running all day. The only time he'd sat down was when he'd been driving the sleigh for an hour in the middle of the day.

He'd brought over some walkie-talkies from the ranch for him and Lainey to use to stay connected throughout the afternoon, and he was surprised the things had any batteries left, the way they'd fired exchanges back and forth to each other all day. They needed more cups at the hot chocolate station, someone had spilled a whole container of silver glitter in the barn, one of the cows had got out of the pasture and was standing in the middle of the Christmas tree maze, and a kid had stuck a gumdrop up his nose at the ginger-bread house decorating booth.

Thankfully, he'd been able to handle all the crises, and even more thankfully, the kid's dad had extracted the gum-drop before he'd made it to the gingerbread booth.

He was also thankful it was almost five when he sank onto the bench next to Stan Gardner to inhale a grilled cheese sandwich one of the food vendors had just handed him. "How'd the booth go today?" he asked between mouth-fuls. He'd caught a glimpse of Copper earlier and noted the tinsel and Christmas ribbon braided into the horse's mane and tail. The horse seemed to be a hit because Holt had seen a line for photos with him all day and a few times when a brown-haired girl was leading the horse around the corral with a kid on his back.

"Great," Stan said. "I don't know how much money we've made, but I can't remember the last time Sarah and I have had so much fun together."

They hadn't told him yet about Maxton and Raine's donation to the horse's fund and were still talking about just slipping it into the girl's donation bucket anonymously. But it was enough to keep the horse in feed and hay for at least the next six months.

"I'm glad," Holt said, and meant it. "How's the job hunt going?"

Stan's smile fell. "Not so great. There's just not a lot of jobs out there for middle management guys like me."

"What kind of work did you do before?"

"I was manager of an auto parts store. But so many people are buying things online now, and the shop was over in Woodland Hills, which you know is even smaller than Creedence, and the shop just wasn't making enough money to keep the lights on. The owners had been wanting to retire anyway, so they just closed up shop and let the five employees go. They hadn't planned for it to be right before Christmas, but their accountant wanted to keep everything in the fiscal year, so they closed down the first of October."

"That stinks."

"Yeah, it does. It was a great little shop. Damn shame to see it close. Buying things online might be convenient, but you just can't beat the personal touch of talking to someone in person and having them find that exact thing you need." Stan shook his head in disgust. "Nobody values customer service anymore."

Holt grinned and clapped Stan on the shoulder. "You know, Stan, I think I may have just the solution for you. You know Sam who runs the Creedence Country Feed & Supply?"

"Sure. I buy our feed from him."

"He was just telling me the other day that he'd like to retire, but he can't until he finds someone he can trust to run the store for him. I seem to recall he was looking for a guy who could manage employees, handle ordering and maintaining inventory and who cared about customer service and taking care of people."

Stan's face lit up brighter with each qualification Holt ticked off. "I can do all those things. I'd love to manage that store. And it would be so great to work in town and not have to commute forty miles every day. Do you think he'd consider me?"

"I think it's worth the phone call to Sam to find out. And I'd be happy to put in a good word for you."

"You would?"

"Sure."

"Why? I've been kind of a jerk to you, showin' up at your house to yell at you and all."

Holt shrugged. "We all have bad days. But I've seen you with your daughter today, and I think you're a good man." He looked across the farmyard to where Lainey was laughing with Aunt Sassy. "And I guess I'm just feeling in the Christmas spirit."

"You fillin' in for Santa Claus this year?"

Holt chuckled. "No, apparently I'm just one of his elves."

Lainey came hurrying toward them, a wide grin on her face. "I saw you two laughing over here," she said. "You must have told him about the money."

Holt shook his head quickly, trying to signal that he hadn't mentioned it, but it was too late.

Stan frowned. "What money?"

Holt spoke out of the corner of his mouth. "I thought we were going to anonymously stick that in Sarah's cash bucket."

"I was worried it was too much to trust just dropping it into her bucket," Lainey told him.

"Will somebody tell me what in the dickens you two are talking about?"

Lainey scooched onto the bench in between them and explained about the visit from Maxton and Raine and the way they hadn't thought twice about passing her a handful of cash for Sarah and Copper. She pulled the folded over hundreds from her pocket and handed them to Stan.

He stared incredulously at the bills in his hand. "How much is this?"

She leaned closer to whisper. "Eight hundred dollars."

"The hell?" He reared his head back, then pushed the money back toward her. "I can't accept this."

Lainey held her hands up so he couldn't put the bills back in them. "You sure can. And you *will*. That money will feed Copper for months. And might help feed your family too. There's no shame in using some of it for groceries or to pay a bill." She closed Stan's hand around the cash. "Those kids didn't even blink at this amount. They told me this was less than they spent on their *bar tab* last weekend."

He frowned. "You're kiddin' me?"

"She's not," Holt told him. "Those kids gave the horse rescue a sizable donation too. And they also dropped off their pet like it was a disposable toy they'd bought and didn't know how to return. Take the money, Stan, and don't lose a wink of sleep over it."

Stan looked down at the money one more time, then folded the bills again and stuck them in his pocket. He let out a long breath, then took out his handkerchief and wiped at the corners of his eyes. "Thank you," he said, his voice hoarse with emotion.

He gave Lainey a hard hug and stood to shake Holt's hand. Stan grinned as he winked at Holt. "I guess you are an elf."

CHAPTER 26

The last event at the festival was judging the Christmas tree contest. It was one of Lainey's favorite parts. Contestants had to sign up in advance and pay a forty-dollar entry fee, then bring their chosen decorations out to the ranch with them. They had all day to work on their tree, and she'd noticed one mother-daughter team had spent almost four hours on theirs.

A couple were sponsored by local businesses and were more of promotional tactic than a real play to win. There was a cash prize taken from a portion of the entry fees, but the real prize was the bragging rights and the gorgeous wooden Christmas tree trophy her grandfather had carved that had passed from winner to winner for over twenty years.

They had twenty-one entries this year, six more than last, thanks to Lainey's social media posts and a little arm-twisting she may have done the night of the bonfire.

There was a Disney tree, a Harry Potter–themed tree, and a John Deere one decorated in green and yellow with a little tractor on top. There was an outer space–themed one with a rocket zooming around the tree and all the balls painted to look like planets and a Halloween-inspired one decorated in orange and black with spooky bats and skulls and little witches' hats for ornaments.

As she walked through the contestants' tree master-pieces, Lainey didn't envy the judges. The trees were all so good. She had no idea how they would choose. But the panel of five took their jobs very seriously.

Aunt Sassy had put together the judging panel, and it included herself, Ida Mae Phillips from church, the mayor's wife, Lyda Hightower, and her bestie, Evelyn Chapman. Sassy had frowned a little on that one since Carley's Cut & Curl had entered a tree and Evelyn was the hairdresser's ex-grandmother in law, but Evelyn had sworn she could be impartial in her judging. Sassy's big achievement this year was bringing in a "celebrity" judge. Her nephew, Rockford James, played hockey in the NHL for the Colorado Summit, and she'd talked him into helping. Although Rock might be a star on the ice, Lainey had a feeling those older ladies would devour him if they had to face off during a power play to pick the winning trees.

The group of judges now stood at the edge of the trees with their heads bent together, clipboards up, as they deliberated the winners. At well over six feet tall, Rock towered over the little old ladies, and Lainey could see him chuckling good-naturedly, but it didn't look like he was getting a word in edgewise.

Holt had taken her grandpa back to the assisted-living center. She still couldn't believe he'd managed to get him out here. And Gramps seemed to have had the best day. Two of the ladies from church took charge of him not long after he'd arrived, and throughout the day, Lainey had seen them wheeling him from one thing to the next, one time with a bag of kettle corn in his arms, another when he was holding a greasy paper container of ribbon fries. But he was always laughing, and the two women seemed to be taking good care of him. Lainey wondered if they might be looking to fill the role of *Mrs.* McBride.

She shuddered, then smiled as she saw Holt walking toward her. "How'd it go?"

"Good. The nurses forgave me for getting him back twenty minutes late, and he couldn't stop talking about what a great job you did today and how proud he was of you. But he also looked tired by the time I got him back to his room, and I'd bet he's gonna sleep pretty good tonight."

She wrapped an arm around his waist and gave him a tight hug. "Thanks for bringing him. That was just the best surprise."

"It was no biggie, but I'm glad it made you happy." He grinned down at her. "The real surprise is gonna happen later tonight when we go to get undressed."

She raised her eyebrows. "Oh yeah?"

"Yeah, after messing with all these glittery decorations and cleaning up two glitter spills this afternoon, I seem to be covered in the stuff. I went to take a leak earlier and even found it on my underwear. So you never know where I'm going to sparkle."

She laughed. "Sounds like I'm getting an early Christmas present then."

A cheer went up in the crowd of people left as Aunt Sassy called out the winner of the Christmas tree contest.

Two sisters (one in fifth grade and the other in sixth) had decorated their tree in ice blue and white, using blue tinsel and white and silvery glittery ribbons and balls to create a *Frozen*-inspired tree with the theme of sisterly love. Second place went to the outer space tree, and Carley's Cut & Curl took third.

Once the Christmas tree contest ended, the festival finally wound down, but the volunteers stayed and helped Holt and Lainey clean up. They left some of the displays up for the Ho-Ho-Hoedown the following night, but the craft stations were dismantled and cleaned up, and the extra supplies were packed away to be used next year. The hot chocolate had run out for the day, but the cocoa bar was cleaned and ready to be restocked for the following night.

"We need to make sure we lock up Santa's workshop extra tight," Lainey told Holt as she walked into the barn to drop off a stack of craft supplies.

"I already did. And I'll be on the lookout tonight for a raccoon wearing a Santa hat whose breath smells like chocolate and peppermint."

She laughed. "If you see him, tell him to buzz off."

He grabbed her by the waist as she walked past him and pulled her in for a kiss. "Hey, remember the other day when you came over to borrow an extension cord?" he said, then nodded to the spot on the wall where at least five extra extension cords hung.

She lifted one shoulder in a shrug as she offered him a sheepish grin. "I just wanted to see you, and that was the only thing I could think of to come over and ask to borrow."

"I'm glad you did," he said, then showed her how glad he was by kissing her again.

With so many people helping, the cleanup went quicker than she'd thought, but it was still almost ten o'clock by the time Lainey and Holt crashed onto the sofa in her living room.

"We did it," she said, curling into Holt's side.

"You did it," Holt said, squeezing her to him.

"You helped. I couldn't have pulled this all off without you."

He brushed a lock of hair from her forehead. "You never seem to give yourself enough credit for the things you can do. I wish you believed in yourself more."

She had good reason to think of herself as never being good enough. She hadn't been enough to have her real dad stick around for, and Randy pretty much hated her, and the only boy who she'd believed had truly loved her had abandoned her and stood her up after she'd asked him to marry her. No wonder she never felt settled in a job or a place. She never believed she fit in or that she could trust people not to let her down, to leave her again.

But these last few weeks had started to feel different. She'd started to feel like maybe she did have a place to belong, that maybe Creedence was where she'd belonged all along, and that it had just taken her a whole lot of years and heartache to find her way back to it.

She looked over at Holt. To find her way back to *him*.

That old feeling of panic twisted in her gut. Could she really believe in him again? After he'd shattered her heart and practically broken her. Tomorrow night was the dance, and it somehow felt like a climactic moment for them, like they were getting a cosmic do-over, but this time they had a chance to show up, to finally get it right.

They had to talk about it sometime though. Or was she just supposed to *assume* they were going together? Why hadn't he asked her? Maybe he wasn't even planning to go. Maybe that night was too big of a reminder of how she'd stood *him* up and changed everything, and he didn't want to relive that.

There were so many questions racing through her mind. She should be exhausted. She was—her body felt like a balloon that had deflated. But the hoedown was tomorrow, and her brain was still busy trying to figure out how they were going to handle it.

There was only way to find out.

She sucked in a deep breath, then let it out slowly. "So I guess we need to talk about the dance tomorrow."

"What about it?"

"Are we going? Together, I mean. Like, were you ever going to ask me to go with you?"

"Like I was inviting you to the prom?"

"Well, no. Not exactly. But yes, maybe."

He nodded. "You've cleared that right up."

She blew out a frustrated huff. "It just feels like tension or something between us when the subject of the dance comes up. And I wasn't sure if you were going or if you wanted to go together or..." She left the next choice up to him.

"I don't know. But you're right. There is tension when it

comes up. It brings up a lot of stuff for me from the last time we tried to go to this dance together. That was a really bad night for me, and I guess I was afraid to ask you because I didn't want to get stood up again."

"I know. It was a terrible night for me too. And I'm sorry. Again. But if you thought getting stood up for a dance was hard, imagine how I felt when you didn't show up on my birthday."

"Your birthday? What birthday?"

"Oh come on, Holt. You know what I'm talking about. My eighteenth birthday when we were supposed to meet at the cabins at the base of Pikes Peak. I always kind of figured you didn't show up because you were getting back at me for standing you up at the dance."

He jerked his head back. "Hold up. I have no idea what you're talking about. What cabins at Pikes Peak?"

"*The* cabins. The Sunrise Cabins. The ones we used to dream about going to for our honeymoon. But that turned out to be a joke. Only the joke was on me. Because I was the only one who showed up." She didn't understand why he looked so confused. "Why are you looking at me like that? I explained it all in my letter. And *you said* you got my letter."

"I did. I got it in the mail two weeks after you left. It was real moving too. Three whole sentences. Let's see, how did it go? Oh yeah… 'Dear Holt, Sorry I missed the dance. Things are moving too fast for me, and this just isn't working out, so I need to break things off. Please understand my needs and let me go. All my best, Lainey.'"

Her mouth dropped open as she stared slack-jawed at

him. "That wasn't me. I never wrote those things to you. And I never mailed you anything. I couldn't."

"You don't need to deny it. It was a long time ago. I told you, we were kids, and I got that we were pretty intense—talking about marriage at seventeen. I understand why you got scared and broke it off. I just figured you would have called and talked to me instead of having your grandmother tell me you didn't want to see me anymore, then sending me a 'Dear Holt' letter and cutting me completely out of your life."

"I didn't cut you out of my life."

"Lainey, I get it. You don't have to lie. I know your handwriting."

A wave of nausea swept through her, and her stomach felt like she'd just been sucker punched. There were only a few people in her life who she totally trusted—her mother, her grandmother, and her grandpa. And one of them had betrayed her. One of them had changed everything.

"Holt, I swear. That wasn't me. I *did* write you a letter. But I never mailed it."

He frowned. "Then how was I supposed to have gotten it?"

"I left it for you at the tree. *Our* tree. I wedged it between the branches, up where we used to sit. It was in a pink plastic shopping bag. There was no way you could have missed it."

"I never got anything in a pink bag. And there was nothing at our...the tree."

"I put it there the night before the dance, the night my mom and I ran away. It explained everything—how we had to run and why I couldn't contact you. And it asked you to meet me at the Sunrise Cabins on my eighteenth birthday, but you never showed up." She decided to leave out the part about bringing a pink rose if he still wanted to marry her.

"I don't know what you're talking about. What does that mean you *had to run*? Like an errand?"

"No. Like for our lives."

He shook his head, the confused look back. "Lainey, what the hell are you talking about?"

She let out a sigh, then looked away as the old shame came back again. "I explained it all in my letter. The one in the tree."

"I just told you I never got a letter in the tree. So I think you need to explain it again."

Her gaze dropped to the floor, and she rubbed at an old spot on the carpet with her toe. "You remember my stepdad, Randy?"

He shrugged. "I guess. I think I only met him once. And I didn't like the guy. I probably never told you that, but there was something about him that bothered me."

"You had good reason not to like him. He used to…" She let out a shaky breath. "He used to hurt my mom."

Holt stiffened. "What do you mean *hurt*?"

"You know what I mean. He was a mean drunk, and when things weren't going great for him, which they seldom did, he took it out on my mom. He beat her, sometimes with his fists, sometimes with whatever was handy, a frying pan, the TV remote. Sometimes he'd slap her, then other times he'd punch or kick her. It usually depended on how much he'd had to drink and how well she'd done at staying out of his way or not pissing him off."

"Did he hurt you too?"

"Only once, and that's what made my mom finally find the courage to leave him. That, and the fact that the beatings were getting worse every time the police were called."

Holt's fingers had curled into fists at his sides, and his expression had hardened as his eyes narrowed. "Tell me where to find him. I'll kill the bastard."

"He's in prison. Now."

"Did you help put him there?"

"No, but I would have testified against him if given the chance because he *did* kill the next woman he was with." She held up her hand as he started to say something more. "Just let me get through this."

He nodded, but his posture stayed erect as he leaned toward her.

"A few weeks before that Christmas break, he and my mom got into a big fight. He usually hit her when I wasn't home or after I'd gone to bed. But that night, I was in the room, and he was mad because she'd put too much salt on the mashed potatoes. He flung the bowl across the room and lifted my mom out of her chair by the throat. I tried to stop him, and he backhanded me across the face and split my lip open."

An angry growl sounded from Holt's throat. "I remember your lip being busted, but you told me you fell off your bike."

"I was ashamed to tell you what really happened."

"*Ashamed?* What the hell did *you* have to be ashamed

about?" Then he pressed his lips together as if to keep from saying anything more. "Go on."

"I think my mom had been working on a plan to get away from him for a while. She'd asked me before if we had a chance to get away from him, if I would be willing to go, and I'd always said yes. Plus, she had a lot of things in place when we finally ran. After he hit me, my mom sent me to my grandparents. Looking back, I think she did that a lot after he'd hurt her, like to give herself time alone to heal. I just didn't get what was going on. But that night, the night before the dance, I knew the time had come. They'd shown up early, Randy had lost his job, *again*, and my mom had a swollen eye, a split lip, and bruises all over her torso. It was after supper that night that she finally came clean to my grandparents and asked them for help."

"They didn't know?"

Lainey shook her head. "Nobody knew. Although I guess they had suspected for a while because they had a bunch of cash they gave to us and my grandma had duffel bags packed and ready with clothes and toiletries. My grandpa came down the stairs with a loaded shotgun and told Randy he had two minutes to get the hell out of his house and that if he ever touched his daughter again, he'd kill him. Randy acted all tough and like it was his idea to leave, telling my grandpa that it didn't matter, my mom would come crawling back to him anyway. He drove off, and we packed up my grandparents' car—they made us take that too—then we just ran."

"Where did you go?"

"Lots of places. We first went to California thinking we

could get lost in a big city, but it was too expensive, so we backtracked to Kansas. We could afford to live there, but it felt too close to Randy, so we headed up to Montana. At first, we were just living in cheap hotels, but then we found a small apartment to rent. The last hotel we'd stayed at was run by this older woman who hired us to clean the rooms and paid us cash under the table. My mom had always loved to garden, and she eventually got hired on with a small landscaper who paid her in cash and didn't require a social security number. I stayed with the hotel and saved every penny I could. Then that summer, the day before my eighteenth birthday, I took a bus back to Colorado and booked a week at the Sunrise Cabins, then I waited for you. But you never came."

"I didn't know."

All the old feelings of hurt and abandonment were coming back, forming a nauseous swirl in her stomach. "I can remember being so excited to see you, then being crushed and humiliated when you didn't show up. I waited the whole week. But you never came." Her voice shook as she fought the tears forming in her eyes. "You didn't just break my heart. You broke *me*. You were one of the few people who I trusted, who I knew wouldn't let me down, yet in the end, that's just what you did."

"You let me down too," Holt said, his voice hard.

She blinked at him, surprised by his harsh tone. "Are you *mad*? At *me*?"

"Damn right I'm mad."

"Didn't you hear what I just told you?"

"Yeah, I heard it. *Now*. But it sure as hell would have been better to hear it back then. Holy hell, Lainey. All it would have taken was a phone call. You say you left me a letter, but I never got it, so all I knew was that this girl, who'd been my best friend *for years*, who'd said she *loved* me and wanted to *marry* me, just up and left without a freakin' word. Stood me up for a dance she'd acted like she was excited to go to, then had her *grandma* tell me she'd left town and didn't want to see me anymore. You think your heart was broken? I didn't know what the hell to think. I went from confused and sad to frustrated and mad. Then I got your letter, and you talk about something that broke you. That damn letter *destroyed* me. I couldn't eat. I couldn't sleep. I damn sure couldn't imagine ever falling for another girl."

His anger was fueling her own resentment. "You think it was any different for me? I haven't had a normal relationship in over a decade. Even if I did meet a nice guy and we started to get close, I'd break up with him before he had a chance to dump me."

"Oh, boo-hoo. You think my relationships were any better?"

"Yes. I saw the pictures of you with some woman plastered all over Facebook."

"Oh yeah, she dumped me on Christmas Eve too."

"I *didn't* dump you."

"Yeah, you're right. You had your grandma do it for you. Then it sure as hell felt like it when I got a breakup letter from you in the mail."

"At least you *got* a letter. Talk about getting dumped. I sat at the stupid hotel waiting for you for days and never heard a thing."

He threw his hands in the air. "Then why didn't you *call* me?"

"Because *you didn't show up*. I was humiliated and heartbroken and figured either you didn't want me anymore or had moved on and found someone else or you were getting me back for standing you up for the dance."

His voice was getting louder and laced with steel. "I didn't show up because I didn't *know*. And I didn't know because you left me a note—*in a fucking tree*—instead of just *trusting* me to tell me what was going on in your life and that your asshole stepdad was abusing your mom."

She reared back, feeling as if she'd been slapped. Holt would never hit her. She knew that in her soul. But his words cut her to the quick. How had she become the bad guy in this situation?

Her mouth had gone dry, and an ache had formed in her stomach. She tried to swallow, struggled to keep from sobbing, as she felt everything around her crumbling in. Everything except her walls of defense. Those were going right back up and were higher than ever.

Her voice was hoarse, her throat tight as she told him, "I think you should go."

His eyes widened, then narrowed into a hard stare. She thought she saw hurt in them, but it was quickly replaced with fury. "Yeah, I think I should go too."

He stomped across the room, ripped his coat from the rack, and yanked the door open. A gust of cold air blew in as he turned back to look at her, staring into her eyes as if waiting for her to tell him to stay.

She bit the inside of her lip, trying to keep herself from saying anything. Then she put her fingers to her mouth, pressing hard, holding in the sob that was trying so desperately to escape. She dropped her gaze to the floor, unable to look at him.

All these motions took seconds to complete, but they conveyed her message, and she jumped as she heard the door slam.

Her sob finally broke free as she looked up and he was gone.

CHAPTER 27

HOLT KNOCKED ON LAINEY'S DOOR EARLY THE NEXT morning. He hadn't been able to sleep, had tossed and turned all night, then got up with the sun to get the ranch chores out of the way before heading to Mountainside.

He shouldn't have left the night before. He was mad and hurt and probably a little in shock, but he should have stayed. Even when she'd told him to go, he should have stayed and talked it out.

Not talking to each other was what got them in this mess in the first place.

He knocked again. It was just past eight. She should be up by now. He'd brought the dog, hoping the cuteness factor of the mutt might soften the mood *and* his apology. But he couldn't apologize if she didn't open the door. Lou sat next to his leg, staring at the door, then looked up at him. She let out a whine and one sharp bark, then jumped up on the door, scratching at it with her paws.

The latch must not have been set, because the weight of the dog pushed the door open, and Lou went running inside. She raced down the hallway and disappeared into Lainey's bedroom. Holt ran after her, calling out, "Sorry, Lainey, the door was open."

He heard the dog start to bark again as he rounded the corner. She was sitting in the same spot as before, in front of the hope chest, but this time she wasn't barking at the suitcase.

Because the suitcase was gone.

Holt sucked in a breath as he looked around the room. The bed was neatly made, and all the surfaces were clean. No half-empty water glass sat on the nightstand, no sneakers lay kicked off at the end of the bed, no loose change or jewelry covered the top of the dresser, and no pajamas lay cast off in the chair by the window.

All traces of Lainey were gone.

He sagged against the doorframe. She was gone. She'd left—again—without telling him goodbye.

Just like last time.

He pressed the pads of his fingers against his eyes. He couldn't freaking believe it.

He stormed back into the living room, searching for any signs of her, but the living room was neat and looked as if it had been freshly vacuumed. The kitchen was the same. The counters had been wiped down and there were no dishes in the sink and no scent of morning coffee having been brewed in the air. He checked the coffeepot just to be sure, but it was empty and cool, and there were no damp grounds in the filter.

Everything was spotless. It was like she'd never even been there.

He whistled for the dog and pulled the front door shut behind him. He checked his phone on the way to the barn. No missed calls. No texts. Her car wasn't in the barn.

Lainey had left. Again.

The sound of a door slamming startled Lainey awake. She was slumped over, and her back ached from sleeping in a chair for the last several hours. Rubbing the grit from her eyes, she peered toward her grandfather's bed, where Walt was sitting up and looking back at her.

He set the book he was holding down in his lap. "Good morning, sunshine."

"Good morning," she said, sitting forward and stretching her arms above her head. "How are you feeling?"

He waved a hand in the air. "I'm fine. They shouldn't have called you."

"I'm glad they did. You fell and hit your head. There was blood everywhere."

He gingerly touched the butterfly bandage covering the cut on his forehead. "You know how head wounds bleed. This is nothing. And I just stumbled getting out of bed on my way to the john. It's not like I had a heart attack or anything."

"Don't even say that," she told him. "And this is probably my fault anyway. I should have insisted we get you back earlier yesterday."

"I appreciate the sentiment, darling granddaughter, but this had nothing to do with how much time I spent at the festival yesterday, and it certainly was *not* your fault. Not unless you have some control over my damn prostate that wakes me up in the night and has me racing to the toilet. Which is not easy with a broken hip and trying to use that durn fool walker."

"Okay, I don't need to know any more about your 'damn prostate.'" She smiled to show she was teasing him, then searched the floor for her purse. She pulled out her phone, then swore at the blank screen. "Damn. My phone is dead. I didn't get a chance to charge it last night."

He narrowed his eyes. "That seemed like kind of a big reaction for a dead battery. You okay?"

She sighed and slumped back in the chair. "I don't know."

"What's going on?"

"I got in a fight with Holt. Well, not really a fight. More like a heated discussion, but I told him to leave."

Walt struggled to sit up straighter in the bed. "Did he lay his hands on you?"

"What? No. Of course not. Holt's not like that." She reached out and patted his leg. "I promise. Holt would never hurt me. Not like that."

"So what happened?"

"The truth, I guess. We've basically been pretending the past never happened. We've been trying to live in the moment and enjoy being together. But last night the past caught up to us, and we hashed out everything that happened all those years ago."

"Why bring all that back up now?" he asked, and Lainey thought he may have squirmed a little.

"Because apparently, I've spent the last decade thinking he stood me up and broke my heart, and he spent the last decade thinking I broke his. I left him a letter asking him to meet me on my birthday, but he never got it. Instead, he got a letter in the mail that *looked* like it was from me, breaking up with him and basically telling him not to contact me again." She narrowed her eyes at her grandfather. "You wouldn't happen to know anything about that letter, would you?" This time, she knew he squirmed. *And* he looked guilty as hell. "I've already figured out it was Grandma who wrote it. I just don't understand why. She knew how Holt and I felt about each other."

"Aww, honey, that's why she sent it. Because she *did* know. And she was trying to protect you both."

"How did breaking up with Holt and telling him never to contact me again *protect* us?"

"I know it may be hard for you to understand, but you should have seen that boy the night he showed up to take you to the hoedown, and she had to tell him that you'd left and weren't coming back. Damn near broke our hearts. We always thought highly of him, of all those Callahan kids. And we knew how devoted you and Holt were to each other. So did your stepdad. Which was why your grandma knew she had to do something to break things off with you two. We didn't know how much you'd told him, but we were afraid Holt would start digging into why you'd left and that he would somehow lead Randy to you and your mom. Not on purpose. But we knew the lengths that bastard would go to in an effort to find you and that he wouldn't think twice about using Holt or *hurting* him to get him to divulge your whereabouts."

Lainey sucked in a breath. "I never even considered that."

"Your grandma tried to let him down easy the night of the dance. I can't remember what she said, but she made it clear you didn't want to see him anymore. But apparently he was having a hard time buying it. Your grandma talked to his, and she told her that he wasn't eating or sleeping and that he was making himself sick with trying to figure out where you'd gone and why you'd left him without a word. We never knew anything about a letter in a tree."

"Apparently neither did he. He never found it."

"Your grandma figured if he got some kind of message directly from you telling him you wanted to break up, then he would stop looking for you. Your handwriting was similar to hers, and she thought if she kept it short enough, he'd believe it was really from you. It would be tough on him, but at least it would be a clean break, and he could grieve you, then get on with his life. Teenage girls break teenage boys' hearts all the time. Folks get over broken hearts. You don't believe me, just turn on the radio and listen to just about any country song."

He looked at her and tried to tease a smile, but she wasn't amused. "I'm sorry, honey. We thought we were doing him a favor and giving him a chance to get over you. And we figured if you ever wanted to get back in touch with him, then that would be up to you."

"When he didn't show up on my birthday, I just thought he'd abandoned me. That he'd never loved me, just like my dad."

"Aww, sweetheart, now you're breaking my heart. What can I do to help fix this?"

"Nothing. I don't know if it can be fixed. I probably shouldn't have told him to leave last night. But he didn't have to go. If he really wanted to work this out, wouldn't he have stayed and fought for us or at least tried to convince me that he really does love me? I've spent the better part of my adult life thinking that I'm not worthy of love and definitely not worth sticking around for, and Holt proved that again last night when he just got up and walked out the door."

"Don't say that. Of course you're *worthy* of being loved. You're a wonderful person, and you've always been so good to your grandma and me."

"Being a good granddaughter isn't usually on the top of the list for desirable qualities you look for in a life partner."

"Well, if that boy can't see what a gem you are, then he can go jump in a lake."

"Yeah, I thought about that option for him too last night when I was stress cleaning your house to within an inch of its life. I hadn't even made it to bed when the nurse called me."

"Listen, honey, I don't know if you want to take advice from an old man, but I know that love, real love, doesn't come around that often. And I think that's what you and Holt have."

"I think so too. I know that *I* love him, and I have since I was ten years old. And I think that he loves me too. But he doesn't have a real great track record for sticking around either. He's bounced around the last ten years from place to place, just like I have. Neither one of us can seem to find a place to settle where we feel like we fit."

Walt shrugged. "Maybe that's because you've both been trying to get back to the only place you felt loved and like you truly belonged—with each other."

———

Holt's boots churned through the dirt and melted snow as he sprinted across the pasture.

After he left Lainey's, he'd brought Lou back to the bunk-house, but he couldn't sit still. He needed to do *something*.

He'd tried to call her several times, but she never answered. Then he'd fired off a text saying he couldn't believe she'd left him again. Then another one that asked her to call him. Then he'd fumed at her not responding, then he'd regretted sending the texts at all. But he'd been mad at her the night before for not trying to call him all those years ago—so he had to at least make an effort to try to get ahold of her.

He'd paced the length of the bunkhouse and back again several times, then got frustrated and stormed outside, deter-mined to find something to do—some activity that would burn off this angry frustration.

Behind the bunkhouse was a stack of logs that needed to be chopped for firewood, and he grabbed the ax and set to splitting them. Swinging the ax with all his might, he chopped his way through a dozen logs. He'd checked his phone again—nothing, no missed calls, no replies to his texts—so he'd chucked the damn thing into the woodpile and gone back to hacking up the biggest logs he could find. But nothing—no amount of pacing or splitting firewood was cutting through his pain.

Which was how he suddenly found himself sprinting through the pasture, the handle of the ax still clutched in his fist. His lungs burned, and his breath was heaving in hard pants by the time he made it to his and Lainey's spot.

It was such a pretty area—the water and the huge cotton-wood tree, its long branches spreading out above the creek and the bridge. It was no wonder it was their favorite place.

Despite its beauty and tranquility, he'd avoided it for years, and now he remembered why. Because seeing this place and recalling the memories swirling around it caused a hard ache in his chest.

He leaned forward and tried to catch his breath as he stared at the massive cottonwood. He considered chopping the whole damn thing down. He was that out of his mind with frustration and turmoil over what to do. But the rational part of his brain told him that it would take hours to actually chop it down and then reminded him that he also loved trees.

But he needed to hack into something.

He looked from the tree to the bridge he'd just repaired, then back to the tree. His gaze moved up the trunk to the branch he and Lainey used to sit on—the one she claimed she'd left him a note in. The branch was at least seven feet off the ground, and he would have to swing *up* to hit it, but he didn't care. He hauled back the ax and took a mighty swing at the spot where the branch met the tree. He swung again, sending chips of the wood flying as the blade of the ax dug into the soft meat of the wood.

He swung once more, but this time, the ax blade stuck in the tree. He yanked at it but couldn't pull it free. Putting his boot against the trunk, he let out a primal yell as he wrenched once more at the handle. As the blade finally came free, it pulled something out with it—something white.

No. Holt peered closer at the plastic sticking out of the new cut. It wasn't white. It had just faded in color. It was actually *pink*.

CHAPTER 28

"Dammit," Holt yelled into the branches of the tree. Then, with the ax still in his hand, he climbed up the tree and onto the branch.

There was a crack where the branch met the tree that had formed a foot-wide cavity. And sure as freaking enough, there was a pink plastic bag that had fallen into it and was wedged in the crevice.

Using the ax, he chipped away at the wood until he could yank the bag free. Then he climbed back down and sank onto the top step of the bridge to examine the contents of the bag.

Lainey's grandpa had smoked cigars for years. The summer when he and Lainey were getting ready to go to high school, Walt had brought all the kids into his study and let them each pick out a cigar box from the stacks of them he'd collected. Holt still had his. He kept the most memorable mementos of his life in it—including Lainey's letter—which he had now come to suspect had actually been written by her grandma.

He remembered that he, Cade, and Bucky had all chosen cedar wood boxes, while Bryn and Lainey had wanted the smaller cardboard ones. He couldn't recall which color Bryn had picked, but he knew Lainey's had been white.

Wrapped inside two Ziploc bags was that same white cigar box, surprisingly dry, and he recognized Lainey's initials and the picture she'd drawn of a horse on the left side.

He dropped the plastic bags to the ground and just stared at the box on his lap. Carefully lifting the lid, he saw two sheets of notebook paper, folded into quarters with his name scrolled across the front. *The letter.* The one Lainey had sworn she had written. Holt lifted the pages out and set them beside him. Emotion burned his throat as he examined the rest of the items in the box.

They were all part of his and Lainey's history. There was the small felt snowman he'd given her for her twelfth birthday, a friendship bracelet he'd made her one summer when she and Bryn were totally into them, a movie ticket stub from one of the Harry Potter movies they'd seen together, a valentine card he'd given her, a neat rock they'd found, a silly unicorn necklace he'd won her at the county fair, a magnet with a picture of Pikes Peak, a postcard he'd sent her from a trip to Mount Rushmore, and a Ring Pop, still in the package, that he'd given her with the promise that someday he'd buy her the real thing. There was a pair of cheap sunglasses and one half of a heart key chain she'd given him. He still had the other half at home in his cigar box.

So many memories of the fun times they'd had together. So many relics of their shared life, their history, and their plans for a future spent with each other. Wiping at his eyes with the back of his hand, he set the box down on the step beside him, then opened the letter and began to read.

When he finished, he had to wipe his eyes again.

Everything she'd said was true. The letter was obviously written by a teenager, and he could hear Lainey's younger voice as he read the words asking him to meet her at the cabins, with a pink rose, if he still wanted to marry her. If he'd gotten this note, he would have moved heaven and earth to have been there, and his chest ached at all those years wasted that they could have been together.

Now all he wanted to do was call her, to talk to her, to hear her voice. He checked his pocket for his phone—*aww, shit*—suddenly remembering he'd hurled it into the stacks of uncut wood behind the bunkhouse.

Gathering up the ax and the plastic, he held the box to his chest as he walked back to the bunkhouse, stopping at the woodpile to retrieve his shattered phone. He was surprised to see Doc Hunter sitting on his porch when he got there.

"Hey, Doc, or should I say Santa," he said, gesturing to the elaborate red-and-white costume Doc wore, complete with the black leather boots and the fluffy white snowball on the tip of his hat. "What are you doing out this way? Shouldn't you be busy loading up your sleigh?"

"I'm out delivering Christmas goodies," Doc said, passing him a plate full of cookies and holiday treats. "Sassy spent all last night baking and putting treats together, then tasked me with delivering them all today while she gets ready for the Ho-Ho-Hoedown tonight."

Holt shook his head as it suddenly hit him that it was Christmas Eve. "I forgot that was tonight."

Doc frowned. "You forgot? Aren't you going with Lainey?"

He sighed. "Nope. Or at least I don't think so. It's complicated. And why I hate Christmas. You spend weeks getting your hopes up that it's going to be this amazing perfect thing, then every year, it's just a big fat letdown."

"Sounds like it's a good thing I stopped by. Wanna talk about it?" He nodded to the plate in Holt's hand. "Over a cookie? And I wouldn't turn down a cup of coffee if you've got one."

Holt's stomach growled. It was well past noon, and he hadn't eaten all day. "Sure, come on in."

Doc followed him inside and played with the dog while Holt started a pot of coffee. He opened the refrigerator and pulled out lunch meat and cheese. "Can I interest you in a sandwich, Doc? I've got turkey or ham."

"Turkey would be great, with just a dab of mustard and mayo if you've got it handy. I've been so busy driving around, I never stopped to eat lunch." Doc planted himself on one of the barstools at the kitchen island. "What's your excuse?"

Holt shrugged as he put together the sandwiches, then poured them each a cup of coffee. He put Doc's on a plate but didn't bother with one for himself as he leaned against the counter to eat it. In between bites, he told Doc what had happened between him and Lainey, starting with them as teenagers, then ending with him finding the cigar box and the real letter.

"That's quite a story," Doc said when he'd finished. "So what are you going to do now?"

Holt scrubbed a hand over his face. "That's the problem. I don't know what to do. Lainey's gone. She left. Again. I've called and texted her, but she hasn't answered or texted back. At least I don't think she has." He gestured to the broken phone he'd tossed on the counter. "Apparently chucking your phone into a pile of firewood is a bad idea. The dang thing won't even turn on now."

"Yikes."

Holt shrugged. "Doesn't matter. It was old, and I was due for a new one anyway. And besides, if Lainey's gone, I don't really have anyone I want to talk to anyway."

"Now come on, son. You've got other people in your life who care about you."

"I know," Holt said with a sigh. "I just want this stupid holiday to be over. I always seem to get burned at Christmas." He told Doc about getting stood up with a ring in his pocket the year before. "See why I hate Christmas?"

"No, actually I don't. None of that stuff is the holiday's fault. And if you ask me, it sounds like you dodged a bullet with that last gal. Just imagine if you would have found Lainey after you'd gotten married to someone else."

"Yeah, I guess," Holt muttered.

"Christmas is obviously different for everyone, but I see the spirit of Christmas as a time of giving—and I don't mean just presents. But giving of ourselves. Spending time together and helping others in need. It's a time of grace and forgiveness, and sometimes you have to offer those things to yourself as well to others. We celebrate the birth of Jesus, and with his birth come hope and a chance at new beginnings. It's a selfless time where we work to be kind, to forgive, and maybe to take a little stock of our lives and figure out how to do better, to give more, to be better versions of ourselves. Christmas is about salvation and love and joy."

Holt swallowed, surprised at the lump in his throat. "I think Lainey has been trying to show me all those things."

"Have you been seeing them?"

"I do when I'm with her. She *is* all those things, selfless and kind and giving. She makes me believe love and joy and second chances are possible. Or she did. Until she left." Despair spiraled through him and settled in his gut.

"So what are you going to do about that?"

"I don't know what to do."

"First you have to decide if you're going to fight for her or if you're going to let her get away again. Christmas isn't over yet, son. I've still got a good feeling that things are going to work out. Oh, I almost forgot. I've got something else for you." Doc reached into his pocket and pulled out a small red drawstring bag and handed it to him.

Holt loosened the drawstring and pulled out a small pine cone covered in silver glitter.

"Sassy made this for you. She made one for Lainey too. The pine cone is a great example of regeneration and second chances. And according to Sassy, it's supposed to be good luck if you put it on your mantel."

Holt stared down at the pine cone, ignoring the little flakes of glitter that now clung to his hands. "Yes, I've heard that." He raised his gaze to peer at Doc. "Are you *sure* you're not really Santa?"

Doc let out a hearty laugh that sounded a little similar to a ho, ho, ho. "No, but I will admit to being one of his helpers."

From somewhere in Doc's coat, the song "Santa Claus Is Coming to Town" suddenly blared out. "Here comes Santa Claus, here comes Santa Claus, right down Santa Claus Lane…" He pulled the phone from his pocket and squinted at the screen. "Hold on. I gotta take this. It's Sassy," he said, tapping the phone, then holding it to his ear. "Hello, sugar cookie." He chuckled at what must have been her replying with a cute nickname in return. "Yes, I delivered everything. I'm out at the Callahan ranch, and Holt was kind enough to make me a turkey sandwich."

Holt stared at the pine cone, not listening as Doc spoke to Sassy. What *was* he going to do about Lainey?

Doc finished his conversation, then stuffed the phone back into his pocket. "You know those second chances we were just talking about?"

"Yeah."

"You're about to get yours. Lainey didn't leave town. Sassy's at her place now. She volunteered to help with the hoedown, and she said Lainey just had her run into town for more chocolate. Something about a stupid raccoon finding a way through a window."

Hope bloomed in Holt's chest. "So she didn't leave?"

"Doesn't sound like it."

"You think we've got a shot at another chance?"

"That's another great thing about Christmas—you always get another chance. Now, you'd better quit standing there and get yourself in the shower. You got a dance to get to."

CHAPTER 29

LAINEY SURVEYED THE SCENE IN THE BARN. EVERYTHING
was ready for the dance.

Everything except the fact that Holt hadn't shown up.
And she *still* hadn't heard from him.

She'd ended up staying with her grandfather until after
lunch, so it had been midafternoon by the time she got home
and was able to charge her phone. That's when she'd seen
the eight missed calls from Holt and his messages about her
leaving again.

She wished she would've tried harder to reach him
that morning. He must be going crazy. How could he have
thought she'd left?

The only thing she could think of was that he must've
come over earlier and seen the way the house was spotless
and that her car was missing and thought she'd gone back to
Montana. That'd teach her to clean the house so well.

He wouldn't have known about her weird habit of cleaning the life out of her place when she was upset. Stress cleaning hadn't really been her thing when she was a teenager. It
was a weird habit she'd acquired as an adult.

As soon as she'd seen Holt's messages, she'd tried to call
him, then texted him that she hadn't left town and wanted to

talk. But he hadn't answered her calls or texted her back. She was getting ready to get in her car and go find him when the band and her group of volunteers started showing up to set up for the dance that night.

She hadn't exactly *forgotten* about the Ho-Ho-Hoedown. She'd maybe just pushed it out of her mind and kept thinking she had more time before it started. But she was out of time now. People would start arriving within the hour, and she hadn't even showered.

So instead of getting in her car and driving to the bunkhouse, she texted Holt that she hoped to see him at the dance instead. He hadn't texted back. Not then or any of the million times she'd checked her phone while the band was getting set up and while she was hurriedly doing her hair and makeup and getting dressed.

She'd found a gorgeous holiday dress online that was a robin's-egg-blue color in a velvet A-line style. It had thin, white fur trim around the hem and the bottom of the sleeves, making her feel a little like a princess from *Frozen*. She paired it with her white cowboy boots—it was a hoedown, after all—and a shimmering silver necklace and rhinestone earrings that looked like miniature Christmas trees. She left her hair down, taking a few extra minutes to try to tame her curls into submission before misting them with hair spray and racing back out toward the barn.

It was barely six, and the townsfolk of Creedence had already started filing into the barn and heading for the punch and cookies table. The dance was scheduled to finish around nine, giving them all enough time to clean up and still make it to most of the late Christmas Eve services that started at ten.

Lainey drew in a breath as she looked around the barn. All the hard work she and Holt had done to prepare had been worth it. The hay bales they'd set up formed seating around the dance floor, and the lighted ten-foot-tall Christmas tree in the corner combined with the twinkle lights strung from the rafters gave the old barn a cheery, festive look.

And she wasn't the only one who thought so. She could feel the joy of the holiday spirit in the laughter ringing through the air. Then the band began to play, and couples were already heading toward the dance floor. The scent of warm mulled cider and cinnamon sticks mixed with the fresh pine smell of the tree.

Everything was perfect.

Everything except the fact that Holt still wasn't here. And she hadn't heard a word from him.

As the minutes ticked into one hour, then two, a hard ache settled into the pit of her stomach. This was starting to feel all too familiar, bringing back memories of waiting for him at the cabins, sitting on the porch steps, her gaze trained to the entrance as she prayed for his truck to drive in.

But this wasn't like before. Because back then, Holt hadn't known she was waiting. Tonight, he knew. He had to know she'd be at the dance, wondering where he was. He'd been mad last night, and in some ways, she could understand that. She *hadn't* trusted him with the truth about Randy, and looking back, putting a letter in a tree might not have been the best form of communication. But she'd been a dumb teenager, and she'd had the romantic notion of him finding her letter and moving mountains in order to meet her.

They had spent so much time at that tree, sitting up on the very branch where she'd left the box, that it had never even occurred to her that he wouldn't find it.

But she couldn't change the past. And apparently she couldn't control the present either. She'd thought things with Holt were going so well, that they'd rekindled the love they had always had for each other. That they finally had a chance at the future they'd both wanted so long ago. That she finally had a chance to find that place where she felt she belonged.

She forced a smile and a thank-you as a neighbor walked by and told her what a great job she'd done with the festival. She'd spent the last two hours doing the same thing, making small talk, shaking hands, sharing holiday greetings, all while trying not to notice how the minutes kept ticking by without the one person she wanted to see the most at the dance.

She pressed the back of her fingers against her heated cheeks, the crowded barn suddenly feeling too warm. Making her way across the floor, she headed for the doors, needing to get some air.

Those old feelings of not being enough crowded in on her as much as the crush of people. She'd always thought Holt was different. That he'd been *the one* who had seen the real her and had really loved her. No matter what.

I guess I was wrong. About Holt. About everything.

She swallowed at the burn in her throat as she reached for the barn door. But it was yanked open before she got to it, and Holt stepped in, a smile on his face and his arms full of dozens of pink roses.

Lainey stumbled back, unable to believe what she was seeing.

It really *was* Holt. But he looked different. He was dressed in jeans and his cowboy boots, but he wore a new red button-down shirt that still had the lines pressed into it from the packaging, and he'd pulled a red-and-green elf hat down on top of the crown of his black cowboy hat.

"I'm sorry I'm late," he said loudly, to be heard over the band, as he reached out to take her hand. "By a decade or so."

She pressed her lips together, not sure if she was going to smile or cry.

The band must have picked that very moment to take a break because the music stopped, and Holt didn't have to raise his voice any longer. "I came to your house this morning to talk things out, but you were gone."

"My grandpa fell last night. He's okay, but he hit his head and he was bleeding. They called me, and I went into town and spent the night in his room at the assisted-living center."

"But the dog pushed the front door open, it wasn't latched, and there wasn't a trace of you anywhere. Your things were gone, and your bed hadn't been slept in."

"That's because I was so upset last night after you left that I spent three hours stress cleaning the entire house. I hadn't even made it to bed when the nurses called me."

"But your suitcase was gone."

Now she did smile, hoping her next words would make him happy too. "That's because I unpacked it and *put it away.*" She squeezed his hand. "Because I'm going to stay. Here in Creedence." *With you.* She wanted to say it, but she couldn't yet.

She thought she knew the significance of the pink roses he held—it had to be—but she was waiting for him to say it.

"You're staying?" he whispered.

She nodded.

He shook his head. "It doesn't matter."

Oh. Maybe she *didn't* get the pink roses thing after all. "It doesn't?"

"No. I mean, I'm glad you're staying. It makes all this a hell of a lot easier, but it doesn't matter if you *had* left. I would have tracked you down this time. I would have found you and fought for you. For us."

She squeezed his hand. "Me too. I'm not going anywhere this time."

"I found your letter."

Her eyes widened. "You found it after all this time? How?"

"I'm not sure you want to know. There may have been an ax involved. But I found the box. It was just like you said. It had fallen down into a cranny of the tree. And I read your letter." His voice broke on his last sentence, and he swallowed, then sucked in a deep breath and bent down to one knee, which seemed to appear quite difficult as he still held on to her hand while trying to cradle the huge bouquet of roses in his other arm.

"Are you kidding me?" A growl came from his throat as he let go of her and set the roses on the floor next to him. He carefully pulled one long-stemmed flower out of the bunch then took her hand again as he held the single rose up to her. "Lainey, I have loved you from just about the very first moment we met. I'd never known anyone like you—so brave and kind and so full of life and adventure. You saw the good in everything, even in me. And you still do. I made a mistake all those years ago of giving up on us, but I will never make that mistake again. From this day forward, I will always find you, I will always love you, and I will spend every day trying to be the man you believe I can be. Lainey McBride, will you marry me?"

She smiled down at him, her heart so full it felt ready to burst from her chest. "Took you long enough to ask."

His lips tugged in a grin. "Hey, I had to go to three stores in two different towns to find this fancy shirt and this many pink roses. I was going to bring you one for every year we missed out on being together, but that just didn't feel like enough. And it took longer than I thought to buy a new phone." He looked sheepishly at the ground. "I may have smashed mine earlier today, but that's a story for another time." He tugged at her hand. "So is that a *yes*?"

She took the rose from his hand and held it to her chest as she peered down into the eyes she'd known and loved since she was ten years old. "Yes, Holt Callahan, that is a definite and forever yes."

He pushed to his feet and swooped her into his arms, hugging her tightly as he swirled her around. He set her back down on her feet and leaned in to kiss her as the room around them broke into applause and congratulatory whoops.

Not letting him go, she looked around the room at all the people cheering and clapping for them. People she'd known since she was a girl and people she'd just met. Her heart swelled in her chest, and she knew this was the place she belonged.

The music started again, and Holt kept his arm around her as he leaned close to her ear. "You wanna dance?"

She nodded then followed him out to the floor. Yes, she did want to dance with him—tonight and for the rest of her life.

━━━━━━━

Later that night, Holt held Lainey's hand as they sat next to each other in his grandparents' favorite pew at church. Everyone had pitched in to clean up the barn, and they'd made it to the Christmas Eve service with minutes to spare.

He looked around the church, at the community of people who he and Lainey had become a part of, then down at the beautiful woman sitting next to him and couldn't believe this was his life.

They stood as the organ began the first notes of "Silent Night." The deacons filed down the aisles of the church, lighting the candles of the person at the end of each pew, who would in turn light the candle of the person next to them. The sanctuary lights dimmed as their voices joined together, and they raised their candles as the chorus began.

Silent night, holy night, all is calm, all is bright…

He could hear Lainey's sweet voice singing the beloved carol and looked down at her to see tears shimmering in her eyes. He understood the feeling. Squeezing her hand, he lowered his candle and peered toward the huge Christmas tree sitting at the front of the church.

Doc had told him that Christmas was a time of new beginnings and hope, and for the first time, he felt that hope and joy were possible in his life. He wouldn't go so far as to say his heart grew two sizes just then, but as he lifted his candle and his voice once more, Christmas suddenly didn't seem so bad.

It had started to snow while they were in the church, and they walked out to see the town covered in white. Carols playing softly from hidden speakers along the street and the bright moonlight and the twinkle lights shining from the lampposts gave Creedence an even more magical Christmas feeling.

"I like your hat," Holt told Lainey as they walked toward his truck. She had gone inside before they'd left for church and come out wearing the elf hat she'd had on the first day they'd seen each other again.

"I like yours too," she said. "It makes me feel like you may finally be feeling the Christmas spirit."

"Let's just say I'm embracing my inner elf." They laughed together as he pulled her to him in a hug.

With the snow falling around them and Christmas music playing in the background, he leaned down and pressed a kiss to her neck. He was feeling more than just the Christmas spirit as he gruffly whispered, "I'm takin' you home, and maybe if we're *both* naughty, we can save Santa the trip to our house tonight."

CHAPTER 30

CHRISTMAS MORNING BROKE BRIGHT AND SUNNY, AND the sunlight twinkled off the fresh landscape of snow as Holt poured a cup of coffee to take in to Lainey. He'd let her sleep while he'd worked on a surprise for her.

She came down the hall as he was walking out of the kitchen, her hair mussed and her eyes still sleepy. She wore one of his flannel shirts but had only done a couple of the buttons, and catching glimpses of her bare skin had him wanting to pick her up and carry her back to bed.

"Coffee," she said, holding out her hands for the cup. She closed her eyes and took a sip as Lou jumped off the sofa and came to circle her legs. After another sip, she sighed and opened her eyes as she reached down to pick up the dog with her free hand. "Thanks. I needed that."

"Figured you would." He waited for her to turn toward the living room and see what he'd been working on since he'd been up.

Her eyes widened as she took in the Christmas tree they'd set up in the corner. But instead of having only a few strands of lights and one measly Christmas ball, the tree was now wound with more strands of brightly colored bulbs and decorated with the two boxes of shiny balls he'd grabbed from a holiday display during his shopping expedition the night before.

But the best part was the ornaments, and he watched her face as she crossed to the tree and peered at each one. He'd bought a few—the small dog one, the green Christmas tree, the cup of hot cocoa, and the wooden Nativity scene. Even a goat ornament. He still couldn't believe he'd found that one. But the best ones were the mementos he'd taken from her cigar box and placed in spots of honor within the boughs of the tree—the friendship bracelet, the key chain, the valentine, the postcard, the unicorn necklace.

Her eyes brimmed with tears as she picked up the magnet from Pikes Peak and clutched it to her chest. "You did all this? For me?"

He nodded.

"I thought you hated all this stuff."

"A guy can change," he said, with a shrug, then touched the magnet. "I googled the Sunrise Cabins, and they're still around. I thought for your Christmas gift, I'd get us a week's stay there, if you want."

She laughed. "I would love that. But you don't have to. You've already given me everything I've ever wanted." She wrapped her arms around him. "You've given me a forever home."

"Speaking of a home, we've got some logistics to figure out," he said. "You can move in here with me, or we can look for a place together. But we've got time to figure all that out."

"Not that much time," she said. "I just realized I forgot to tell you that Mayor Hightower offered me a job working for the county as an event coordinator. I start next week."

"No way. Congratulations. That's awesome. And sounds right up your alley."

"Yeah, it does. I think I've finally found something I'm *good at* and that I *want* to do."

"I'm really proud of you." He went to hug her again but stopped as his new phone buzzed in his pocket. He pulled it out and saw a text from his cousin. "*I* just realized I forgot to tell you that Bryn and Zane got home late last night, and they've invited everyone over to their place for Christmas dinner. Are you good with that?"

She nodded. "Yes, that's perfect. But I'm not even dressed. How much time do we have before we need to leave?"

"We don't have to be there until noon," he said, reaching for the buttons of her flannel shirt. "So we've got plenty of time for me to unwrap *you* as my Christmas gift. And the good thing about me being a grinch is that I've got something that'll grow three sizes."

She let out a loud laugh and pulled him to her. "Come here then, you grinch, and kiss me like you mean it."

He leaned in and spoke against her soft lips. "I always mean it when I kiss you."

And he did.

———

Holt wasn't kidding when he said Bryn had invited "everyone" to her house for dinner. The living room and kitchen were filled with people and laughter rang through the house as he, Lainey, and Lou came through the door.

Aunt Sassy, who was wearing a red sweater with a green Christmas tree on the front that lit up, was sitting on the sofa talking to Cade and Nora. His brother wore a new blue flannel shirt that must have been a Christmas gift and a smile that seemed to come so easily to him now.

Sassy had an adorable blond preschooler sitting on her lap, and Holt was glad to see her parents, Stef and Logan, standing at the island in the kitchen laughing with Jillian and Ethan while they noshed on the spread of appetizers. Holt had told Bryn about their new neighbors, and it didn't surprise him a bit to see she'd invited them to the Christmas festivities.

Allie was sprawled out in a mess of pillows on the floor, her head buried in a book she probably got for Christmas that morning. She was in the center of a cuddle puddle of animals. Tiny was wearing a pink poinsettia and stretched out next to her, a dog was curled around her legs, and Esme the goat was tucked under her arm.

Lainey had been worried about how Bryn would react to seeing her, but Holt had already filled his cousin in on all that had been happening. So, in typical Bryn fashion, his cousin screamed when she caught sight of them and flew across the room to launch herself at Lainey, throwing her arms around her. "It's so good to see you. I've missed you so much," she gushed, then pulled Lainey into a tight hug again. "We'll have tons of time to catch up, but for now, you all need to grab some plates and start digging into this food."

"Before we do," Holt said, pulling an envelope from his pocket. "I've got a little Christmas present for you." He and Lainey had decided to wait to tell Bryn the news about the donation until today. Lainey had made a little certificate on the computer to share the news.

Bryn frowned as she took the envelope, but her eyes widened as she read the postcard inside. "Is this for real?"

Holt nodded, a grin breaking out on his face. "It's in the bank, and the check's already cleared."

She threw her arms around him and hugged him tight enough to crack a rib. "This is amazing."

"We've got a present for you too," Zane said, coming up to shake his hand. "That horse you've been riding, Bristol. She's yours if you want her."

Holt blinked. A sharp pang of grief squeezed his chest at the loss of his own horse. "Really? Are you sure?"

Zane nodded. "Seems like you two have already bonded. And a cowboy needs a horse."

Holt laughed as he hugged Bryn again, this time squeezing her tight, then—*what the hell*—he was feeling festive, so he hugged Zane too. It was a quick manly hug, but Zane got it. He understood how much his horse had meant to him and how much he appreciated the gift.

The door opened behind them, and Santa Claus, a.k.a. Doc, walked in, pushing Walt McBride in a wheelchair.

"Gramps," Lainey squealed and ran to hug him. "I can't believe you're here."

Walt chuckled as he squeezed her to him. "I wouldn't miss Christmas with my best girl."

"I wasn't sure they'd give you the all clear to leave today."

He jerked his thumb over his shoulder at Doc. "Santa showed up and broke me out."

Doc chuckled. "I am a doctor, you know. And besides, nobody argues with Santa."

Holt and Lainey had planned to take some turkey leftovers and spend Christmas evening with Walt at the assisted-living center. But the beaming smile on both their faces told him this was so much better.

Lainey looked up at Doc. "Thank you so much for bringing him over."

Doc nodded, then pulled a long wrapped present from the back pocket of Walt's wheelchair. "I brought you this too. I took my woodburning tools with me this morning, and your grandpa and I just finished it."

She clapped her hands together, then took the gift and handed it to Holt.

He looked down at the present. It was about three feet long and almost a foot wide and had a heft to it. "What's this?"

"It's a present. For you. From me. I asked Doc to help me with it."

He tore the wrapping paper away and then his heart swelled as he looked down at the board that had their initials wood-burned into it—*HC + LM = 4ever*. A pine cone was etched into one corner.

"It's a new step," she said, tears shining in her eyes. "For our bridge."

"Yeah, I know what it is," he said, smiling as he leaned down to kiss her. "I love it. Thank you. It's perfect." He kissed her again. "Just like you."

The front door opened once more, and Brody, Elle, and

Mandy walked in, the new baby cuddled in Elle's arms. Everyone gathered around to see the sweet baby boy, who they'd named Tyler Nicholas Tate, ahhing and cooing at the precious bundle.

"He's so adorable, Elle," Nora said, then grinned at Cade before looking back at her friend. "I know you got a ton of cute baby clothes, and I think he'll be growing out of them just in time to hand them down to me." The room went silent as proud smiles spread across both Cade's and Nora's faces.

"I'm not so sure about that," Jillian said. "We may have to arm wrestle for them."

Elle's mouth had dropped open, and she looked at Nora. "You mean...you're pregnant?"

Nora nodded.

Elle's head swiveled to Jillian. "And you're pregnant too?"

Jillian laughed as she nodded as well.

Then the room erupted into laughter and cheers as they all took turns hugging each other.

"This calls for a toast." Doc already had a glass of eggnog in his hand, and he raised it to the room. "Here's to old friendships and new beginnings. To hope and love and second chances." He looked toward Holt and gave him a wink. "Here's to a new year filled with love, laughter, friends, and family. May you all have the best year yet. Merry Christmas."

"Merry Christmas." The cheer went up in the room, which must have startled Esme, who had gotten up and was headed toward Lainey, because she stiffened and fell over.

As more laughter rang out, Holt put his arm around Lainey and pulled her close to his side. He looked around the room at his family and all the new friends he'd made. He felt so different from the angry and depressed man he'd been last year at this time. He'd been given a second chance, and he wasn't going to take it for granted. Doc had told him Christmas was a time to take stock of their lives and to figure out how to be better versions of themselves, that Christmas was about salvation and love and joy. Lainey's love and joy had saved him, and he was determined to be a better version of himself, to let himself love and trust and be happy.

He looked over at Santa, and it was almost as if he could read his mind as he nodded and winked at him again.

Lainey laughed as she reached to pet Esme, who had finally made it over to her. Then she picked up Lou, who had also run over to them, and cuddled the little dog to her chest.

Winnie ran across the room and crashed into Holt's legs, hugging them as she peered up at him with an adoring smile. "Merry Christmas."

He bent down to her level. "Merry Christmas, Winnie. Did you get a mini-horse for Christmas?"

"No, but I feel good about next year," she said, grinning. "'Specially now that I know one of Santa's elves."

Holt laughed. Maybe he didn't hate Christmas so much after all.

THE END...

AND JUST THE BEGINNING...

Can't get enough of Creedence Cowboys?

Read on for an excerpt from Book 3 in the Creedence Horse Rescue series.

CHAPTER 1

CADE CALLAHAN STOOD IN THE HOSPITAL GIFT SHOP staring at the colorful display of get-well tokens. A fluffy white unicorn with a purple horn and a glittery pink-and-purple mane caught his eye. Allie had loved unicorns as a little kid—she'd called them "princess ponies." But he was wrestling with the notion that now she might be too old for a stuffed animal.

If she was, she could always toss it. At least he was trying, he thought as he snagged the unicorn from the shelf. He considered a card but figured that might be a little too much. Besides, he doubted he'd find a card that read, *Sorry I was a shitty dad. Get well soon.* For now, the unicorn would have to do.

He grabbed two bottles of water and threw a couple of Reese's Peanut Butter Cups onto the counter, thinking they might want them on the drive up the mountain. He was already dreading the trip. His back hurt from sleeping in the chair next to her hospital bed, and between the two of them, they were grumpier than a grizzly who'd stepped in a hornet's nest.

I'm the grown-up, he reminded himself. Which meant he needed to be the better person, no matter how many of his buttons his thirteen-year-old daughter pushed. And if there were an Olympic event for pushing a parent's buttons, Allison Raye would take home the gold *and* the silver.

As the teenage cashier rang up the items, his eye caught on the shelf of paperbacks behind her. He gestured to the books. "Do you have any YA?" he asked, recalling the conversation he'd had earlier with his daughter about the Kindle app on her phone. It was probably the longest one they'd had yet. Even though she'd rolled her eyes at his lack of knowledge of the young adult genre, he'd still gleaned three important pieces of information from the conversation: one, her phone was at home on the charger; two, her Kindle took the place of any real friendships she might have; and three, she was still a bookworm who loved to read.

The cashier turned to peruse the shelf and pointed to three books along the bottom. "It looks like we only have these three."

"Okay, I'll take them."

"Which ones?"

"All three."

"Sure." She added the books to his total, then slid them into a bag.

Allie was asleep when he got back to her room. He paused in the doorway to look at her and had to swallow back the emotion burning his throat. He and her mother had had their share of struggles, but he couldn't believe Amber was gone. And the thought that Allie could have died in that car accident too hit him like a punch to the gut.

He blinked back the sudden burn of tears as he peered at

the dark purple bruises around her eyes and along one of her cheeks. A thin line of stitches ran next to her hairline—they weren't sure if she'd hit her head or something in the cab had flown by and cut her when the car rolled. Her right arm was bandaged and secured in a cream-colored splint, and her left leg was constrained in a blue boot, only sprained and thankfully not broken.

She looked so small, so young, like the little girl he remembered. He hadn't seen his daughter in almost a year. He'd contacted Amber a few years back, told her he wanted to try to see Allie more often, but she'd stalled and always seemed to have some excuse for why it wouldn't work. When Allie got a cell phone, he'd tried to call her, but the few times they'd talked had been stilted and awkward with neither of them knowing exactly what to say.

That's bullshit, he thought as he forced himself to step into the room. *I should have tried harder.*

Her eyes fluttered open, and a hard knot tightened in his chest as he saw the array of emotions flash in her eyes with each blink. They changed from almost glad to see him to confused to angry, then to agonizingly sad as the realization of her mother's death must have hit her again.

She winced as she tried to push herself up in the bed with her good hand but waved Cade off as he took another step toward her. "I got it."

He stayed where he was, not sure how to help her and knowing she wasn't ready to accept his help yet anyway. It used to feel like walking on eggshells around each other— now it felt more like land mines.

The nurse had said she'd be able to leave before lunch, and she'd changed into the shorts and one of the T-shirts his cousin Bryn and neighbor Elle had bought for her when they'd come down to Denver after they'd heard about the accident. The T-shirt was red and yellow and referenced being a Gryffindor on the front.

"Nice shirt," he said.

"Thanks. Cousin Bryn and your other friend Elle bought it for me. Apparently they stalked me on Insta and figured out my size and that I love Harry Potter."

"I don't know what Insta is, but I'm glad you like the things they brought." He held out the unicorn. "Here, I got you something too."

"What's this?" she said, peering down at it.

"A peace offering. And an apology, I guess. And just something I thought you'd like."

"Wow. That's a lot of mileage to get out of one stuffed animal."

He shrugged. "I like to consolidate. I also mix my peas into my mashed potatoes and gravy."

She wrinkled her nose. "Gross."

"What? It keeps them from rolling off the plate." He'd been trying to make her smile—just one instant of her lips curving up—and he thought he might have had it. But then her face shut down again as she pushed the unicorn into the tote bag with the rest of her things. "They gave me a bag with my stuff in it, but I don't know if I want it anymore."

The hospital had given him a bag with his ex-wife's things as well. He'd taken a quick look inside—enough to see some clothes, a pair of sneakers, and a streak of blood across the front of Amber's purse. Being on the rodeo circuit, he was no stranger to blood, but it was different when it belonged to the mother of his child who had been alive and breathing less than twenty-four hours ago. He'd twisted the bag closed and stowed it behind the seat in his truck.

He picked up the plastic bag with his daughter's name written on the front. "I'll take care of it." He passed her the bag of books, as if in trade. "Here. I got you these too. The cashier said they were all YA."

A hint of a smile pulled at her lips as she peered into the bag. "They are. I've read one of them already."

He held out his free hand. "That's okay. I can take it back."

She shook her head and pulled the bag of books to her chest. "No, I'll read it again." She narrowed her eyes, then barely lifted one eyebrow. "The unicorn is cute, but you should have led with the books."

He turned away to hide his smile. At least he'd gotten something right.

A nurse pushed a wheelchair into the room. "You ready to break out of this joint?" she asked Allie.

"So ready." The girl pointed to the chair. "Do I have to ride in that thing?"

The nurse crossed her arms over her chest. She'd been with them since the night before and most of the morning and seemed immune to his daughter's snark. "First of all, yes. It's a requirement. And second of all, you're not going to be walking anywhere today. We're sending you home with crutches, and you'll be using those and that boot you're wearing for the next few weeks at least."

"Fine." Allie plopped down in the seat.

They had already completed the paperwork for her release, and Cade had taken a load of stuff down to the truck earlier that morning. He picked up the rest of her things and followed them down the hall.

═══════════

The drive up the pass took just over an hour but felt like five. The cab of the truck was thick with awkward silences and uncomfortable attempts at conversation. Mostly his.

To say Allie wasn't thrilled about heading to Bryn's ranch was an understatement. She'd assumed they were going back to her house, but Cade wasn't ready for that. And he wasn't sure Allie was either. He promised her they'd go by her house on their next trip down, but for now, he was trying to keep her mind on her recovery.

Cade's efforts to ask about her school or how she was feeling were met with wisecracks or exaggerated shrugs, so he'd finally just turned on the radio and let his daughter sulk.

She wrinkled her nose at the country music station. "Is this the only kind of music you listen to?"

"No. I'll listen to whatever. You can choose."

She shook her head. "I guess I don't really care either. You can leave it, SD."

He furrowed his brow as he turned the volume down. "So, what's with this SD business?" She'd used the initials several times.

Allie lifted one shoulder. "It's just a nickname I have for you."

"What does it mean?"

She shrugged again and kept her gaze trained out the window.

"I don't think I like it," he told her.

"Oh well."

"Can't you just call me Dad?"

She turned back to him, her eyes narrowed as she leveled him with a cool stare. "No. I can't. You haven't earned that title in a long while. I haven't even *seen* you in close to a year."

He swallowed at the guilt churning its way up his throat like a bad bout of heartburn.

"That wasn't my—" He stopped. He was going to say it wasn't his fault—that Amber had moved them again and hadn't given him her new number for months. And that even when he'd called, she'd always had a reason why he couldn't talk to his daughter. But telling Allie that wouldn't do any good. He didn't want to speak poorly of Amber, especially right now, and it probably was his fault too. He should've tried harder, pushed Amber to put Allie on the phone or insist she return his call. "How about you just call me Cade? I didn't earn it either, but that's my name."

Slumping further into the seat and turning back to the window, she offered him that slight lift of her shoulders coupled with a mumbled "Whatever." Which he now took as her way of agreeing with him.

Glad that's settled. He glanced at the dashboard clock before returning his focus to the road. Only forty-five more minutes of awkward silence to go.

Close to an hour later—traffic up the mountain had been a bear—he turned the truck into the driveway of the Heaven Can Wait Horse Rescue.

ACKNOWLEDGMENTS

As always, my love and thanks go out to my family! Todd, thanks for always believing in me and for being the true romantic hero of my life. You make me laugh every day, and the words it would take to truly thank you would fill a book on their own. I love you. *Always*.

A special thanks and acknowledgment goes out to one of my writer besties, Anne Eliot, for your constant and consistent encouragement and support both in my writing journey and in making this book happen. And this is the book that finally got the fainting goat! Yay! I loved our writing retreat in the mountains, plotting at the hot springs and writing until one in the morning. You are always willing to listen and talk through plotting struggles and character crises, and we always have the most fun doing it. Thank you for your steadfast belief in me and for alternately holding my hand and lovingly pushing me to the finish line of this book.

This writing gig is tough, and I wouldn't be able to do it without the support and encouragement of my writing besties who walk this journey with me. Thank you to Michelle Major and Lana Williams for all the encouragement and the hours and hours of sprints and laughter. Thanks to Sharon Wray for always being in my corner and for being with me for that final sprint-a-thon push to the deadline of this book. You all are just the best.

I can't thank my editor, Deb Werksman, enough for your grace and support, for believing in me and this book, for loving Holt and Lainey, and for making this story so much better with your amazing editing skills. I appreciate everything you do to help make the town of Creedence and my motley crew of farmyard animals come to life. Huge thanks to Susie Benton—for your steadfast support and for giving me the opportunity to write a Christmas book. I love being part of the Sourcebooks Sisterhood, and I offer so many thanks to the whole Sourcebooks Casablanca team for all your efforts and hard work in making this book happen.

Huge thank you to my agent, Nicole Resciniti at The Seymour Agency, for your advice and your guidance. You are the best, and I'm so thankful you are part of my life.

Big thanks goes out to my street team, Jennie's Page Turners, and for all my readers: the people who have been with me from the start, my loyal readers, my dedicated fans, the ones who have read my stories, who have laughed and cried with me, who have fallen in love with my heroes and have clamored for more! Whether you have been with me since the first book or just discovered me with this book, know that I write these stories for you, and I can't thank you enough for reading them. Sending love, laughter, and big Colorado hugs to you all!

ABOUT THE AUTHOR

Jennie Marts is the *USA Today* bestselling author of award-winning books filled with love, laughter, and always a happily ever after. Readers call her books "laugh out loud" funny and the "perfect mix of romance, humor, and steam." Fic Central claimed one of her books was "the most fun I've had reading in years."

She is living her own happily ever after in the mountains of Colorado with her husband, two dogs, and a parakeet who loves to tweet to the oldies. She's addicted to Diet Coke, adores Cheetos, and believes you can't have too many books, shoes, or friends.

Her books range from western romance to cozy mysteries, but they all have the charm and appeal of quirky small-town life. She loves genre mashups, like adding romance to her Page Turners cozy mysteries and creating the hockey-playing cowboys in the Cowboys of Creedence. The same small-town community comes to life with more animal antics in her new Creedence Horse Rescue series. And her sassy heroines and hunky heroes carry over in her heartwarming, feel-good romances from Hallmark Publishing.

Jennie loves to hear from readers.

Website: jenniemarts.com
Facebook: JennieMartsBooks
Instagram: @jenniemartswriter
Twitter: @JennieMarts

Also by Jennie Marts